Meadville Pa. 16335

High Spirits

HIGH SPIRITS

ALICE DUNCAN

FIVE STAR
A part of Gale, Cengage Learning

Detroit • New York • San Francisco • New Haven, Conn • Waterville, Maine • London

GALE
CENGAGE Learning

Copyright © 2008 by Alice Duncan.
Spirits Series #3, featuring Daisy Gumm Majesty.
Five Star Publishing, a part of Gale, Cengage Learning.

ALL RIGHTS RESERVED
This novel is a work of fiction. Names, characters, places and incidents are either the product of the author's imagination, or, if real, used fictitiously.

No part of this work covered by the copyright herein may be reproduced, transmitted, stored, or used in any form or by any means graphic, electronic, or mechanical, including but not limited to photocopying, recording, scanning, digitizing, taping, Web distribution, information networks, or information storage and retrieval systems, except as permitted under Section 107 or 108 of the 1976 United States Copyright Act, without the prior written permission of the publisher.

The publisher bears no responsibility for the quality of information provided through author or third-party Web sites and does not have any control over, nor assume any responsibility for, information contained in these sites. Providing these sites should not be construed as an endorsement or approval by the publisher of these organizations or of the positions they may take on various issues.

Set in 11 pt. Plantin.
Printed on permanent paper.

LIBRARY OF CONGRESS CATALOGING-IN-PUBLICATION DATA

Duncan, Alice, 1945–
   High spirits / Alice Duncan. — 1st ed.
     p. cm.
   ISBN-13: 978-1-59414-695-4 (alk. paper)
   ISBN-10: 1-59414-695-0 (alk. paper)
   1. Majesty, Daisy Gumm (Fictitious character)—Fiction. 2. Spiritualists—Fiction. 3. Pasadena (Calif.)—Fiction. I. Title.
   PS3554.U463394H54 2008
   813'.54—dc22   2008031599

First Edition. First Printing: November 2008.
Published in 2008 in conjunction with Tekno Books.

Printed in the United States of America
1 2 3 4 5 6 7 12 11 10 09 08

In loving memory of Edwin O. Hammer,
who was very fond of Daisy.
I wish he could read her further adventures.

Chapter One

If it had been anyone else in the world who asked me, I wouldn't have done it. As it was, I turned down Mrs. Kincaid several times before I finally capitulated to her entreaties. I didn't want to do it even then. And, in spite of the fact that I made Mrs. Kincaid's son (and my best friend) Harold, accompany me, the job turned out to be every bit as bad as I'd anticipated. Maybe worse.

I suppose I'd better elaborate. My name is Daisy Gumm Majesty. In 1921, when all of this took place, I lived with my husband in a pretty little bungalow on South Marengo Avenue in the lovely city of Pasadena, California. Back then Pasadena was a haven for wealthy people from back East and from the moving picture industry. The two privileged groups didn't always spin in the same circles, but they all *wanted* me.

The above isn't a boast. It's a cold, hard fact. You see, at the time I earned my living (and that of my husband) as a spiritualist medium. I don't think there were more than a couple of wealthy matrons in the whole city who didn't call on my services at least once.

When they did, most of them wanted me to get in touch with dead relatives through my spirit control, a Scottish chap named Rolly who couldn't spell very well because he'd never attended school. Rolly's one more aspect of my career I'd thought up when I was ten, and he'd served me well since, although I sometimes wished I'd given him a more dignified name. I also read tarot cards, the Ouija board, crystal balls, and palms, although turning tables and blathering to dead people were my specialties.

My husband Billy would have been more than happy to bring home the bacon for the both of us, but he couldn't. In 1917, only a few weeks after he and I were united in holy matrimony, Billy went off to war. Before he left for the front, we thought fighting for the freedom of Europe against the wicked Kaiser and his German incursions was a brave and romantic thing to do.

Our enthusiasm didn't last long. Not only did I miss him terribly, but he hadn't been in France for more than a month before the Germans gassed him out of his foxhole on the frontier and then shot him when he tried to crawl to safety. Billy almost died. I know for a fact that he often afterwards wished he had. When he finally came home to me, he was a wreck of his former self and confined to a wheelchair.

I haven't had much use for Germans ever since, although I'm sure that bespeaks an illogical prejudice on my part. On the other hand, if prejudices weren't illogical, they wouldn't be prejudices, would they?

Billy didn't approve of the way I earned our living. He let me know it every chance he got. He even went so far as to call me wicked on occasion. According to Father Frederick, a very kind Episcopal priest with whom I was acquainted, this was only Billy's way of demonstrating how helpless and hopeless he felt.

That made sense to me since I felt the same way. I did my best to be charitable about Billy's fits and tantrums, but *you* try living with someone who's always berating you and see how understanding *you* are.

This was especially true since I made good money as a spiritualist, more than most men I knew and *much* more than I'd have made if I'd been someone's housemaid or secretary or

High Spirits

if I'd worked as a clerk at Nash's Dry Goods and Department Store. What's more, I'd created my job out of whole cloth. You don't honestly suppose I believe in spirits, do you?

You'd think my husband would at least have given me credit for ingenuity.

Not Billy. He carped and complained every time I so much as read a palm.

I worried a lot about Billy, and not merely because he fussed at me. His lungs had been damaged beyond repair by mustard gas, and his legs had been severely injured by grapeshot and shrapnel. He was, therefore, in constant pain, and he had to take far too much morphine for my peace of mind. I'd spoken to our family doctor about his morphine use, and Dr. Benjamin had more or less convinced me that addiction was better than incessant agony. I guess I agreed with him, but that didn't mean I had to like it, or didn't wish there were more than those two alternatives for alleviating Billy's pain.

My mother and father and aunt lived with us on Marengo. My sister Daphne and brother Walter were married and living elsewhere, although we all got together for holidays. Fortunately for those of us in the bungalow, Aunt Vi did the cooking. If either Ma or I had been charged with feeding the family, we'd probably have starved to death or been poisoned long since.

I was a crackerjack seamstress, though. When I was a little girl, I, like most of the other girls I knew, had possessed two skirts and approximately four blouses. That was before I learned how to sew. By 1921, my spiritualist wardrobe was superb. Maybe even a trifle elaborate. Heck, everything else in my life stank; I figured I deserved nice clothes.

For the job Mrs. Kincaid talked me into doing, it probably didn't matter much that I always wore sober-hued, refined costumes of the latest mode and of a tasteful length when I worked. None of your short and sassy "flapper" skirts for me, thank you very much. I trod a fine line in my job and made a tremendous effort to preserve my dignity and discourage people from believing me to be what Billy called me. Shoot, I even sang alto in our choir at the First Methodist Episcopal Church, North, on the corner of Marengo and Colorado. Choir service didn't matter for that blasted job, either.

1921 had come in with a whimper. My whole family, including Billy, whom I'd pushed in his wheelchair, had walked up to Colorado to watch the Rose Parade on New Year's Day. Now the city fathers were planning to build a new stadium for sporting events, to be called the Rose Bowl.

As for the rest of the world, Babe Ruth was expected to whack home runs by the score when the baseball season began. Russians continued to starve to death in droves, and people in Pasadena continued to collect funds to send to them. A rich young Pasadena fellow had died of ptomaine poisoning in January (which made me sad because I'd met him once or twice and liked him). "My Gee Gee (From Fiji Isle)," "Mandalay," and "When Autumn Leaves Begin to Fall" were popular songs—I'd play them on our old upright piano on dull evenings when nothing else was going on. Billy and Pa were champing at the bit for someone to perfect the radio signal receiving set so we could get one.

Women had been allowed to vote in a national election for the very first time the year before, in 1920, but I'd missed out since I wasn't twenty-one yet. I resented that, although there wasn't anything I could do about it.

The *Pasadena Star News*, one of our daily newspapers, had run an article about the Senate Chaplain being a Baptist, which, claimed the newspaper, should make our new president happy. It didn't make Ma happy, since she considered Baptists only slightly less pernicious than heathen savages.

As well, most of the country had been dry—or was supposed

High Spirits

to have been dry—for nearly a year by the time 1921 rolled around, although that didn't seem to be stopping anyone from consuming booze. The police were raiding speakeasies and smashing illegitimate stills with alarming regularity. What's more, the unlawful liquor-running business was getting deadlier with each passing day. You couldn't pick up a newspaper without reading about gun-toting cops raiding speakeasies in Chicago, rumrunners shooting it out with G-men near the Canadian border, booze-smuggling sailors exchanging gunfire with coastal guards from Mexico or Canada, or New York bootleg gangsters killing each other off to gain control of the city's streets. The bootleggers were a bold and deadly lot.

We on the West Coast didn't have quite as much trouble with that sort of violence as they did back East. Still, we had our share of bathtub gin, illegal liquor, and people who fancied themselves "bright young things" because they drank and smoked and danced their lives away at illicit speakeasies. Mrs. Kincaid's daughter, Stacy, was a perfect (or, rather, a particularly imperfect) example of this phenomenon. Naturally, as long as there was a demand for liquor, somebody would always be willing to supply it.

None of my friends frequented speakeasies, mainly because *they* all had sense. They also had to work for a living and didn't have the time, inclination, or money to fritter away doing anything so useless. That went for me, too. I wouldn't have gone to a speakeasy, even if I could have afforded to, because I judged the speaks to be a pestilential waste of both time and money. And can you imagine what people would have thought of a medium who drank outlawed liquor. I can tell you: not much. I'd have been out of business in less than a heartbeat.

On a personal level, I was glad the nation had gone dry. I worried plenty enough about Billy's morphine use. If he'd had access to liquor, too, I'd probably have gone nuts.

When Pasadena first incorporated in 1886, it had been a dry city that didn't even boast a saloon to call its own. People had been forced to go clear to Arcadia, twelve miles east, if they wanted to booze it up among like-minded folks. That state of affairs changed after a while, but there still wasn't a lot of riotous living being carried on in Pasadena in the twenties. For the most part, we were a tasteful, temperate, well-behaved community. Even the moving-picture people who lived there knew better than to outrage civic morality within the city limits.

I knew of at least one speakeasy in, or near, town, because Stacy Kincaid had been arrested there once during a raid. I'd heard rumors that the place was run by an Italian gentleman from back East, but I didn't know anything for a fact. Every time the coppers raided the place, it shut down and opened up again somewhere else. It was kind of like a rash that wouldn't go away, but spread to a new location every time you thought you had it whipped.

Which is where Mrs. Kincaid's request of me came in. She'd already telephoned me three or four times in the past couple of months, asking if I wouldn't please hold a séance for the man in charge of the speakeasy Stacy frequented.

"I'm so worried about her, Daisy!" she wailed. She was a first-class wailer. To give her credit, I'd probably have wailed, too, if I'd had a daughter as awful as Stacy. Because of Billy's injuries, I didn't have to worry about that since he was unable to father children. Darn the blasted Germans to heck and back.

"I'm very sorry, Mrs. Kincaid." I told her, but I still wasn't about to set foot in a speakeasy.

"She begged me to ask you."

If I recall correctly, I took the receiver from my ear and stared at it in bemusement. Not only was the request an odd one to begin with—how many times do you suppose people are asked to conduct séances in speakeasies?—but the fact that Stacy Kincaid had asked her mother to telephone me was almost unbelievable. Stacy Kincaid had as much use for me as I had for her, which was none at all. I thought she was a spoiled brat, and she thought I was a fraud. We were both right, but at least I was good at what I did. Stacy was good for nothing.

Mrs. Kincaid had been my best customer for years. She had, moreover, got me started in the spiritualist business, sort of, when she gave my aunt Vi, who was her cook, an old Ouija board. Therefore, rather than holler at her, I stated politely that Rolly was extremely particular about the venues in which he manifested himself, and he didn't care to work in unlawful drinking establishments. I refrained from making any puns about Rolly being one spirit too many in such a place, and I believe my restraint should be applauded.

To my dismay, Mrs. Kincaid persisted. She called me every day for a week before I finally caved in. I only did so because she started crying at me. I hate it when people do that.

"Oh, but Daisy, you'd be doing me such a favor if you could hold a séance for those creatures."

Those creatures? If she really thought of them as *those creatures,* why did she let Stacy haunt their dens of iniquity? But that's a stupid question. I doubt that Mrs. Kincaid had ever forbidden Stacy to do anything at all—or that Stacy would have obeyed such a command if it were given.

"Um, why is that, Mrs. Kincaid?" That's when she started sobbing over the telephone. I hope I suppressed my sigh.

"Stacy has taken up with the most horrid woman, Daisy! She calls herself *Flossie!*"

She'd told me that before, and I hadn't yet been able to figure out what she had against the name. Maybe because it was a couple of vowels and a consonant away from "floozy," which is what her daughter was, but Mrs. Kincaid surely didn't blame Stacy's hideous behavior on Flossie. Did she? Shoot, maybe she did. People aren't always enamored of rational thought. This was particularly true of Mrs. Kincaid. I said only, "Mmmm." Soft murmurs go a long way in my trade. They're expected, in fact.

"And she's begun seeing a terrible man called Jenkins!"

Most of the bootleggers I read about in the newspapers had a million vowels in their names and were Italian. This fact sat ill with Billy's best friend (and my mortal enemy) Sam Rotondo, who was Italian *and* a police detective.

"Ah, yes," said I in my silkiest mystical tone. "That's the gentleman she calls Jinx, if I recall correctly."

"Yes." Mrs. Kincaid paused to blow her nose. "Can you imagine such a thing?"

Well, yes, I could, but only because I have an excellent imagination. I gave her another "Mmmm."

"The man's employer—the man who runs the speakeasy—is determined to hold a séance there. He wants to get in touch with his uncle. He calls him his godfather, although I doubt that he has anything at all to do with God. I think that's some sort of thing gangsters have. Godfathers. Oh, Daisy!" Again she wailed. I repressed another sigh. "The man was *murdered!*"

I gathered from this speech that the murdered man was Jinx's employer's uncle, although I didn't attempt to clarify the matter. I'd become accustomed to interpolating Mrs. Kincaid's garbled communications years earlier.

"And I *need* for you to go there and make sure the place is suitable for my daughter! Harold won't do it."

Perfectly understandable. Harold and I harbored similar opinions about his sister. I wanted to ask Mrs. Kincaid how any speakeasy could be a "suitable" place for a young woman from a wealthy family—or any other young woman, for that matter—to frequent, but didn't. As already mentioned, Mrs. Kincaid had never been a strict disciplinarian or a devotee of rational thought. Also, her old man had been a crook and a bounder, so there you go. Maybe Stacy came by her unpleasant tendencies naturally. Mrs. Kincaid and Harold were both sweethearts. It's odd how such disparities can exist in families, isn't it?

Feeling more than slightly beleaguered, as well as awfully guilty (after all, Mrs. Kincaid had been the rock and the mainstay of my career for years), I attempted to demur gracefully. "I wish I could help you, Mrs. Kincaid, but Rolly simply refuses to manifest himself under certain conditions."

"But are you *sure*, dear? Won't Rolly do it for *me?*"

Crumb. I wish she hadn't put it that way. With an awful feeling of impending doom, I hesitated. I knew it was the beginning of the end, but I refused to give up yet. "Um . . . perhaps I can meditate on the problem and consult the spirits, Mrs. Kincaid."

"Oh, Daisy!" She knew I was done for, too. I could hear it in the joyful tone of her voice. "Thank you so much! I'm sure Rolly will understand how much this means to me."

I was sure he would, too, darn it.

Chapter Two

The next Friday, the evening of the speakeasy séance, Harold Kincaid came to call for me up in his low-slung, snazzy, bright-red Stutz Bearcat. Billy and I had been sitting on the front porch, the February evening being unseasonably balmy, awaiting his arrival.

Billy wasn't happy that I was going away, but Spike, our almost-grown-up, black-and-tan dachshund, was doing his best to cheer him up. Spike had been one of my more inspired acquisitions. There's just something about a puppy that makes the world a brighter place. This holds true even if you're Billy. I know it for a certified fact because my husband had been much happier since Spike joined the family. He'd even decided to try to walk again.

Actually, Billy had always been able to walk a little bit, but his legs were badly damaged, and his lungs were half eaten away by the gas. He'd talked to Dr. Benjamin, however, and they had come to the conclusion that if he went slowly and I helped him, the functioning of his lungs and legs might improve with time and exercise. Therefore, we went for tiny walks every day. He put his arm around my shoulder, and I supported him, and we walked at least as far as our neighbors', the Wilsons, house to the north of us. I don't know if Billy felt any improvement in his mobility, but I was getting shoulders like a line backer. I sure hoped it would help him, though.

I truly believe Billy's new-found interest in improving his

High Spirits

health sprang directly from the influence of Spike who, being a dog and not beleaguered by the prejudices we humans have, loved Billy and me uncompromisingly, was never persnickety or depressed, and never looked down on Billy because he was crippled. Or me because I was a medium, God bless the beast.

What's more, Spike was a most discerning doggie. He'd actually piddled on Sam Rotondo's shoe the first time they met. You've got to love a dog like that.

Anyhow, back to the porch where Billy, Spike, and I awaited Harold's arrival. I was as nervous as a prairie dog in a cage full of rabid coyotes but didn't dare let my anxiety show. Billy didn't know where I was going that evening. If I had my way, he never would know, either.

When Harold pulled up in front of our house, Spike announced his presence with gusto. Billy condescended to allow me to roll his wheelchair down the ramp Pa had built for him so he could admire Harold's jazzy automobile. Billy was always polite to Harold even though he didn't like him, and he was wild about motorcars.

I'd recently purchased for the family's use a perfectly splendid, closed-in, battery-operated Chevrolet sedan with a self-starter and a driver's-side door as well as one on the passenger's side, as a replacement for our old 1909 Model T Ford that had given up the ghost right around Christmas time. We all loved the Chevrolet, but it sure wasn't a bright-red Stutz Bearcat.

Before the war, Billy had been primed to become a motorcar mechanic. The automobile industry had become a huge employer countrywide, and mechanics who could work on motorcars were much in demand. Billy had always been fascinated by automobiles and was a crackerjack mechanic. He'd been all set to start work at Hull Motor Works when he came home from the war. Thanks to the Kaiser, my husband's

17

mechanical skills with automobile engines had become moot. The war had left him with a paltry pension, a ruined body, a generally bad mood, and a beleaguered wife.

Poor Billy.

Poor me.

"Beautiful machine, Mr. Kincaid."

"Call me Harold," Harold said to Billy. He winked at me to let me know he doubted Billy would take him up on the offer.

I knew my husband, though, and was pleased when Billy proved me right. "Thanks, Harold. I'm Billy, as I'm sure you already know."

"Yes, indeed. I hope you don't mind that I'm in love with your wife, Billy."

Billy let that one pass, and I tapped Harold lightly on his shin with the pointy toe of my left shoe. Harold winked at me again. Billy ran his hand over a glossy painted fender. "This is a real beauty, Harold. I used to like working on machines like these."

"It's a whiz to drive."

As for me, I wasn't all that interested in motorcars, although I was pleased that Billy and Harold were talking. That didn't last long. After Billy had looked his fill at the machine's outsides and inspected the motor, which enthralled him, he bade me a short farewell and wheeled himself back to the porch, Spike trotting at his wheels.

Harold opened the passenger's door and I climbed into the motorcar, hoping my hat wouldn't fly off. Harold must have anticipated this problem because he presented me with a scarf with which I tied it down.

"I don't want to do this, Harold," I muttered, not sure the words could be heard over the racket the motor was making.

They must have been because Harold said cheerfully, "Everything will be fine, Daisy."

"Hmm." I was glad I'd worn my black wool coat. Even

though the night wasn't yet cold, the breeze whipped up as the auto sped south on Marengo was chilly. I watched gloomily as lawns and houses seemed to fly by, becoming sparser the farther south we went. Harold turned right on Glenarm Street, then south on Fair Oaks Avenue, and my heart started thumping out a funereal dirge in my chest. I felt as if I were headed to my own execution—and not your quick beheading, either, but a slow, painful death by torture.

The winter night, while moderately mild, was black as the pit from pole to pole. The electrical streetlights ended approximately a mile north of where Harold finally parked the Bearcat. I saw nothing but trees when he and I set out to cross Fair Oaks Avenue, unpaved since this part of the street was well south of Pasadena's city limit. I think it was close to Cawston's Ostrich Farm because I detected the faint aroma of poultry in the air. Actually, it was more of a stench.

The new moon grinned at us. Stars twinkled innocently down from the heavens. Innocence sounded like a good idea to me, but it was too late. I think I must have groaned.

"Don't be frightened, Daisy. This will be fun."

Harold was all set to enjoy himself, at any rate. As for me, I had grave doubts about the evening's agenda. For one thing, I lied to Billy, and I hated doing that. But if you think my husband would have countenanced my visit to a speakeasy, even to do something as blameless as conduct a séance, you don't know my Billy. Well, of course you don't, but . . . Oh, you know what I mean.

I muttered, "Sez you."

"I've always wanted to visit a speak," Harold went on, his relatively high-pitched voice even squeakier than usual due to his state of excitement. "Del won't go to one with me, even though I have the passwords to a dozen of them in Los Angeles. He's very religious, you know."

Del was Delroy Farrington, Harold's boyfriend.

That sounds odd. Perhaps I'd better explain. You see, Harold and Del were what my husband and Sam Rotondo called "faggots." I called them friends.

They were both perfect gentlemen: kind hearted, generous, well behaved, and well dressed—and Del even had a religious streak. Both were employed at high-paying jobs (Harold worked in the moving pictures, and Del and another gentleman had saved the Kincaid bank when Harold's father ran off with a pile of bearer bonds). Both men had exquisite taste in home decoration.

But did Billy and Sam ever mention *those* pertinent facts? Facts that would, if they didn't know about the one little eccentricity Harold and Del shared, have lifted the two men out of the realm of masculine mediocrity and to the heights of respectability and praiseworthiness?

Of course not. Men are like that. One little thing reduces two exemplary fellows to the status of freaks in a sideshow.

Okay, so maybe it's not exactly a little thing to prefer people of one's own sex to those of the opposite one, but golly, I thought Harold and Del were both swell, and Harold had saved my own personal hide more than once. I resented it that Sam and Billy overlooked all of their sterling qualities and concentrated on that one blot, if it can be called a blot, on their characters.

But that's neither here nor there. Harold had agreed to go with me to the speakeasy, a condescension I truly appreciated. In spite of that, I was scared to death.

Not only had I lied to Billy, but I was going to work for a bunch of vicious criminals, one of whose progenitors had been murdered. My imagination, which is sometimes too vivid for my own good, had already created hundreds of scenarios for the evening. They all ended with me lying dead in a pool of gore, the victim either of gangs of rival bootleggers or overzealous policemen.

Perhaps I hadn't really *lied* to Billy. I'd told him I was going to do a job for Mrs. Kincaid, which was the absolute truth. But I'd committed a sin of omission at the very least, and the criminal part still held true. If Billy had known what I'd intended to do that evening, he'd have pitched a fit. And I wouldn't have blamed him.

I dug in my heels. "Harold, I don't want to do this. I'm scared. I don't care what you say. This is an awful place, it's run by a bunch of murdering hoodlums, and we could get arrested. Or even shot." I squinted across the expanse of dirt road at what looked like a large bunch of trees, probably sycamores since there were a lot of them down that way, although it was too dark to tell for sure. "Besides, I can't even see it. Maybe it's not there after all. Maybe they moved it." That was an almost-comforting thought, and it lasted approximately five seconds, until Harold spoke again.

"It's there. You're not supposed to see it, sweetie. It's illegal. They try to hide them." He tugged on my arm, but I didn't move.

"Oh, Lord, Harold, I don't want to do this!"

"You're such a pessimist, Daisy. Can't you look upon it as an exciting new experience?" Harold laughed merrily.

I didn't. "No. I almost wish there was another spiritualist medium in Pasadena. Maybe your mother would have hired her to do this instead of me."

"No she wouldn't. You're the top of the line when it comes to spiritualists, my dear, and Mother would never hire another one. You're the epitome. Top of the trees. A mistress of your art. Why, even your name is perfect. Desdemona Majesty."

I rolled my eyes and said, "Huh."

"Nonsense. You're brilliant at your line of work, Daisy!"

"Yeah, you've said that before." I know I sounded grouchy. I felt grouchy. "But I don't like breaking the law, whatever I am. Especially for your sister's sake."

"It's not for Stacy's sake, sweetie. I don't like her any better than you do, but I do love my mother, and the poor dear is worried sick about Stacy."

"I know, I know." What I wished was that someone would drive a stake through Stacy's heart and rid the world of a blight. Sure, her daughter's death would make Mrs. Kincaid sad for a while, but ultimately I'm sure we'd all be better off. Problems are seldom solved so handily, however, and I didn't expect Fate to stick an oar in and help me out with Stacy. Fate wasn't exactly my bosom pal. Nevertheless, I gave in and resumed walking.

My persona couldn't be faulted, considering I was a soon-to-be felon—unless it was a misdemeanor to frequent speaks. I was dressed in a dark green silk suit that I'd made for Christmas. It had satin edging around the collar and a low waist with a satin belt that tied on the side at my hip. It complemented my dark red hair and was gorgeous, and I usually felt good when I had it on. I'd decided to wear it that evening, knowing I'd need all the help I could get in the feeling-good department. The dress wasn't working.

"Well," Harold said, continuing our conversation as we walked through a sycamore grove (they *were* sycamores) in the dark, "at least you won't have to do this more than once."

"Sez you," I retorted crossly. Not only was I stumbling over roots and leaves and things, and probably snagging my best pair of black silk stockings—thanks to the rum-running gangsters' need for privacy—but I had no faith whatever that Mrs. Kincaid would let me off the hook after only one séance. I did, however, have infinite faith in her daughter's ability to thwart anyone who attempted to help her. Therefore, I feared Mrs. Kincaid's entreaties that I appear at the speakeasy were destined to continue. The notion filled me with a sensation I still find difficult to describe. Dread and terror come close, with a liberal dose of resentment thrown in. "Where the heck is this place, anyhow?"

"It's in this grove. An old ranch house, I understand."

"I don't like breaking the law, Harold."

He laughed. Big help. Suddenly I saw, tucked away among some trees, a faint light shining from a lamp mounted on the pillar of a porch attached to what looked like a barricaded building.

It turned out to be an old ranch house, just as Harold had predicted. Its windows had been boarded up, and the porch looked rickety. I'd have been willing to turn tail and run away and tell Mrs. Kincaid that Jinx and his cronies must have moved quarters, but Harold remained undeterred. Retreat probably wouldn't have worked anyhow since Stacy would have pointed out my mistake. I supposed it was as well to get it over with tonight; surely I'd be able to think of an excuse to get out of coming here again.

As if he'd done this before, Harold led me along a path through a jungle of weeds and to a back porch that looked to be in an even sorrier state of disrepair than the front one. He tripped agilely up the scarred wooden stairs and rapped on the door as if he belonged there. I followed in his wake, looking over my shoulder, expecting to see uniformed coppers following us with their guns drawn.

No such luck. I heard something that sounded like a bolt being lifted, and a gimlet eye appeared at a small hole in the door. A gruff voice said, "Yeah?"

Harold whispered, "Oh, you kid."

The eye disappeared, and the door opened. My heart was heavy when I trailed after Harold into the house.

Golly, what a difference between the outside and the inside!

I'm not sure what I expected, maybe a continuation of the shabbiness exhibited by the exterior of the place. Instead, I stepped into what looked like a bordello designed by a color-blind seventeenth-century French courtesan. Not that I know what that would look like, but it's the closest I can come to describing my impression of the place.

Red-and-black flocked paper covered the walls. Plush red carpeting had been laid upon the floor beneath our feet. The decor was undoubtedly meant to impart the impression of opulence, but it gave me a queasy feeling in my tummy (although that might have been a result of my state of trepidation). Crystal chandeliers with dangly ornaments were supposed to shed light on all below, but the cigar and cigarette smoke was so thick, everything looked merely fuzzy. A jazz band blared away in the main room, which lay straight ahead of us. I remember my footsteps dragging; I didn't want to go forward.

Harold grabbed my hand and yanked, and I had no choice. "Come along, dearie. Let's see what my sister finds so fascinating about this place and these people."

I'd never before wanted to do anything Stacy Kincaid did, so Harold's reasoning left me cold. But it was too late to back out now. I'd already committed myself. Nodding, I would have followed Harold, except that the man who'd opened the door to us, a bruiser of a fellow in a yellow-checked suit who must have been nearly seven feet tall and almost as wide, stopped us by the simple expedient of holding out an arm as big around as a tree trunk. We couldn't move.

"Hold it a minute." He sounded as if somebody had sandpapered his vocal chords. "I gotta tell Jinx youse guys is here. Wait a minute."

Harold and I exchanged a glance. "Um . . . sure," I said.

The noise was ghastly. While we waited for the monster to deliver his message and return to us, I gazed glumly into the main room. A long bar had been built parallel to the far wall, behind which stood what looked like a battalion of bartenders mixing and shaking and handing out drinks, all of which I presumed contained alcohol. A huge mirror backed the bartenders, reflecting the revelry going forward in the main room. Girls in skimpy outfits, net stockings, and shingled hair walked here and there with trays strapped to their shoulders that were supplied with cigarettes and cigars and matchboxes.

Leaning close so that I could whisper directly into Harold's ear, I asked, "Where does it all come from?"

He shrugged and shouted back. "No sense whispering. Nobody can hear us anyway."

He was probably right, but I didn't want to raise my voice. I was scared, darn it. "Where does all the liquor come from?"

"Beats me."

"Oh." Since he didn't seem to know any more than I did about the mysterious world of speakeasies, I let my question ride and stared some more, wondering if any of the scantily clad cigarette sellers were girls I knew from school. None of them looked familiar, and I was glad. I'd be done for if anybody besides Harold and Stacy recognized me.

Approximately three hundred people swarmed around the place, dancing to the music, laughing, chattering, and screaming. I think they were only screaming because it was the one way they could make themselves heard over the band, which was playing "Honolulu Eyes." Almost everyone who wasn't actively dancing held both a drink and a cigarette or a cigar. Most of the ladies (I use the word loosely) used holders for their cigarettes. I guess that was supposed to be sophisticated. I knew for a sinking certainty that I was going to smell like an ashcan when I got home.

The atmosphere was supposed to be festive, but it appeared only sordid to me. Maybe that's my Methodist upbringing talking, but I don't think so. I doubted that any of those people were truly happy. Then again, neither was I, so I guess I shouldn't talk.

Whatever the mood of the attendees, you should have seen their clothes. I've never beheld so many beads in my entire life. Or so many rolled stockings and knees, most of which were rouged, I'd bet. In a couple of years, a dance called the Charleston was going to sweep the country, but most of the people in that room were foxtrotting. I think. Whatever dance they were doing, they were doing it with an air of devil-may-care abandon.

All the band members were dark-skinned and appeared a good deal happier than the people dancing and drinking, although that impression, too, might have been colored by my sense of unease. I surveyed the band in wonder, until I got to one particular face.

Then I gasped, grabbed Harold's arm, and cried, "Good heavens, Harold, that's Jimmy, Mr. Jackson's son!"

Squinting into the melee, Harold said, "Who? Where?"

"That one, playing the trumpet. Over there." I didn't want to make any large movements—God alone knows why—so I jerked my chin toward the band.

"There are five men playing trumpets, Daisy," Harold pointed out.

"Maybe, but there's only one who looks like he's ten years old."

"Oh, yes. I see him now. So he's Mr. Jackson's son, is he? Who's Mr. Jackson?"

"Who's Mr. Jackson?" I stopped gaping at the band and gaped at Harold instead. "He's your mother's gatekeeper, for heaven's sake! He's manned the gate at your mother's estate for years."

"Oh." Sheepishly, Harold muttered, "I don't keep close tabs

on Mother's servants."

I shook my head. "It's got to be against the law for a boy that young to be playing the trumpet in a place like this."

Harold shrugged. "It's against the law for all of us to be here, if you want to get picky."

I could tell Harold didn't share my outrage. But Jackson was a friend of mine. He'd instructed me in many aspects of Voodoo and Caribbean spiritualism. I liked Jackson a lot, darn it, and I wondered if he knew about his young son's career as a trumpet-player in a speakeasy jazz band.

Probably. Some people don't care how they make money, as long as they make it. Look at me, for Pete's sake.

"Do you see Stacy anywhere?"

I squinted into the swirling smoke. "Not yet. Did you tell her we were coming?"

"Mother did. Stacy and I don't chat on a regular basis."

Perfectly understandable. I didn't say so because the monster came back. "Follow me," he rasped.

So we did.

Chapter Three

Although I hadn't believed it to be possible, I became even more uncomfortable as Harold and I approached a knot of people on the far side of the main room. The knot contained Stacy (oh, joy), another woman, and two chaps who didn't look as if they believed in brotherhood and tolerance toward their fellow men. One was an oily specimen with his curly brown hair slicked back, and the other was Italian. I could tell because he looked a lot like Sam Rotondo.

From what Mrs. Kincaid had wailed at me, I presumed the woman who wasn't Stacy to be Flossie, the oily man to be Jinx, and the Italian to be either Jinx's boss, whose name I didn't know, or another gangster whose name I didn't know. I didn't want to know them. In fact, I didn't want to meet any of those people. Neither did Rolly.

"Harold!" Stacy screeched. She ignored me, which was okay by me. She rushed to her brother and made a show of being pleased to see him. I knew better. Stacy and Harold got along like lions and lambs before Christmas was invented, although I couldn't honestly have told you which one was the lion. Probably Stacy.

"Stacy," Harold mumbled, trying to avoid her hug. He couldn't do it, but he didn't hug her back.

I suppose Stacy could be called a good-looking girl. She had a pretty face with delicate features, and she dressed in the latest modes. Well, I did, too, but Stacy favored the most radical of modern fashions, the ones that bring to mind the phrases, "flaming youth" and "flappers." Her skirts were always too short, her accessories too jangly, her lipstick too flashy, her hair too short (and too blond), and her voice too loud. Invariably, too, she held a cigarette in a long, shiny black holder and blew smoke in everyone's faces. Her total air was that of a brat of a girl who was trying too hard to be something she wasn't: the heroine in *This Side of Paradise*. That goal would have been impossible for any of us. Stacy was too stupid to know it.

"Jinx! Jinx!" she shouted, hauling Harold over to the group. "This is my brother Harold! And this"—her enthusiasm chilled, although mine was equally frigid—"is Daisy Majesty." She flapped a hand in my direction.

"Mrs. Desdemona Majesty," Harold corrected. He was such a pal.

Stacy sniffed and said, "Desdemona Majesty."

I probably ought to explain that "Desdemona" thing. It wasn't really part of my name at all. When I was ten years old and first introduced to the Ouija board, I decided Daisy was too pedestrian a name for a spiritualist, so I opted to become Desdemona. I wouldn't be forced to read *Othello* until I was in the ninth grade, or I probably would have borrowed some other literary character's name, preferably one who wasn't murdered by her husband.

Jinx looked me up and down as if he were assessing me for the tax collector. "So," he said, "dis is da medium, eh?" He stuck out his hand.

Honest to goodness, I didn't know people really talked like that until I met James Leroy Jenkins, "Jinx" to his friends—and probably his enemies, too. I didn't figure among either of those select groups, thank God. The closest to his accent I'd heard up till then was that of Mrs. Barrow, our nosy party-line neighbor who hailed from Brooklyn. And Sam Rotondo, but his accent wasn't like this. Although it pains me to give Sam credit for anything, his New York accent had more class than Jinx's or Mrs. Barrow's.

"How do you do?" I muttered, keeping my chin high and my hand at my side. That was probably a foolish thing to do given the violent predilections of Jinx and his cronies, but I didn't fancy shaking hands with a bootlegger who might well be a killer. I mean, they all were, weren't they?

I never did find out if Jinx would have taken my unwillingness to shake hands amiss because Harold grabbed the hand hanging there in the air and shook it, making me feel small and petty—until I remembered the killer part of this equation, and then my sense of self-righteousness kicked in again. That was absurd since I was there in the speakeasy and was, therefore, just as bad as Jinx was, except for the killer part.

Stacy noticed, however, and huffed in my direction. Jinx either didn't take offense or didn't pay attention to me. He greeted Harold, took his arm, grinned at me, and said, "Lemme take youse guys to da boss."

"Da boss," I presumed, was the one whose godfather had died. Been murdered. Oh, Lord.

My heart started battering against my ribcage in fright. I didn't want to meet any more gangsters. Jinx was plenty enough. Nobody had introduced me to the blond woman or the Italian man. I glanced at the woman and gave her a small smile, but she was studying her bright red fingernails, so I don't think she noticed.

"It'll be fine, Daisy," Harold whispered in my ear.

I doubted that. Stacy had latched on to Jinx's arm. Jinx didn't seem particularly ecstatic about this sign of affection, although he didn't shake her off. He knocked on the door, using the time-honored if trite rhythm of "shave and a haircut, six bits."

A voice from beyond the door said, "Yo!" and the door was

yanked open so fast, I jumped. Harold patted my shoulder. Another bruiser, not quite as large as the monster but every bit as scary, said, "C'm in, youse two. Da boss is waitin'."

I was too terrified to apologize for my jumpiness, which was okay, since we weren't late or anything. Gee, but those people frightened me! I wasn't sure Rolly would be able to show up even if he was me, if you know what I mean. I'm no prima donna, but shoot, I need to have *some* kind of peace of mind and freedom from panic when I work. Then the door closed behind us, and absolute silence filled the space in which we stood.

Shocked by the sudden stillness, I turned to stare at the door. It looked just like any other door in the world. A chuckle at my back startled me, and I spun around.

"Da doors and walls is soundproofed, Mrs. Majesty." The words came from the mouth of a large man standing at the other side of the room. In spite of his accent and grammar, he looked as if he'd just stepped out of a gentleman's fashion magazine. His smile made my stomach hurt, probably because it didn't go with his eyes, which were cold, and black, and small, and reminded me of the eyes on a cobra I'd seen at the Griffith Park Zoo the previous November.

"Oh."

"Dis," said Jinx with a smirk of pride, "is da medium, boss."

"You should oughta interduce me to da lady, Jinx, not da lady to me," the boss said.

"Oh, that's all right," I said in a rush. "I don't mind. Really. It's fine. Truly. I—"

Harold took my arm, and I realized I'd started babbling. I swallowed, and Harold said, "It's okay, Daisy." After clearing his throat, he said, "Mrs. Desdemona Majesty, please allow me to introduce you to . . ." His voice trailed off, I guess because he didn't know "da boss's" name.

"Da name's Vicenzo Maggiori, Mrs. Majesty. Pleased ta meetcha." His voice was deep and oily and kind of reminded me of the olive oil Aunt Vi used when she fixed spaghetti.

The feeling wasn't mutual. I said, "H-how do you do?"

"Don't pay no attention to Jinx. He ain't got no manners."

None of these people had no grammar either, apparently. Or maybe that should be neither. Unable to speak because my throat was dry and my tongue had stuck to the roof of my mouth, I nodded and attempted one of my gracious smiles. Gracious smiles were my stock in trade, along with gentle murmurs and Rolly, but I couldn't find one in me to save myself. I hoped the nod would suffice.

It seemed to. Maggiori swept out a well-manicured hand and said, "Please, Mrs. Majesty, sit here." He looked at Jinx. "Tell George to bring refreshments, Jinx. Da lady prolly wants somethin' to drink."

The notion of being served an alcoholic beverage jarred me out of my fear-induced stupor. "No!" I swallowed. "I mean, I don't need anything, thank you."

"Nuts," said Maggiori. "Get da lady a ginger ale, Jinx."

"Sure ting, boss."

"Bring me another drink, too, Jinxy," said Stacy, acting flirty.

"You've had enough," Jinx said with noticeable coolness.

Stacy pouted.

The bottle-blonde I'd assumed to be Flossie sidled up. Actually, it wasn't really a sidle. In fact, she seemed kind of shy. A gangster's moll who was bashful was such a surprising concept, I forgot my nervousness and smiled at her. What the heck. Since we were the only two people present with enough sense to be ill at ease in that environment, we might as well support each other. My friendliness must have given her courage because she moved a little closer.

"Hi," she said, whispering. "I'm Flossie. Flossie Mosser."

Mercy sakes. The poor thing. I stuck out my hand. Why not? Of course, I was only assuming she hadn't killed anybody. What did I know? "Happy to meet you, Miss Mosser. I'm Desdemona Majesty."

"Oh, just call me Flossie. Love your name." She gave me a small smile but still looked nervous. "Desdemona. It's got such class."

"Move it, Floss," Jinx growled. Poor Flossie leaped back as if he'd struck her.

I frowned at him as he handed me my ginger ale but was too intimidated to scold him for being rude to Flossie. In fact, I said, "Thank you." I tried to make it sound cold but knew I was being cowardly.

"Let me know when youse guys is ready, Mrs. Majesty. After you wet your whistle and all."

Maggiori smiled at me, and I felt cold all over. Lord, but the man was terrifying—and all he'd done so far was be polite and smile. I shuddered and hoped he didn't notice. "Thank you," I said again, this time to Maggiori. "I'm ready when you are."

"Good." He rubbed his hands together and looked happy, which made one of us. "Stacy here says you want da room dark with just a red lamp with one candle on da table. Dat right?"

"Yes. Thank you." I told myself to stop thanking the guy every three seconds, but even as I did so I knew the admonition wouldn't work. I was scared spitless and would do darned near anything to keep him from getting mad at me. I stared hard, trying to identify bulges that might signify guns but didn't see any. Well, why should Maggiori carry a gun? He had a herd of goons to shoot people for him.

Egad. I was scaring myself.

"Can you really talk to dead guys?" The question was a whisper, and it came from Flossie, whom I'd forgotten all about in my panic.

Stacy had come closer. I hadn't noticed her do it, or I'd have moved farther away. "So she says," she whined in a snotty tone.

Harold growled softly, "Give it up, Stacy."

His voice sounded fiercer than usual. I glanced over to find him looking more uneasy than he had before. About time, if you ask me. Past it, maybe.

I answered Flossie. "It's my job." I wished I could keep her beside me because I sensed that she felt almost as out of place in that environment as I did. Although I also knew the feeling to be irrational since she was evidently one of these gangsters' lady friends.

"I think that's swell," Flossie said.

"C'mere, Flossie, and leave da lady alone."

Flossie jumped and trotted over to Jinx, who shoved her into a chair. "Keep yer fat mouth shut, too. None of your blabbin', y'hear?"

"Sure Jinx," Flossie said in a tiny voice.

I felt almost as sorry for her as I did for myself, so I rounded up a gracious smile and flung it at her. It probably wasn't a very good one since I was petrified with terror, but it seemed to make her feel better.

"I'll sit here," Stacy said, plopping herself into a chair one person removed from me. I was grateful for that until Jinx sat down between her and me and Vicenzo Maggiori sat next to me on my other side. Harold sat beside him.

Oh, sweet Lord, have mercy, as Aunt Vi sometimes says, I was sandwiched between two murdering hoodlums. I scolded myself for allowing Mrs. Kincaid to talk me into doing this. I should have held firm against her entreaties, no matter what, but by then it was far too late to back out.

I always try to weave a mystical spell during the first few minutes of any séance. That night I was so anxious that it took me longer than usual to relax enough to play my part.

Acting on a nod from Maggiori, the bruiser (as opposed to the monster, who I guess manned only the front door) turned out the electrical lights. The room went dark. It was a few seconds before people began focusing on the feeble light emanating from the cranberry candle lamp in the middle of the table.

Deciding what the heck and that the sooner I got it over with the better, I cleared my throat and spoke in my best, most velvety spiritualistic voice. "Everyone please join hands."

Thus it was that I found myself holding hands with two of the most evil men I'd ever met. Jinx's hands were rough and sweaty. Maggiori's were as soft as a woman's. I suppressed a shudder as I imagined him as a big black spider in the center of a web, directing people to do his malevolent wishes without ever dirtying his own hands.

In an attempt to shake off my sense of impending doom, I began my usual banter. "In order for the spirits to break through from the Other Side and communicate with us, we must maintain absolute silence. No one must speak."

What hogwash. But it worked really well that evening. For the first time in my entire eleven-year career as a medium, honest-to-goodness silence descended upon one of my séances. Gee, those people were much more obedient than most of my clients. I suppose the threat of being shot to death does that to a person, you know, makes him behave.

That thought took some of my satisfaction out of the success of my command. I tried not to let it bother me.

I'd been told, via Stacy through her mother, that Vicenzo Maggiori wanted to get in touch with his dead uncle who'd been a big gangster in New York City. The man's name was Carmine "The Hand" Bennadutto. I don't know why they called him "The Hand," and, frankly, I don't want to. I figured the nickname had something to do with his criminous career.

Therefore, I'd gone to the Pasadena Public Library and looked through old issues of the *New York Times* in search of information relating to Mr. Bennadutto. After all, if I aimed to trick a vicious gangster (Maggiori) into believing I'd called another vicious gangster (Bennadutto) from the dead, I'd better know what Rolly was talking about.

Carmine Bennadutto had been born in Sicily in 1879, had moved to the U.S.A. in 1908, and had risen to a position of great celebrity in certain New York circles—not the kinds of circles in which I personally whirled. His gang was known to supply a section of New York City with liquor. He'd been gunned down in an Italian Restaurant on Mulberry Street in New York City in October of 1920, apparently the victim of a rival gang faction that wanted to take over his territory. There had been a picture of the murder scene, which I regretted looking at afterwards.

So then I read about the rival gang faction. During my research, I gleaned a whole lot of interesting information about the different gangs extant in New York City at the time, and none of it made me view Maggiori's séance with sanguinity. Or maybe sanguinity isn't the right word since it makes me think of blood.

At any rate, I didn't want to conduct the darned séance, but I, stupid to a fault, had agreed to it. So I was stuck, and I aimed to do as good a job as I could, if only not to irritate Vicenzo Maggiori, whose reaction to irritation might prove painful, or worse, to my humble self.

Approximately ten minutes into my act (it usually only takes about five minutes, but I was *really* nervous), I began to exhibit symptoms of falling into a trance. I'd started moaning and groaning a trifle, and allowing my head to droop, and that sort of thing.

In case you've wondered, I never had any truck with

ectoplasm, which I consider merely disgusting. I mean, who wants to have some kind of slimy junk all over his table, or the floor? I know some people thought that producing ectoplasm was a great way to prove you were in communication with the dead, but not me. Ick. However, I digress.

After another few minutes Rolly appeared, God bless him. I love Rolly, and not merely because he'd served me well for so many years. The story between Rolly and me, you see, is that we had been soul mates approximately a thousand years ago in Scotland. His spirit had stayed with me through all my incarnations ever since. You've got to love a guy with that much sticking power. Besides, given the state of my own marriage, it was comforting to think that some man, even if he was a figment of my own imagination and dead for a millennium, would love me through time and all eternity. It sure didn't look as though that sort of love would be mine in this life. Not only that but Rolly, who was ostensibly a Scotsman, had an accent all his own, which I'd pretty much mastered. Because of his built-in accent, I didn't have to fiddle with other types of accents. I wasn't sure how I'd handle an Italian mobster, for example.

Anyhow, Rolly had showed up, and we were just getting into the meat of the séance, during which Carmine "The Hand" Bennadutto was going to speak through Rolly to his godson, Vicenzo Maggiori, when a door opened, completely shattering the mood.

Maggiori said, "Huh!"

Totally disconcerted, I didn't know what to do, so I just sat there, sagging. It was a most uncomfortable position. Until that evening, none of the séances I'd ever conducted had been interrupted at just that point—the point at which everything's going to begin to happen but hasn't yet.

A man silently slithered over and bent to whisper in Maggiori's ear. I felt the big boss stiffen and wondered what the heck was going on and when it would stop. And *then* something happened that totally floored me. Maggiori released my hand, which flopped onto the table, and stood up.

He said softly, "I'm awful sorry, youse guys, but Jinx and me, we gotta go. But I want to do dis again later." On my other side, Jinx, too, let go of me, and there I was, supposedly in a trance and communing with spirits, but with no living human being connected to me.

Well, golly! Since, to all intents and purposes, the séance was over, I made up my role of a medium deserted in mid-trance extemporaneously, having had no practice in the part. No one was seated next to me, so I remained slumped over, wondering how long I should take to recover my senses.

The matter was taken out of my hands when all of a sudden the door burst open, lights flared on in the room, and a booming voice hollered, "Cheese it! Da cops!"

In less than a second, Harold, Stacy, Flossie, and I were alone in the room, blinded by a flood of light, and trying to shade our eyes against it. I don't think I spoke a single word, being too astounded by events. I remember Harold saying something like "Shit!" or "Damn!" but I didn't hold his bad language against him. If I'd thought of it, I'd probably have sworn, too.

The lousy place was being *raided!*

Approximately an hour later, Harold, Stacy Kincaid, Flossie Mosser, and I sat in Detective Samuel Rotondo's office at the Pasadena Police Station, which was situated behind the Court House on the corner of Fair Oaks and Walnut. I was still shaking with leftover panic and trying not to cry. Harold was grinning, Stacy was pouting, Flossie seemed resigned to her fate, and Sam looked like a volcano about to erupt. Where Jinx and Vicenzo Maggiori were was anybody's guess.

High Spirits

And I was done for. My goose was cooked. I was a goner.

"I-I thought you didn't get involved in County matters." My teeth chattered, my voice shook, my heart raced like a greyhound chasing a rabbit, and I was pretty sure I was going to die from fright any minute. I didn't feel like fighting with Sam. But darn it, it was the Los Angeles County Sheriff's Department that was supposed to watch out for things in the area where we'd all been arrested. Yet here we were, in the Pasadena Police Station, being glowered at by Sam Rotondo, my worst nightmare.

"We cooperate," he growled. "Which is more than I can say for some people."

Meaning me. I'd have argued, but I was too rattled. Plus, I was still straining not to cry. We Gumms are made of tough stuff. If I cried in front of Sam, I'd hate myself. Of course, since I already hated myself, there was probably no point to the struggle. Nuts.

After skewering me with a hideous frown fully long enough for me to wish I was dead, or at least visiting my father's relatives in Massachusetts, Sam jerked his head at a policeman who stood behind Stacy and Flossie. "Take those two to the lobby, Joe. I need to talk to Mrs. Majesty and Mr. Kincaid for a minute."

Oh sweet heaven. I watched them go, wishing for the first time since I'd met her that Stacy wasn't leaving a room in which I existed. As soon as the door shut behind the two women and the copper, Sam turned on me.

"Damn it, Daisy Majesty, does Billy have any idea where you were and what you were doing tonight?"

"St-stop shouting at me." My protest was feeble. I'd done a terrible thing that night and deserved to be shouted at. Sam was quivering like the aspic on one of Aunt Vi's preserved chickens. Ignoring Harold in favor of berating me, he loomed over me like a mountain, and he was doing a darned good job of making me feel like a crawling bug or a plague-infested rat.

"Damn it, how could you do this to your husband? Don't you feel any sense of responsibility at all?"

That hurt a lot, mainly because my sense of responsibility regarding Billy was as large as an alp—and also because I thought I'd treated my husband shabbily by agreeing to help Mrs. Kincaid. I didn't want Sam to know how much his words stung. Still, the shock of hearing him shout them made me suck in a gulp of air.

"Really now, Detective Rotondo. There's no need for that sort of thing. Daisy has felt terrible about this job ever since my mother talked her into accepting it. She was absolutely petrified the whole of the evening and could speak of nothing but how ashamed she was to have misled her husband."

Bless Harold Kincaid's sweet heart. Sam didn't buy it, which is no less than I'd expected of him, but I appreciated Harold's attempt to make him see the truth.

Sam swung around to face Harold, making poor Harold start. "*Misled?* That's a fine word for it, I'd say. She lied to him! Damn it, why did she do it, if she was so damned miserable?"

"Because she's a kind-hearted woman who tries to help people. She feels obliged to my mother—don't ask me why—and she agreed to take this job even though she didn't want to."

"Nuts. Your mother's got more money than God. Mrs. Majesty's got a family that needs her a lot more than Mrs. Kincaid does."

"I'm sure that's true. But don't you see that working at her job as a spiritualist *is* taking care of her family?" Harold sounded irritated, which was unusual for him.

"*She doesn't have to work in speakeasies, for God's sake!*"

I flinched. Harold proved his mettle. He hollered right back at Sam, "*She had to work in a speakeasy this time!*"

I'd covered my ears at Sam's bellow. With Harold's, I decided

I'd cowered enough. Gumms aren't supposed to cower. Lifting my hands (which still trembled, by the way) from my ears and sitting up straighter, I frowned at Sam. "Stop shouting, both of you." I turned to Harold. "I appreciate the support, Harold, but Sam knows darned good and well that I have to work for a living. He just doesn't like how I do it."

"No more does your husband," Sam said, shoving the words through his clenched teeth. I'd seen Sam angry lots of times, but boy, I'd never seen him *that* mad. Unfortunately for my humble self, I couldn't fault him for his ire that night.

Harold tried to help again. "Honestly, you're making a mountain out of a molehill, Detective Rotondo. Daisy was merely performing a séance. Neither of us took a drop of alcohol."

If I hadn't been so upset, I might have found the sight of Sam going through the various stages of fury interesting. I'd noticed before that his olive skin, which wrinkled up as when he pursed his mouth when he got mad at me, made yellowish lines, as opposed to the white lines my own fair skin made when likewise engaged. That night I was too miserable to increase my knowledge of which colors olive-skinned Italians turn when infuriated.

Sam included both Harold and me in his next glower. "And you think that because you weren't drinking, that makes visiting an illegal gin joint right?"

"Oh, stop it! Harold didn't mean that, and you know it. He meant that the only reason we went there was because of the séance. Harold only went because I was too scared to go alone."

The full heat of Sam's continuing fierce glare focused on me. It would. "And why do you suppose that was?"

Crumb, it felt as if a boulder had lodged in my throat. I knew I was going to cry pretty soon, and I just *hated* to show Sam how upset I was. I managed to swallow my lump for the nonce.

"Stop being so darned sarcastic. I'm not an idiot, you know. I didn't want anything to do with those awful people."

I was beginning to remind myself of Mrs. Kincaid. That was bad because I knew Mrs. Kincaid to be a fluffy-headed nitwit. If there was anything on earth that could have made me feel lower than I already did, it was that.

But you did it anyway, Sam said flatly. "How much sense does that show, do you think? Did you give a rap about your family while you were fulfilling Mrs. Kincaid's wishes?"

That was it. The tears came spilling out. I felt *so* stupid. "Yes!" I blubbered. "I knew Billy would hate it! That's why I didn't tell him."

Harold, bless him for a saint, handed me a clean white handkerchief, and I wiped my eyes and blew my nose. I looked at Sam, wishing I was one of those women whom people feel sorry for when they cry—you know, the fairy-tale princesses of the world who look even more gorgeous than usual when teary-eyed. I'm not. My eyes get red, my complexion gets blotchy, and my nose runs. Not a pretty sight.

"I never wanted to hurt Billy, Sam Rotondo, and if you don't know that by this time, you're an idiot yourself."

My pathetic aspect didn't affect Sam noticeably. He frowned at me for another couple of seconds, then turned to Harold. "Would you mind leaving us alone for a few moments, Mr. Kincaid? I need to talk with Mrs. Majesty."

Harold squinted at Sam and then at me. "Daisy?"

What the heck. Maybe Sam was going to shoot me and put me out of my misery, although I didn't expect such a happy ending to that awful day. "It's all right, Harold."

Still, Harold hesitated. "Are you sure?" He cast a glance at Sam that I would have resented had it been directed at me. Sam's hide was tough as an elephant's, and he didn't even seem to notice it. His attention was centered on me—and not in a kindly way, either.

I heaved a gigantic sigh. "Yeah. I'm sure. Thanks, Harold."

"I'll wait for you right outside the door," Harold assured me.

"Great. Thanks."

"I'll take you home," Harold said.

"Not until we've concluded our business here, Mr. Kincaid. Don't forget that you're both still facing booking and arraignment."

I think I whimpered.

"I'll still take her home," Harold said firmly.

"I can take her home, for God's sake," said Sam.

Harold and I exchanged a glance. If I looked as doubtful as Harold, it couldn't have boosted Sam's ego any. Harold said, "I don't know . . ."

The volcano erupted at last. "Oh, for God's sake! Get the hell out of here, Kincaid. I'm going to talk to Daisy whether she likes it or not, and if she doesn't, I may just let the two of you spend the night in the slammer instead of letting you out on bail. It's what you deserve!"

Afraid he might mean it, I said, "It's all right, Harold. Sam will take me home." I made a valiant effort and came up with a grin. "And if he doesn't, please have the coppers scour the foothills tomorrow."

Neither Sam nor Harold thought that was funny. I guess I didn't, either.

Chapter Four

The door closed with a click, and I was alone with Sam. Abandoned. Bereft. Scared out of my wits. Although I was pretty sure he didn't have one, I attempted an appeal to Sam's softer side.

"Do you have to tell Billy about this, Sam?" I sounded pathetic. I *felt* pathetic.

My pathos didn't phase him one little bit, exactly as I'd expected. "I'll be hanged if I'll aid and abet you in deceiving your husband, Daisy Majesty. Billy's my best friend, and he deserves better."

Better than me is what he meant. Fearing I'd cry again, I didn't answer him or try to defend myself. I was well and truly up the creek now. Not only would Billy doubt me forevermore, but I was going to have a criminal record, and my career as a spiritualist to wealthy Pasadena matrons would be ruined. Since I was the chief breadwinner in the family, this was a true catastrophe. What's even worse was that it was all my own fault, and I couldn't blame it on a single soul but myself.

And my only hope of escape from vilification, condemnation, and poverty was Sam Rotondo, a man who considered me only slightly less noxious than cholera. I was done for.

Silence filled the room like an evil emanation. Unless that was my guilty conscience. While I continued to cower in my hard wooden chair, Sam stood on the other side of the room, his arms folded across his chest, his bushy black eyebrows almost meeting over his dark, angry eyes, which were, naturally, fixed upon yours truly.

He stood there like a rock, immobile, furious, glowering, until I finally got too antsy to take it any longer. I straightened slightly—my energy level had slumped like a deflated balloon, probably due to my mood of total despair. "What? Why are you staring at me like that?"

Silence.

My perturbation finally burst out into words. "Darn it, Sam, *what?* Stop staring at me! If you're going to lock me up, just go ahead and do it! I'm sick of this room and of being glared at by you! I feel bad enough without that!"

He moved so quickly, I cringed back in my chair, thereby loathing myself as a coward and a craven. Grabbing another hard-backed chair, Sam plunked it down right in front of me with its back facing me. Then he straddled the chair, sticking his face close to mine. This time, with reason, as opposed to the first time when I was merely being cowardly, I recoiled as if he were a bulldog about to attack. "Don't *do* that! You startled me!"

"Listen, Daisy, maybe there's a way out of this for you— without your having to go to jail. And without ruining Billy's life."

What about my life? I wanted to ask but didn't, knowing Sam didn't give a fig about that. Instead, I muttered, "I'd never ruin Billy's life," still sounding pitiful. I was also afraid I was lying, so I added, "On purpose."

"Huh. Maybe not on purpose. But the way you persist in doing stupid things isn't geared to help him any."

"I'm not stupid!" I cried, stung.

He said "Huh," again. Clearly he didn't believe me. I didn't either, for that matter. Not after this evening's debacle.

I knew I wouldn't win a verbal battle with Sam, so I said

resentfully, "Well? What can I do?"

"You can help the Pasadena Police Department shut down Vicenzo Maggiori and his outfit."

I know I blinked at him. Probably my mouth dropped open, too, although I don't remember that part. I do know I couldn't think of a thing to say.

"Well?" he asked. He did it snappishly, too, as if I was supposed to know what he was talking about, which wasn't fair.

I cleared my throat. "Um . . . how?" I had a mental image of me strapped with those crisscrossing bandolier things and shooting it out with Jinx and the monster. Machine guns at thirty paces. I couldn't think of another way I could help. Giving me a gun wouldn't help, either, of course, unless I used it on Stacy Kincaid, and I was pretty sure Sam didn't mean that.

He waved a hand in my face, as if to shut me up, which I thought was rude although I didn't point it out to him, thereby showing good sense for perhaps the first time all day. He was in a bad enough mood already. "I'm thinking."

All sorts of testy retorts sprang to my mind. I didn't utter *them,* either. I did murmur, "Let me know when you're through." *If your brain doesn't explode.*

He shot me another frown, which I didn't think I deserved. Much.

I'm not sure how long we sat there, me quivering with dread inside and Sam thinking so hard I expected to see smoke plume out from his ears, but it seemed like forever. After the end of time or maybe a little longer, he sat back, pressed his lips tight, and took to glaring at me once more. I endured this as long as I could, but I finally blew up.

"Doggone it, stop staring at me! I'm not a fiend, Sam Rotondo, and you know it! I'm only trying to earn a living. And I don't know what you think *I* can do to stop those lousy bootleggers!"

"I do."

I blinked again. "You do?"

"Yes. Now shut up while I think it through." He gave me an especially hot scowl. "It'll do you good to stew for a while longer. Think about Billy and what you're doing to him while you're out consorting with criminals."

"I wasn't consorting," I keened, crushed.

"Like hell. Shut up."

Although I didn't appreciate being told to shut up, and I *really* hated that he thought I was a bad wife, even though I thought it, too. I shut up, understanding that discretion was, under the circumstances, the better part of common sense. I did huff once or twice. Couldn't help myself. Sam didn't seem to notice, which was probably just as well.

After another eternity or two, he looked me in the eye and said, "All right, here's what I want you to do."

I swallowed hard and didn't speak. Every once in a while reason will overtake my innate Gumm passion for expressing myself.

"You need to hang out with Maggiori as much as you can for as long as you can."

My eyes popped wide open, and I regret to say I screeched at him. "*What?* I can't do that! I hate that man and never want to see him again! You just accused me of being a criminal and a bad wife because I did exactly that!"

He flapped his hand in my face again. This time I swatted it away without giving a thought to discretion. "Stop doing that!"

"I'm not through explaining my plan to you yet," he growled.

It was my turn to "Huh," so I did.

"What I want you to do is gain the confidence of Maggiori and Jenkins and their hoodlum cronies and tell me everything—and I mean *everything*—you learn while in their company."

I sucked in approximately ten gallons of stuffy police-department air and let it out in a whoosh. "You're crazy."

His grin made my stomach ache. "It's the only way you're going to get out of this without a criminal record, Daisy. You don't want Billy to think you're more of an idiot than he already does, do you?"

I gasped. "Stop it! Billy doesn't either think I'm an idiot."

"He certainly doesn't approve of the way you work."

"The *way* I work is totally aboveboard and always has been, darn it. I'm good at what I do."

Sam looked at me with such a sour expression on his face, I'd have sworn he'd been drinking vinegar. "You're quibbling, and you know it. Billy disapproves of what you do to earn money."

My gaze dropped. "I know it." What's more, up until that evening, I'd thought Billy was being too hard on me. After what I'd done that night, I wasn't so sure any longer.

"Then you can think of this as a way to redeem yourself."

"Redeem myself?" I tried to give Sam a cynical grimace, but it didn't work the way I wanted it to. "I'll probably end up dead."

"Nonsense. I'll be working closely with you, and I'll make sure nothing bad happens to you."

Right. The man who hated me more than he hated Vicenzo Maggiori, Al Capone, Jack the Ripper, and the Kaiser combined. "Billy won't like it if my helping you gets me injured or killed," I pointed out.

"You won't get injured or killed." He sounded disgusted.

"No? I thought that's what those guys did: kill people."

"That's not their primary business. Their main reason for operating illegal drinking joints is to make money."

Made sense to me. I didn't say so.

"And we haven't been able to put them out of business because somehow or other, they've been able to anticipate every single one of our raids. Maggiori, Jenkins, and the rest of the leaders of the gang always manage to get out of the joints before we come in."

"Poor planning on somebody's part." Okay, I know it was snide. It was the meanest thing I could think of to say, and I admit I shouldn't have said it. I wasn't in any position to make sarcasm advisable.

"Good planning, is more like it, on their part," he said, giving me another hideous scowl. "They're getting inside information somehow, and you're going to find out how they're getting it and from whom, and you're going to tell me all about it."

I pointed at my chest. "I am?"

"You are."

I gulped. "How?"

"By sticking close to those guys and keeping your ears open. And *telling* me what you learn."

"That's nuts, Sam! If they don't kill me, Billy will. I thought you were such pals with him."

"I am, damn it! I'll take care of Billy for you. *You* take care of gathering information for me."

I wailed, "But I don't want to!" I guess I'd learned well from Mrs. Kincaid because it was a super wail.

"Would you rather have a criminal record?"

My head drooped so low, my chin darned near bumped against my chest. He had me. I was a dead duck. I felt as I had that day when I'd caved in to Mrs. Kincaid's request that I conduct a séance in a speakeasy, only worse. I couldn't see any way out of the mess I'd made for myself except for the one extremely frightening—and, I'd swear, dangerous—way Sam was giving me. He was probably only doing it because he knew I'd be offed by the bad guys and then Billy wouldn't have to put up with me any longer. It was all a big plot, and I'd stepped right smack into the middle of it like the sucker I was.

Knowing I was licked didn't mean I had to give in without consequences to Sam Rotondo, darn him. Retrieving my self-possession, which had sunk into my once-lovely and now-scuffed black shoes, I lifted my chin and stared back at Sam with almost as much heat as he'd flung at me. "If I do this for you, you've got to do something for me."

He lifted an eyebrow, which made him look even more derisive than he had before. "I should think keeping you out of the clink would be enough."

My chin jutted out farther. "It's not."

His other eyebrow went up to join the first one. "Oh?"

"You have to let Harold and Flossie go. They didn't do anything wrong. Harold only accompanied me to the speakeasy because I was afraid to go alone. And Flossie's just a sweet kid who hangs out with the wrong kind of people. She's really nice, Sam." In truth, I didn't know that for a fact, but I sensed a certain goodness about Flossie. Even as I begged for her life (so to speak) I figured I was wrong about that, too. My judgment had been really, really bad of late.

He pinched his lower lip between a thick finger and a meaty thumb. "Hmmm."

"Please, Sam. They shouldn't suffer because I did Harold's mother a favor. It's not their fault I'm a fool." Boy, I hated saying that—the fool part—mainly because I knew Sam agreed with me.

Sam frowned. Since the frown wasn't directed at me, I didn't take it personally for once. "I don't know. I'm not all that fond of floozies and faggots."

I *hated* it when he called Harold a faggot. Since I wasn't in a position to chide him, I held my tongue. "They're less guilty than I am," I pointed out.

"Stupidity and gullibility aren't very good excuses for wrongdoing," he pointed out back at me.

"They're not stupid." I didn't say it with much fervor since I wasn't sure about Flossie. And she *was* gullible, or she'd never have become involved with Jinx and Maggiori and their crew. Kind of like me.

"Well . . ." He eyed me, squinting. "What about Miss Kincaid?"

"Who? Oh, Stacy. Shoot, I'd forgot all about her." I shook my head, trying to clear it of irrelevancies. Since visions of prison, my bullet-riddled body, and an outraged Billy kept swirling in my head, shaking didn't help a whole lot. I didn't like Stacy. In fact, I disliked her and figured she was the ultimate reason for the mess I was in—and deserved to be locked up behind bars—unlike me. After all, she'd gone to the speakeasy because she'd wanted to. I'd only gone there because I was foolish and weak-willed. Still . . .

"Mrs. Kincaid will be happy with me if I spring her kid from the slammer, I suppose."

"I suppose." Sam's tone was extremely dry.

"Okay, let her go, too. No booking. No arraignment. No record."

"She already has a record."

That's right. I darned near smiled. "No more of a record than she already has, I mean."

He thought. And thought. And then he sighed deeply. "All right. The two Kincaids and Miss Mosser can go. And so can you, with the stipulation we agreed to—and you have to promise you won't tell a soul about any of this. That would defeat the purpose."

Tell anybody I was hanging out with gangsters and spying for the coppers? Who did he think I'd tell? Maggiori? Jinx? Did the man think I *wanted* to end up in the Pacific Ocean wearing cement overshoes? "I promise."

"That includes Billy."

If Sam Rotondo thought I'd ever tell Billy about this night and the results thereof, he was insane. "I promise."

"Very well. I'll allow the four of you to go without consequences. This time."

"There won't be another time," I muttered.

"We'll see."

He didn't sound the least bit confident in my declaration, the rat. Nevertheless, my heart felt infinitesimally lighter. "Do I have to sign anything? A legal document or anything?"

"No. If you don't do what you've agreed to do, I'll just lock you up. I expect you'll cooperate."

"Thanks heaps."

Sam went to the door and opened it for me. Gentlemanly of him. When I joined Harold, Flossie, and Stacy, Harold and Flossie jumped to their feet and rushed over to me. Stacy remained in her chair and continued to sulk.

Somehow or other, I managed to smile at Harold and Flossie. "It's all right. I'm fine."

But I didn't get to break the good news to them. Sam did that, telling them that he'd let them go this time, but if he ever caught them in an illegal situation again, he wouldn't be so nice.

Nice? Ha! I burned to reveal all, at least to Harold. He'd have sympathized with me. But I couldn't. The burden was mine alone to bear. Mine and Sam's. Whoop-de-do. Somehow, that knowledge didn't significantly lighten my load.

Harold and Flossie took taxicabs from the police station, and Sam drove both Stacy and me home after that. None of us said a single word until we got to Mrs. Kincaid's mansion and Sam drove through the big iron gate, which was manned by Mr. Jackson, whose son had probably escaped the same raid in which I'd been snagged, and to the front of the house. Then Sam took Stacy by the hand, told me to wait in the motorcar, and led

High Spirits

Stacy to her mother's front door.

I watched as Featherstone, Mrs. Kincaid's butler, opened the door. I stared hard in order to see if he showed any reaction. He didn't. Featherstone was the most professional person I'd ever seen in my life. I tried to emulate him in my own work. Not that I wanted to look like a butler, but I always tried to keep my spiritualist image intact under all circumstances during which I might possibly be observed by clients or potential clients.

Although Featherstone didn't bat an eye, I think I heard Mrs. Kincaid screech—and that was after the thick oak door closed behind Sam and Stacy. A screech from Stacy's mother was no more than typical, and I thought morosely that I could expect a telephone call from her in the morning.

Sam didn't spend very long in the Kincaid house, but came back to his car after no more than ten minutes. I eyed him without favor. "Have fun?"

"Oh, sure. Tons of fun."

"Is Mrs. Kincaid hysterical?"

"What do you think?"

I couldn't quite make myself smile. I truly did feel sorry for Mrs. Kincaid. Sort of. She might have done a better job with her daughter, although her son was a peach. I got kind of tired of her hysterics, too, having felt for some time that a swift kick to Stacy's rear end would do more to straighten her out than tears and tantrums. On the other hand, what did I know? I didn't have any kids and never would, thanks to the lousy, stinking Germans, so I wasn't exactly an expert on childrearing.

"That girl's going to get herself in real trouble one of these days," Sam growled, punching the Hudson's self-starter viciously.

"Probably." And what did I care if she did? Not a thing, that's what. In fact, I hoped she did, which goes to show what a bad mood I was in. I don't usually wish evil upon people, even people I don't like.

I was surprised it wasn't later than it was, but when Sam pulled his Hudson up to the curb, it was only about eleven. There was still a light on in the house. My heart didn't exactly sing when I saw it, mainly because it no doubt meant Billy was waiting up for me.

Now, here's the thing: if Billy had been healthy and whole, I'd have thought it was sweet that he stayed up to greet me when I came home from a hard evening's work conducting séances or whatever. But when my poor mangled leftover-from-the-War Billy waited up for me, it almost always meant he was in more pain than usual, angrier than usual, or had gone to sleep and been awakened by a terrible dream—and I hadn't been there for him.

Then again, maybe he and Pa were playing cards.

Naw. My luck was never that good.

Therefore, I turned to Sam. "Let me out. I don't want Billy to know you brought me home. He's expecting Harold to drive me home in his Bearcat. He'll know I've done something wrong if you show me to the door."

"At least you admit it was wrong." Ignoring my wishes, Sam opened his door, climbed out of the car, and started walking to the passenger side to open my door.

I opened my own darned door, furious with him. In a hissing whisper, I said, "Darn it, you said you wouldn't tell Billy about the speakeasy if I did what you wanted me to do! I agreed to do it, so get back in that car and go away before Billy sees you!"

"It's all right, Daisy. I'll just tell him I drove by when you were leaving . . . whose house? Where did you tell him you were going to be working?"

I sighed, perceiving he wasn't going to give up. "Mrs. Kincaid's, darn you."

"Perfect," said he. "I'll just say I brought Stacy home after she was arrested, and then offered to bring you home. It's almost the truth."

I saw his white teeth flash against his Italian skin and wanted to kick him.

"Cheer up," he said. "At least Billy won't have to visit you in jail."

True. The knowledge didn't cheer me up one tiny little bit.

Spike announced us before we got to the door.

"Good watchdog," Sam growled.

"Yeah."

I held my breath, fearing the worst, as I pushed the door open and stooped to greet Billy's dog. "Don't eat the shoes, Spike. They didn't cost much, but they're one of my favorite pair." Only then did I dare glance up to look for Billy and try to assess his mood.

By gum, something good happened then for a change. Billy and Pa sat in the living room at the card table. They'd been playing gin rummy, and Billy actually smiled at me! I was so relieved, I darned near cried again.

It soon became clear, however, that I wasn't out of the woods yet. As soon as Billy saw Sam, he frowned—not at Sam, but at me. "What are you doing with Sam? I thought you were at Mrs. Kincaid's place?"

I was about to answer with a lie when Sam preempted me with one of his own. Shaking Pa's hand, he spoke to Billy. "I had to take the Kincaid daughter home from a raid at a speak tonight, and your wife was there. I offered her a ride home."

The doubt vanished from my husband's face instantly. It never did that when *I* lied to him. "That kid's a real mess. I don't know why her mother doesn't send her to a nunnery or something."

"Probably because they're Episcopalians and not Roman Catholics," I said, striving to sound light and frivolous, as if I'd just returned home from an evening of jollity and fun.

All three men looked at me as if I was crazy. Fine. I'd just leave them alone, then. "I'm bushed, Billy." I went over and gave him a peck on the cheek. "You going to stay up long?" It was difficult to know exactly how Billy should be treated. I didn't want to nag, but I also knew that he needed his rest. So did Pa, with his weak heart.

Without answering, Billy quirked an eyebrow at Sam. "Want to join us in a couple of games, Sam?"

Sam eyed the table with longing. I've never understood how people can sit and play cards for hours at a time. I'd be bored silly. "Well . . . I've got to work tomorrow . . . Oh, what the heck." He headed to the hall closet where he knew we stored the card table and folding chairs because he and Billy and Pa played cards all the time.

That answered my question, so I left the men and Spike to their game, went to our bedroom, changed into my nightgown, and fell into bed, totally exhausted. That night I slept like the dead. Maybe I was only wishing.

The following morning, dawn broke much sooner than I thought it should, and I awoke before Billy. I did what I always did on mornings when my husband couldn't catch me at it: checked the level of morphine syrup in the bottle he kept in our birds-eye maple dresser across the room from our bed.

My heart always hurt when I saw how much of the medicine he'd had to drink the day before—and I wasn't even sure that was his only bottle. I suspected him of stashing that one bottle in the dresser because he knew I checked up on him. I had a feeling he took even more morphine than I was aware of and that he hid his other bottles because he didn't want me to worry about him. As if I'd ever not worry about him.

The bottle was half-empty. It had been full the day before. I sighed and put it back, wondering why I bothered. Dr. Benjamin was right about addiction being better than pain. I told myself so over and over and over again, and I worried anyhow.

After tiptoeing back to the bed and kissing Billy's ruffled hair—he had beautiful hair; it was the one thing that hadn't changed since the war—I put on my robe and slippers and shuffled out to the kitchen, which connected to our bedroom.

Ma and Aunt Vi were eating breakfast and chatting softly. It always touched me that they took such pains not to awaken Billy and me in the morning. Both women smiled when I joined them, and Aunt Vi said softly, "I made waffles, Daisy."

God bless my aunt. My mouth started watering instantly. "Thanks, Vi."

"There's bacon, too," said Ma.

Better and better. "Yum." Glancing around in search of the missing members of the family, I said, "Where are Pa and Spike?"

"Joe took the dog for a walk," said Ma, smiling. "He said Spike is getting fat and needs the exercise."

"Ha. Pa should talk."

"It's good for the both of them." With a sigh, Ma stood, picked up the hat she'd laid aside, and put it on, stabbing a pin in it haphazardly. "The auditors are going to be at the hotel today. I'm not looking forward to it."

"Bank auditors?"

"Yes. They audit the accounts every year about this time. I'm not worried, but they take so much of my time. They don't usually come on a Saturday. I'm afraid I may be late coming home from work today."

Ma was head bookkeeper at the Hotel Marengo. It was a responsible position for a woman in 1921—or any other time, for that matter—and I was proud of her. She normally worked half-days on Saturdays, and I hoped she wouldn't have to work much longer than that. She deserved her time off.

Pa had worked as a chauffeur for rich movie people until his first heart attack four years before. Now he socialized. And took Spike for walks.

Golly, but I loved my family. Impulsively I gave Ma a hug. She looked at me as if I'd lost my mind, but I only grinned at her. "You'll triumph over those auditors, Ma. I have faith in you."

"Go along with you, Daisy Majesty," she said, borrowing one of Aunt Vi's favorite sayings. By gum if she wasn't blushing when she exited through the side door to walk to work.

"Daisy, you're a caution," Vi said, springing a new saying on me. I'd heard it before, but not from my aunt's lips, and I wondered what a *caution* was, as related to persons. I didn't ask. Vi didn't take things quite as literally as Ma did, but I didn't want to confuse her so early in the morning. She tapped her upper lip with her forefinger. "We need onions and potatoes."

"I'll stop by the store on my way to work," I offered.

"Thank you, dear. That would be very nice of you."

"You sure you trust me?"

Vi chuckled. "I trust you to pick them out, just not to cook them."

I chuckled, too, although I rued my lack of cooking skills. "Thanks for the great breakfast, Vi. Any special occasion?"

"No. I just felt like making waffles."

Boy, I wished I felt like cooking every once in a while. Or maybe it was better that I didn't since I could burn water.

Vi set a plate before me, and I slathered butter on the piping-hot waffle. My father's sister, my aunt Madeline, sent us a big can of Vermont maple syrup every Christmas, and I was about to pour some of the delicious stuff, heated in a saucepan on our lovely self-regulating gas range, on my buttered waffle when Vi interrupted me.

"Is Billy awake, Daisy?"

"I don't think so. Want me to look?"

"Why don't you? I don't want to cook a waffle for him until he's ready for it, but I have to go to work."

She didn't have to add that she didn't trust me to cook Billy's waffle for him. Everyone in the family knew better than to trust me in the kitchen.

"Be right back." I hurried to our room, hoping my waffle wouldn't get cold.

My heart took a nosedive when I saw Billy slugging back the contents of the bottle I'd left in the dressing table drawer. He heard me at the door, but he didn't hesitate to finish what he'd been doing. He swallowed, grimaced, and looked my way. "Stuff tastes vile," he said.

Lots of words bubbled up inside me and danced on my tongue, but I swallowed them all, reminding myself that Billy's pain wasn't his fault and, therefore, neither was his dependence on opiates. Instead, I forced a smile. "Aunt Vi has a cure for that. She fixed bacon and waffles for breakfast."

His eyebrows lifted and for a second, he looked like the man I'd married. I darned near burst into tears.

"Be right there," he promised, smiling at me.

I shut the door, gulped a couple of times, and returned to the kitchen table. Aunt Vi must have read my expression because she patted me on the shoulder. "He was a good soldier, Daisy. Now *you* have to be one. It's a crying shame."

It sure was.

"Thanks, Vi."

She set another plate on the table. "Why don't you butter that one for your husband while it's still hot, dear?"

So I did.

Chapter Five

The telephone waited to ring until Billy and I had sopped up the last of our maple syrup with the last of our waffles, which was a consideration on its part that it didn't generally grant us. Most days the darned phone rang just as I was drinking my coffee or chewing something. That morning I managed to grab the receiver before any of our other party line members picked up theirs.

"Daisy?"

I made a face at Billy and mouthed, "Mrs. Kincaid." She was in a tizzy too. Last night's horrors, which I had conveniently tucked away and not considered yet, flooded back to taunt me. "Good morning, Mrs. Kincaid." I used my soothing spiritualist voice because she needed it. It wouldn't have hurt if someone had used some soothing techniques on me, but, of course, I wasn't as lucky as Mrs. Kincaid.

A party-line person picked up her receiver just then; I heard the click. Since she didn't speak but only breathed in our ears, I knew it was Mrs. Barrow, the premier party-line snoop of all time. At least Mrs. Mayweather and Mrs. Pollard had the grace to hang up when they realized the call wasn't for them. Our other party-line member, Mrs. Lynch, evidently actually listened to the rings and didn't often pick up her receiver if the ring belonged to someone else. Not Mrs. Barrow, who tried her hardest to remain on the wire during my calls. I'm sure my calls were more interesting than hers, but it was still annoying.

"Oh, Daisy!" Mrs. Kincaid sobbed.

I didn't want Mrs. Barrow to hear anything Mrs. Kincaid might have to say, given the events of the prior evening, so I said, "One moment, please, Mrs. Kincaid. We have another person on the wire."

"What? What?" Mrs. Kincaid, who didn't have to worry about party lines since she could afford a wire all her own, sounded confused, which was a normal state of affairs.

"Please wait one moment," I repeated. Then I said, aiming for a tone that combined velvet with sharp spiky needles in an effort to shame Mrs. Barrow (which never worked), "Please hang up your receiver, Mrs. Barrow. This call is for me."

I heard a "Humph" and a click, and Mrs. Kincaid and I were alone on the wire—except, perhaps, for the woman at the telephone exchange, which meant I'd have to persuade Mrs. Kincaid not to carry on about speakeasies or arrests during her call. Allowing my head to fall back, I surveyed the ceiling and sighed silently, wishing *everything* in my life wasn't such a struggle. I mean, wouldn't you think I could at least have had peace on the telephone? But no. Not me.

Pardon me, please. I didn't mean to whine.

In my best, most syrupy medium voice, I ignored the frustration roiling in my breast and spoke again. "I can tell you're upset, Mrs. Kincaid."

"You *always* know, my dear," she sobbed. "It's your particular gift."

I glanced at the ceiling again, amazed that she should consider my knowledge in this instance as a sign of my supernatural powers, completely ignoring the fact that not only was she sobbing into the receiver, but that I'd *been* there when the speakeasy was raided. For Pete's sake, Stacy and I had darned near been arrested. But never mind. I told myself to be grateful for the gullibility of some people since it provided Billy and me with a much better income than we might have had if everyone else in the world had been rational.

"I do my best," I said modestly. Because I didn't want to discuss anything in front of Billy, I said, "But please, let's not discuss this on the telephone, Mrs. Kincaid. You never know who might be listening." I spared a moment to hope that Medora Cox, an old high-school friend of mine, wasn't working the telephone exchange that morning because I'd just maligned all telephone operators.

Mrs. Kincaid gasped. "You're right. You're so wise, my dear."

If that were so, I wouldn't have been in the pickle in which I found myself that day, but I didn't argue with her. "Why don't I visit you this morning? Would ten o'clock be all right with you?"

"Oh, yes, dear. Thank you so much. Please bring your cards. We can use my board."

It had been Mrs. Kincaid who'd been responsible for my career, in a way. She'd given Vi an old Ouija board, and I'd been making a living off it ever since. Therefore, out of a sense of obligation, I always tried to oblige her—and heck, I liked her, too, even if she was a dizzy broad.

"Of course. Try to calm down, and I'll see you at ten."

"Thank you so much, Daisy. I don't know what I'd do without you."

I didn't either. When I turned with a sigh to go back to the table and clean up the breakfast dishes, Billy looked displeased. My heart crunched. Gesturing at the telephone on the wall, I murmured, "Mrs. Kincaid."

"Yeah. I heard." He shook his head. "I don't know how you can put up with those people, Daisy. Most of them are dimmer than a burned-out light bulb."

"I know it. But they're rich. I guess intelligence isn't a prerequisite for inheriting gobs of money."

"Huh." He gulped coffee. "Too bad, if you ask me."

High Spirits

"I don't know." I stacked our plates and carried them to the sink. "It wouldn't make any difference to us if God required brainpower before he handed out money."

"I don't think God's in charge of money."

"Probably not." In fact sometimes I didn't think God gave a hoot about those of us languishing on earth. Since Billy already thought I was wicked, I didn't share that thought with him. I suppressed a whole bunch of sarcastic comments in those days.

"Listen, Daisy, I don't like you hanging out with Mrs. Kincaid."

Lifting a wooden bucket into the sink and turning on the hot-water tap, I said, "I knew that already, Billy. It's not news to me. If you can tell me how to make as much money as I do telling fortunes by working as a housemaid, I'll listen, but I've got to tell you I don't relish getting housemaid's knee." I was trying to keep the conversation light.

Billy didn't buy it. "All those rich people are turning your head, darn it. You're getting to where you aren't satisfied with your station in life any longer."

Dumbfounded, I whirled around, my hands dripping soap bubbles. *"What?"* I was sure I'd misunderstood him.

"You heard me."

"I heard you, but I don't believe you." I was so shocked, and his allegation was so absurd, I actually started laughing. It was an improvement over the stew I'd been in after Mrs. Kincaid's call.

"It's the truth." Billy didn't like it when I laughed. He started getting surly, actually, as if he knew he was being unfair but wouldn't apologize. "And it's not funny."

I should have been used to his moods by that time, but I wasn't. My laughter stopped as abruptly as it had begun. "It is too funny. And it isn't the truth! Darn it, Billy, you know as well as I do that performing for wealthy people is my job. I'm not

63

dissatisfied with my *station in life*. Whatever *that* is. You sound like an English detective novel, for crumb's sake!"

"Right. Is that why you go out with Harold Kincaid all the time? For your job? Don't be ridiculous. Your head's getting turned by all that money and all those expensive cars."

"Harold?" I goggled at my husband. "You're jealous of *Harold?*"

"I'm not jealous of anybody," snapped Billy.

He was lying. He was jealous of everyone who took me away from him. I knew it was only because he was in such sorry shape, but it sure could be a pain in the neck.

"Darn it, Billy, Harold and I are *friends!* I should think you'd be glad I'm friends with somebody like him. I could be running around with someone considerably less safe than Harold, you know." My face felt hot. I'm sure I'd turned a bright red.

Which brings me to an insignificant point. One of the troubles with being a redhead, even if your hair is more auburn than red, as was mine, is that you blush easily. Every darned time Billy started picking on me, I turned red. It was only one more burden to bear, and a small one at that, so I suppose I shouldn't complain.

He stared at me for several seconds. The expression on his face was worrisome, but I was getting angry and feeling burdened, and it didn't dawn on me what inference Billy would draw from my comment until he spoke again. "You deserve a whole man. I know it as well as you do, Daisy. You don't have to rub my nose in it."

My jaw dropped.

He shook his head. "I don't know why you haven't started running around on me before now."

"Running ar—Billy, stop it!" In spite of my drippy hands, I rushed to his side and knelt down. "I'd *never* run around on you! For God's sake, don't you know me better than that?" It

High Spirits

hurt like crazy to realize my own beloved Billy would actually consider me capable of having an affair with another man. "I love you!"

At that moment Pa and Spike came home, and I jumped up, glad our depressing conversation had been nipped in the bud. Spike, his toenails clicking out a fast and jazzy drumbeat on the linoleum floor, raced across the kitchen, his tail held aloft and wagging like an out-of-control metronome.

Pa shouted, "Good morning, you two lazybones! It's a beautiful day!"

Every day was beautiful to Pa, who was one of the cheeriest specimens of mankind God ever invented. My mood improved at once. "Hey, Pa. Did you get some of Vi's waffles before you left."

"Sure did. You don't think I'd walk out on a waffle, do you?"

Spike hurled himself like a torpedo onto Billy's lap, landing so hard the wheelchair backed up a couple of inches. Strong dog. Every time he did that, I cringed, fearing he'd hurt Billy's legs, but Billy never seemed to mind. He chuckled softly and held on to Spike while the puppy washed his face, searching for stray droplets of maple syrup, I guess. Pa and I watched the joyful reunion between the man I loved and his dog, whom I also loved.

When I glanced at Pa, he had a sappy expression on his face. I'm sure I did too. No matter how much Billy and I rubbed against each other—and we did it constantly—I couldn't not love him. When I compared the hunched, unhappy man loving his dog to the man I married, though, my heart nearly broke in half. In other words, everything was normal in the Gumm-Majesty household, more's the pity.

But that was neither here nor there. I went back to the sink, finished washing up the dishes, rinsed, dried, and put them away, and toddled off to the bedroom to select that day's spiritualist costume.

Sometimes, when I felt particularly guilty about my passion for fashion, I'd make the whole family matching outfits, thereby embarrassing Billy, who thought it was silly for us to dress alike, even for church. Maybe it was, but I'd already started on a new batch of pastel spring coats, including a snazzy little overcoat for Spike. That dog was going to look like a million bucks when I got through with him.

After glancing out the window to judge the weather, I decided to wear a black-and-white checked suit I'd made of a lightweight woolen fabric I'd bought on a bolt-end from Maxime's Fabric Store.

I loved Maxime's. They always had the best deals. I'd edged the collar and pockets with black bias tape, and when I wore the suit with a black hat, shoes, and bag, I was the picture of a dignified young matron with a spiritualistic bent going out to chat with ghosts on a crisp winter's day.

I'd recently had my hair bobbed by the barber Billy and Pa frequented, so I didn't have to fuss with my hair, thank God. I just plopped my black hat on my head, stuck a pin in it in case it got windy, and sailed out into the kitchen, where the men in my life waited.

"Think I'll stop at the grocery store and pick up some onions and potatoes before I go to Mrs. Kincaid's place," I said as I shoved my tarot cards into my handbag. "Vi said she needed both."

"Good," said Pa. "Pick me up a can of baked beans while you're there." Pa, a transplanted Yankee, loved his baked beans. He'd made a batch a few months before this, but he wasn't much of a hand in the kitchen, a trait he shared with Ma and me, and Aunt Vi considered baking beans beneath the talents of a cook like her. She was probably right, although those beans had tasted awfully good.

"Will do. I'm also going to the library. Anybody want anything?"

"No thanks," said Billy. "The new *National Geographic* came yesterday. I'll read that."

"I'm set," said Pa.

"Okay." I was hoping a new crop of detective novels had been catalogued. I was friendly with Miss Petrie, who worked in the cataloguing department of the Pasadena Public Library, and the wonderful woman always kept new mysteries back for me before they were put on the shelf. I was blessed in my friends, as I was in my family, two facts I tried always to keep in mind when the burdens of my life felt overwhelming. I wasn't always successful.

Have I mentioned before this that Spike was a cagey little critter? Well, he was. As soon as he saw me emerge from the bedroom all dressed up, he knew I was leaving the house, and he wanted to go too. He hurtled from Billy's lap and dashed to the front door, leaping around like a ballerina in his excitement. Watching his antics, Billy chuckled, which made my heart leap as joyfully as Spike was doing.

"Come back here, boy," he advised his dog. "You've got to stay home with me."

"Here, poochy, poochy," Pa called, waving the cup of coffee he'd poured for himself at Spike, as if as an inducement.

I knew better than to think Spike would prefer coffee to a ride in the motor. "I'll get him." I walked to the door and scooped up the dog and had turned to take him back to the kitchen when a knock came at the door. Still holding Spike, I opened it. At first I couldn't comprehend the sight that met my eyes.

"Pudge?" Pudge Wilson, the neighbor's boy, was clad in his Junior Boy Scout uniform and looking pretty natty considering he was nine years old, skinny, eternally scraped up, and freckled to a fare-thee-well. Pudge (I don't know who'd given him his nickname, but it didn't suit him) adored me, bless him. He also wore an unusually sober expression on his shining, freckled face.

Behind Pudge, whose presence, while unexpected, was at least understandable, stood a woman. It took me several seconds and a lot of brain twisting before I realized it was Flossie Mosser standing on my front porch. Nonplused doesn't half describe the state of my mind at that moment. I'm sure I gaped rudely in my astonishment.

Pudge spoke first. "How do you do, Mrs. Majesty?"

Good Lord. I knew his business was serious when he addressed me so formally. My attention snapped back to the boy. "I'm fine, thanks, Pudge. What's up?"

"I was walking to school when this lady asked me if I knew where you lived," Pudge explained, sober as a judge. "So I showed her the way to your front door." His face broke into an impish grin, and he finally looked like the Pudge I knew.

"Ah." Enlightenment dawned. Pudge took his Junior Boy Scout duties seriously, as did most Junior Boy Scouts and Boy Scouts in those days. What's more, it was only about eight o'clock in the morning, and he'd already accomplished his good deed for the day. No wonder he was grinning. He could spend the whole rest of his day being a normal, everyday nine-year-old boy. "Thank you very much, Pudge."

Pudge saluted me, bowed to Flossie, and bounded down the porch stairs. Flossie and I both watched as he skipped up the street, resuming his aborted walk to school. We turned and looked at each other at the same time. At once she focused on Spike.

"Cute dog," she said.

"Thanks," I said.

And then I didn't know what to do. All I knew for sure was

that I didn't want either Billy or Pa to meet Flossie Mosser. Shoot, if Billy didn't like my friendship with Harold Kincaid, I didn't even want to *think* about what he'd say if he thought I'd taken up with the likes of her.

Still, I didn't want to hurt her feelings. Spike started wriggling, and I was afraid he'd get loose. I reached out and touched her arm, which made her flinch, which puzzled me. "Wait here for a second, please. I'll be right back."

"Sure."

That morning Flossie wore a bright orange dress with bangles, a black fox-fur stole, flesh-colored stockings with high-heeled black shoes, and a black hat with a veil. Her costume most definitely wasn't anything a Pasadena lady would wear during the daytime. Or any other time, for that matter. Pasadena was a dignified, tasteful community. Flossie stuck out like a mud lark in a herd of swans. My heart lurched when I thought I saw black-and-blue bruises and swollen eyes behind her veil.

Maybe I was wrong. I hoped so, as I toted Spike back to the kitchen.

"Who was that at the door?" Billy wanted to know. He would.

"Pudge. He wanted to know if he could do a good deed for us before school." It almost wasn't a lie.

Both Billy and Pa chuckled. "That's Pudge, all right." Pa swallowed the rest of his coffee. "Get it over with first thing, and then cut up for the rest of the day."

"My thoughts exactly," said Billy.

Mine, too. "Here, Billy, hold your dog. He wants to go with me badly."

"Don't blame him," Billy's smile was wistful.

I gave him another quick kiss, wishing it were he leaving the house to earn our daily bread instead of me. Not that I didn't enjoy my line of work, but I'd have preferred being a normal wife. And mother. I tried not to think about never having children, but sometimes I couldn't help it. "I'll be home as soon as I can be, and we can go for a walk, sweetheart."

"That'll cheer Spike up."

True. I only wished our attempts to get Billy's legs and lungs working again did more to cheer him up.

As soon as I shut the front door behind me, I hustled Flossie to our Chevrolet, which was parked in front of the house. "Get in quick." I hadn't been mistaken about the bruises, unfortunately. The poor kid's face was a mess.

She got in, sliding into the machine with great care, as if more of her was bruised than just her face. I suspected it had been Jinx who'd delivered the blows, and my distaste for the man blossomed into full-blown loathing. "Don't say anything until we get away from the house." I don't know why I told her that. Probably too many crime novels. All I know is my nerves were twanging, and I didn't want Pa or Billy—or Jinx Jenkins or Vicenzo Maggiori—to see me with Flossie.

"Sure." She didn't sound happy.

When I glanced over at her, she didn't look happy either. Her hands were strangling each other on her Halloween-orange skirt, and she had her head bowed, staring at her fingers as if she'd never seen them before. Her whole aspect was that of a woman who knew nobody wanted her because she was no good.

My heart gave a hard spasm of sympathy. I told myself not to judge her too lightly too soon. I didn't even know her. And, although I had pegged her the night before as a woman more sinned against than sinning, I might well be wrong. It wouldn't have been the first time my judgment had turned out to be faulty, and that's putting it mildly.

Not to mention the fact that my imagination often soared into incredible flights of fancy. For all I knew, Flossie had just got herself lost and only wanted to ask me directions to the public library. Unlikely, but not impossible.

Besides all that, even if she did turn out to be only a victim—of fate or stupidity, or anything else—I didn't really want to get involved. I'd had experience in rescuing a damsel in distress once before, and it hadn't been any fun. It had also caused me no end of trouble and worry. I sure didn't want to get involved with another one.

The Chevrolet had been aimed downhill when we got into it, so I continued south on Marengo until Bellefontaine hove into view. I turned right, figuring neither Billy nor Pa was likely to catch us there, and pulled over to the curb. Then I turned to take a good gander at Flossie. And then I flinched.

"Gee whiz, Flossie, what happened to you?"

A big sob escaped her before a word did, and then it was, "Jinx."

I knew it. The fact that I was right caused no triumph to rise within me. "The lousy bum."

She nodded.

"Gee, kid, I'm really sorry."

She opened her shiny black bag and pulled out a hankie. Mopping tears from her cheeks, she said, "Thanks."

That took care of that. I didn't know what to say next. Neither, it soon became clear, did Flossie. I knew what I should do, however. So, as much as I didn't want to get involved in anyone else's problems, figuring I already had plenty of my own, I took a deep breath and spoke.

"Is there anything I can do to help you, Flossie?" It sounds mean-hearted and petty, but I was hoping she'd say no.

"I didn't mean to bother you," she said, sniffling pathetically.

I wanted to ask why she'd done it if she didn't mean to, but didn't, knowing such a question would be unkind. "Don't be silly. It's not a bother." *Liar.* But what's a kind-hearted, moral, upstanding spiritualist supposed to do when faced with such a dilemma? If I really *could* chat with spirits, I might have asked one of them to snatch Jinx out of this world and hurl him into Hades, but I couldn't. It wasn't the first time in my career that I'd wished I wasn't a fraud.

"It's only that you was so nice to me last night."

She thought I'd been nice to her? I'd only spoken a couple of words to her. Shoot, how did people treat her normally, if she thought that was nice? Another peek at her veiled face answered that question.

"I probably shouldn't've come."

Her voice had turned thick with tears, and my soft heart squished. I took it as an omen and groaned inside. I'd been gripping the steering wheel with my gloved hands so tightly that my fingers had begun to ache. With a sigh, I released the wheel and sat back. "You'd better lift that veil and let me get a good look at you, Flossie."

She shook her head. Even as she did so, she lifted the veil. When she turned to stare me in the eyes, it was all I could do not to cry out in distress. But honestly! How could Jinx do that to a person who must have weighed a good fifty pounds less than he did and was female, to boot? Both of her eyes were black and swollen, her lip had been split and was also swollen, and there were finger marks on her throat. "Geez Louise, Flossie. Why'd he do that?"

"He was mad about the raid."

"And he took it out on *you?*" My mind boggled. It did that a lot.

"Yeah. He gets mad and hits me. He don't mean it."

Oh, boy.

If he didn't mean it, why'd she look like that? "You'd better stay away from Jinx from now on."

Tears dripped from her swollen eyes. She dabbed at them with her handkerchief. "He's my fellow. I love him."

I gaped at her for several seconds before bursting out, "How can you love a man who does *that* to you?" I made an effort not to shout, but the words came out in sort of a bellow.

Poor Flossie shrank back against the seat of the automobile. Grabbing the door handle, she whispered, "I'm sorry I come, Mrs. Majesty. I should oughta go now."

I reached out and latched on to her arm. "No! No, don't go. Listen, Flossie, I'm sorry. I shouldn't have said that."

"Other people have said it before you." She sounded utterly defeated. "I guess I'm too dumb to believe it."

I didn't want to delve into that subject. "Have you been to a doctor?"

She shook her head. "I'm all right."

Like heck she was. Speaking slowly and thinking a good deal harder than I usually do before I say anything (sad, but true), I said, "Flossie, no man has the right to beat anybody the way Jinx beat you. It's against the law."

Was it? I didn't know. If it wasn't, it should be. I decided to ask Sam. Since I had to deal with him anyway, thanks to our accursed bargain, I might as well get some useful information out of the situation.

She sat like a lump, neither moving nor speaking, so I continued on the same theme.

"You deserve someone who treats you well, Flossie, not some thug who slaps you around."

This time she reacted. She shrugged. "Naw. I don't, really. I'm no good."

Shocked, I shouted. "Nuts to that! You are, too! Everyone's worth being treated well, for heaven's sake. *Everyone!*"

Her poor mouth, which had already undergone tortures, twisted up and she sobbed again. "No I'm not. I'm trash. Jinx knows it. I know it. Everybody knows it."

"That's nonsense." It would take more than a brief conversation in a Chevrolet, however new and shiny, to convince her of it, though, and I had other things to do that morning. Nevertheless, I couldn't just let her go back to Jinx. Not without a fight. Well, I didn't mean a fight, but . . . Aw, nuts.

Thinking fast, I said, "Say, Flossie, I've got to do a job right now, but we need to talk some more. You deserve better than Jinx. Jinx is nothing but a big stinker and a bully, and you're a good person whose shoes he doesn't deserve to lick, and I'm going to prove it to you."

Apparently, nobody had ever mentioned these salient facts to Flossie before or told her she was worth anything and that Jinx wasn't. If her eyes weren't such a painful mess, they'd have popped open wide. She only whispered, "Oh!"

"But I can't talk now because I have a job I have to go to." My hands went to the steering wheel again, and I engaged in another bout of hard thought. "Let me pop into the grocery store and buy some potatoes and onions and beans, and then you can go to the library with me."

"The library?" She said the word as if she'd never been in one and didn't know what a body was supposed to do there.

"Yes. You can wait for me there."

"With a bunch of books?"

"Books are better than Jinx," I pointed out.

She nodded slowly, as if she didn't quite believe it but was willing to give it a try.

"They have lots of magazines there, too."

She brightened slightly. "That's good. I like looking at magazines."

"I'll pick you up there as soon as I'm though with my job, and we can go to the Tea Cup Inn. We can have a bite to eat there and talk." The Tea Cup Inn was a little teashop on North Marengo, close to home. I was pretty sure Jinx wouldn't show up there. It was much too refined for him.

"You're awful kind, Mrs. Majesty," she whispered.

"Nuts. Call me Daisy. You need a friend, Flossie, and Jinx isn't it."

She covered her face with her hankie and her shoulders shook. I sighed, pressed the starter button, drove to the little corner grocery store and then the library, thinking all the way, which did no good, as usual. By the time I left Flossie in the reading room next to the magazine rack, I still didn't have a clue how to help her. She'd seemed to like the idea of magazines. Maybe she could find something interesting to read in one—maybe, say, an article on how to type, so she could get herself a job and give Jinx the boot.

Then I went to the front desk, didn't find any books set aside for me by Miss Petrie, toured the book racks, and picked out two new-to-me mystery books and an old favorite, *The Spiral Staircase*, by Mary Roberts Rinehart. I loved that book; it always comforted me to read it. And, believe me, I needed comfort right then.

As I drove from the library to Mrs. Kincaid's mansion on Orange Grove, I pondered how the heck I was supposed to help Sam Rotondo shut down Vicenzo Maggiori's speakeasy. When I'd worked that one to a standstill without reaching any conclusions, I concentrated on how to instill self-respect into a woman who had none. Sounded like a daunting task, and I was pretty sure I wasn't up to it—and I was even more sure that I didn't want to tackle it.

Chapter Six

Smiling broadly, Jackson waved to me as I tootled on past him and up to the front door of the Kincaid mansion. I was dying to ask him about his son in the speakeasy but didn't dare. If Sam ever found out I'd blabbed, he'd have my hide.

Our shiny new Chevrolet didn't look quite as out of place in such an elegant setting as our old 1909 Model T Ford had, but a Pierce Arrow or a big Packard would have looked better. Or Harold's Stutz Bearcat.

On the other hand, the Chevrolet was a lot better than our old horse, Brownie, who used to haul me around. Brownie had gone to his reward the year before, and I kind of missed him, even though he'd always been a reluctant beast of burden.

Since this was Southern California, even though it was technically still winter, vibrant irises and gladioli lined the semicircular drive in front of the porch. Mrs. Kincaid's gardening staff made sure things bloomed all year long. That day there were even a few early roses showing their pretty blossoms here and there.

Looking around and sniffing the sweet fragrances, I sighed happily, glad that my profession allowed me access to the homes of rich people since they were the only ones who could afford huge fancy gardens—and a full gardening staff. I enjoyed gardening, and our modest home on Marengo boasted a pretty little garden, but it sure wasn't anything like this.

Because I didn't want the Chevy to feel inferior in such grand surroundings, I patted it on its hood before I bounced up the huge marble steps, past the huge marble lions guarding the door, onto the huge marble porch, and pressed the doorbell. The door was huge, too, although it wasn't marble. I think it was mahogany.

Featherstone, Mrs. Kincaid's butler, opened the door to me. I adored Featherstone. He was the most elegant man I'd ever seen in my life, and was absolutely perfect for his job, as stiff and humorless as the marble lions outside. I admired him tremendously. "Good morning, Featherstone." I gave him a broad smile.

He never, ever smiled back. "Good morning, Mrs. Majesty. Please come this way."

The thing about Featherstone that impressed me so much was that he never showed any emotions at all. I'd been in a room with him when Stacy Kincaid was throwing a full-blown temper tantrum, and he'd stood there like a statue, not even watching the action, but staring over it with cool indifference, as if it neither interested nor concerned him. He was, in fact, rather like an automaton. He must have been the most perfect butler God ever created. Sometimes I thought that if old Featherstone ever died, someone ought to stuff him and stand him in the hall. He wouldn't look a bit different. I'd miss his British accent, though.

"Thank you, Featherstone."

His head high, his back straight, his gait steady, he preceded me along the hall to the drawing room. I did my best to perfect my own spiritualistic persona before we reached the door where Featherstone stood aside, held out a hand to accept my handbag, hat, and coat, and marched off to the hat rack while I entered the drawing room.

As soon as she saw me, Mrs. Kincaid jumped to her feet and rushed over to greet me, her hands held out to grasp mine. Unlike Featherstone's, Mrs. Kincaid's emotions were always right there on the surface, often spilling over.

A good-looking, slightly overweight woman, Mrs. Kincaid was always as beautifully groomed and coifed as if she'd just stepped out of a magazine. According to my friend Edie Applewood, who worked as a housemaid for her, Mrs. Kincaid employed a personal maid to do nothing but take care of her person and her clothes. Every single morning of Mrs. Kincaid's life, the maid applied her makeup, fixed her lovely graying hair (which I believe owed a good deal of its beauty to regular bluing), and made sure her clothes were cleaned and pressed. That morning Mrs. Kincaid wore a simply smashing day dress of royal blue silk.

She was also in a frenzy, which wasn't unusual. She had a good reason for it that morning since her daughter had almost been arrested the night before.

"Daisy! Oh, my dear, I'm *so glad* to see you! I've been in such a state!"

I could tell. "I'm so sorry," I purred, trying to waft to the sofa while she clung to me. It wasn't easy since she wasn't a small woman, but wafting was part of my act, so I wafted.

After depositing her on the sofa, I pulled over a beautiful chair, settling it across from her. I don't know what kind of chair it was—one of the French Louis-es, I think—but it had a medallion back and a plush red velvet-covered seat. I wouldn't have minded having a couple of chairs like that, although I'm sure they'd have cost more than our entire bungalow.

"Shall we start with the cards?"

"Oh, yes, please." She hauled out a hankie and dabbed at her eyes. It looked as if my entire day was going to be full of weeping females. At least this one paid me to put up with her tears.

With a quick move, she reached across the table and grabbed my hand just as I was about to withdraw my tarot deck from the embroidered velvet pouch I'd made for it. I glanced at her quizzically.

She swallowed, squeezed my hand, and gave me a deeply penitent look. "First I must apologize to you, Daisy. I'm *so* sorry for all the trouble you've been through on my behalf."

She didn't know the half of it. I smiled with gentle condescension. Clients loved that smile.

"I had no idea that horrid place was going to be raided last night."

That was a darned good thing, for both of us. If she *had* known and hadn't told me, I might just have had to find another best customer, which would have been a real pain in the neck.

"And Stacy said you were already in your trance when the police barged in." She squeezed my hand again, and tears seeped from her eyes. "Oh, my dear, that might have been so dangerous for you. You might have been trapped in your trance. And it's all my fault!"

True. I'd been feeling a little testy about it, too. Smiling graciously, I said, "The spirits treated me better than might have been expected. It's always tricky when a séance is interrupted." Her face was a study in misery, but I pressed on, figuring she deserved it for begging me to break the law in the first place. "My soul might have been lost in the netherworld forevermore." I bowed my head soberly as Mrs. Kincaid gasped, released me, and pressed her hands to her bosom.

"Oh, Daisy!" Her voice wobbled. "I'm so, so sorry. It was outrageous of me to ask you to risk yourself that way."

Now, here's the thing. I'd had a rough night, and it had been followed by a rough morning. I was sick of Stacy Kincaid, annoyed with Mrs. Kincaid, apprehensive on my own account, mad at Sam Rotondo, sorry for Flossie, and worried to death about Billy. Therefore, my mood was neither jolly nor forgiving.

Because that was the case, and because I couldn't shake the

selfish notion that many of my problems were basically Mrs. Kincaid's fault, I said in my softest, most serious and portentous medium's voice, "I must tell you that which was brought home to me last night, Mrs. Kincaid. Rolly has told me that I must divulge *all* to you. That speakeasy is an evil place. The people who operate it are vicious criminals who deal in crime and murder. The emanations are wicked there. Rolly hates it."

I took a deep breath and then went farther than I'd ever before gone when dealing with a client. "I don't want to worry you unduly, but I must say this. Rolly has spoken to me. Other spirits have spoken to me. If Stacy doesn't stop mingling with those people, something terrible will happen to her."

Madeline Kincaid's scream nearly ruptured my eardrums. I know I winced, which is very unspiritualist-like behavior, but I doubt that Mrs. Kincaid noticed, being involved in her own problems at the moment. "I knew it!" she wailed. "I knew it! I told her! Oh, Daisy, *please, please* say that you'll help us avoid this catastrophe!"

And here I'd been hoping she'd call on somebody else—say Father Frederick or even an alienist—to help her out with Stacy. I should have known better. Mrs. Kincaid didn't trust alienists, and Father Frederick always told the truth, which she didn't want to hear. She preferred to deal with me, a phony spiritualist. You figure it out; it's beyond me.

I started feeling guilty. I'd browbeaten, in my own gentle way, a woman who was extremely kind, if stupid. She'd always been nice to me, and she'd paid me heaps of money over the years. She didn't deserve having her legitimate problems added to by me, someone who was only miffed. Or maybe she did, although her heart was in the right place. All I knew for sure was that I felt awful for having upset her so badly. I put my arms around her, but she kept weeping.

"Oh! Oh! Oh! I knew it!" she cried. "It's all my fault! Oh,

High Spirits

Daisy! Oh, Stacy! I should have been firmer with her! I should have left Eustace years earlier!" Eustace was her no-good crook of a husband and Stacy's father. "I should have made her go to college! I should have done so many things differently! What's going to happen to her?"

Beats me. I clucked soothingly. Far from being comforted by my presence, Mrs. Kincaid seemed to be getting more hysterical. Increasingly desperate, I looked toward the door, praying that a maid or a friend would pop in and offer a suggestion. It didn't happen. I'd heard that one was supposed to slap the faces of sufferers from hysteria when they were in the throes of an attack, but if you think I was about to slap Mrs. Kincaid, the mainstay of my professional career, you're crazy.

At last someone showed up: Featherstone, who appeared at the door sort of like my own spirits never do. He must have been lured by the sounds of distress. I beckoned to him, and he walked over to the sofa, his nose in the air, as stiff as ever.

I stood up, hauling Mrs. Kincaid with me. And then I did something I'm sure Featherstone will never forgive me for if we both live to be a hundred years old. Thrusting Mrs. Kincaid at him, thereby forcing him to lift his arms and catch her or let her fall to the floor, I said, "Hold on to her! I'm going to get a posset!"

Whatever a posset is. But even if I didn't know a posset from a peacock, I knew my aunt Vi. She'd be able to give me something for her boss's frenzy. Forsaking dignity, I raced down the hall, ignoring a startled housemaid along the way.

Bursting into the kitchen, I slammed a hand over my heart and stood there, panting. Aunt Vi whirled around. She'd been doing something with flour, and it puffed up around her. "Daisy Majesty! What in the name of Glory are you doing, barging in here like that? And what's that dreadful noise? It sounds like someone let a banshee in."

"I'm sorry, Vi."

Vi lifted her chin, squinted, and aimed her gaze at the pantry door, through which I had just erupted. Muffled wails and sobs emanated from the drawing room. I pictured Featherstone, stoic in his butler suit, holding Mrs. Kincaid up by the armpits and gazing off into some middle distance, emotionally apart from the chaos surrounding him.

"What's going on in there?" Vi's face took on a worried expression. "Has something happened to Mrs. Kincaid?" She made a lunge toward the door.

"No!" I held out my hands and made patting motions to calm her down. "She's not sick or anything."

"Has that dreadful daughter of hers finally gotten herself killed, Daisy? If that child—"

"No!" Oh, Lord. "Please, Vi, it's all right. Mrs. Kincaid just got a little . . . upset, is all."

"Upset?" Vi's eyes narrowed and she put her floury fists on her hips. "Daisy Majesty, if you've said anything to distress that poor woman, I'll . . . I'll . . . well, I don't know what I'll do, but you ought to be ashamed of yourself."

"I am," I said miserably.

"What did you say to her?"

"I only said that if Stacy doesn't straighten up, something awful will happen to her." Defensively, I added, "It's the truth! You don't have to be a spiritualist to figure that one out."

"It was a cruel thing to say to a fond mother, Daisy Gumm Majesty." Vi's voice was severe. She walked over to the sink and washed her hands. "How could you? I'm ashamed of you."

"I'm sorry." And I was. It wasn't Mrs. Kincaid's state of upset that I was sorriest about; it was Aunt Vi's displeasure. She'd never said she was ashamed of me before. I can't remember very many times when I've felt so low-down and worthless. "But I can't take back what I said, Vi. And now I need a posset. Something to calm her."

Vi glared at me over her shoulder from the kitchen sink. "You wouldn't know a posset if you tripped over one."

"I know it." Humbled and abashed and completely cowed, I grasped my hands behind my back and stared at the floor. "Please, Aunt Vi? You know everything about food. Surely you know something to feed someone who's hysterical."

"Hmph. And whose fault is that, I want to know."

"Mine." My own eyes began to drip.

"I'll fix something," Vi said with a longsuffering sigh. "Just a minute." And she put the kettle on, Probably for chamomile tea or some other soothing beverage that I, being myself and a nincompoop, knew nothing about.

So I waited in the kitchen, thoroughly ashamed of myself and feeling miserable, as yowls and moans continued to come to us from the drawing room. I pictured Featherstone in my mind's eye. He'd never forgive me for this. Probably Vi wouldn't, either. And they'd both be right not to do so.

Redemption for Daisy Gumm Majesty seemed a long way off at that moment.

By the time I finally walked into the reading room at the Pasadena Public Library to fetch Flossie Mosser and attempt to rescue her from the toils of Jinx, I felt about as low down as a person could get. My spirits didn't rise appreciably when I couldn't find her in the reading room.

Mentally wiping my brow in relief, I turned to leave the library, Flossie, and her problems behind. I longed to crawl home and hide under the covers. I told myself that Flossie, who obviously wasn't a big reader, had become bored and left the library, deciding not to wait for me. It was *such* a good excuse, and it would have been *such* a relief not to have to deal with Flossie's problems.

But I couldn't make myself do it. Not after observing her unhappiness—and her injuries—that morning. Besides, I'd promised. A Gumm keeps her promises. My mother would have told me that this was exactly what principles were for: to make sure you do the right thing even when you don't want to.

Boy, I tell you, a strict Methodist upbringing can create problems that last a lifetime.

So I searched for Flossie. Everywhere. Upstairs and downstairs. Into the fiction stacks and through the non-fiction stacks. (I got stalled in the 92s, when I remembered I wanted to read a biography of the Fox sisters, but I couldn't find one). Through the children's room, where I admired some of the lovely prints hanging on the wall. No Flossie.

I finally found her in the restroom, applying makeup to her purple eyes. I regret to say that I wanted to screech at the woman for making me search for her.

However, since I knew my bad mood was my own fault and not Flossie's, I braced myself and smiled at her reflection in the mirror. "I'm back."

She must have jumped a foot, and she spun around so fast, she dropped her powder, which was compressed into a small, newfangled, purse-sized compact. "Oh! Oh, Lord, Mrs. Majesty, I thought you was Jinx!"

"In the ladies' restroom at the public library?"

Her terror was unfeigned, and I regretted my sarcasm. Poor Flossie was spooked, and obviously for good reason.

"He . . . he has his ways," she whispered. She started to bend over to pick up her compact, but I beat her to it, recalling her painful condition.

"I'm sorry, Flossie. I didn't mean to sound so snotty. It's been a rough couple of days." It was a gold compact, beautifully crafted, and probably cost somebody (Jinx?) a pretty penny. "Here. I hope nothing's broken."

She shook her head and jammed the compact into her handbag without looking inside to check it for damage. "It don't matter. It's just a compact."

I softened my voice. "How do you feel, Flossie?"

She started to cry, although I sensed she didn't want to. "Lousy." After digging in her handbag for a couple of seconds, she drew out what must have been the same handkerchief she'd used since that morning because it was crumpled and stained with makeup. "I'm sorry. I'm so stupid."

"Nuts. If anyone had beaten me like that, I'd be crying too. Have you taken a powder or anything?" In those days, aspirin didn't come in pill form. You had to stir powder into a glass of water and drink it that way. It tasted awful, but it helped when you had aches and pains.

Shaking her head, she murmured, "I didn't want to walk to the drug store and miss you."

That made me feel even guiltier, if such a thing was possible. Here the poor girl had suffered through an entire two-hour period of waiting for *me*, of all worthless specimens, without even taking some salicylic powders or even a cup of tea to ease the pain of her injuries. Thoroughly remorseful for a whole day's worth of bad behavior, I took her arm gently. "Come on, Flossie. Let's get you a powder and some lunch and a cup of tea, and have a girl-to-girl talk."

"You're too nice to me," she whispered, allowing me to lead her out the restroom door.

I only wished that were true. I wouldn't have felt so rotten. "I hope you weren't bored. Did you find anything to read?"

"Oh, yeah. Tons. My eyes was hurting a little, though, so mainly I just sat there."

I should have taken her inside our house, to heck with Billy and Pa, given her some medicine for her pain, and made her lie down and rest with a damp cloth across her forehead. Guilt gnawed at me like mice at a sack of meal. "Well, are you hungry at all?"

"Oh, sure. I haven't eaten nothing today."

Egad. I wondered if it were possible for a person to die of guilt poisoning. "I'm *so* sorry, Flossie. I should have made sure that you ate something before I left you by yourself."

We were walking through the main reading room of the library, and a man seated at a table glanced up and glared at us. I glared back, figuring helping Flossie was more important than whispering. Nevertheless, I gestured to Flossie that we shouldn't talk anymore until we were outside in the pretty garden in front of the library's arched doorway. "It was unforgivable of me to whisk you off the way I did and then abandon you. I'm sorry."

"It's not your fault. I coulda eat something while you was gone. I just didn't want to miss you." She sniffled wretchedly. "Nobody's ever told me I was worth anything before you."

Oh, boy. I was stuck for good and all now. I couldn't abandon the poor thing after a declaration like that. With a sigh, I opened the door to the Chevrolet and gestured for Flossie to get in. I stopped by a pharmacy to buy some powders before driving us both to the Tea Cup Inn.

Mrs. Geraldine McKenna, a childhood friend of my mother's, managed the Tea Cup Inn. She and her sister, Susan Fincher, had opened the shop about five years earlier, when Mrs. McKenna's husband passed away and Mrs. Fincher's husband ran off with another woman ("Which was the nicest thing he ever did for me, and I feel sorry for *her*," according to Mrs. F).

It was a tidy, genteel place, where a lady could eat a small meal without feeling uncomfortable. In those days, women weren't encouraged to be independent.

I parked across the street and Flossie and I waited for a couple of cars and a doctor's buggy to pass before we could

High Spirits

cross the roadway. I noticed Flossie looking doubtfully at the small, neat teashop.

"What's the matter, Flossie?"

"Nothing." But she hung back when I stepped off the curb to cross the street.

I turned back to her. "Aren't you hungry?"

"Yeah." She slowly stepped down to catch up with me, but I drew her back onto the sidewalk.

"Listen, Flossie, if you want to eat somewhere else, just tell me. We don't have to eat here. It's just that it's so close to home." For me. It wasn't for Flossie. At least I assumed it wasn't.

"It's not that." She drew in a big breath, straightened her shoulders, and took a strong step forward. She looked as if she were heading out to face a battalion of armed enemy soldiers, or a pack of rabid hounds.

Odd. I didn't say anything until after Mrs. McKenna greeted me, nodded happily to Flossie without appearing too startled or appalled when she noticed her bright orange costume or her veil-covered bruises, and led us to a quiet table in a back corner.

"We have a lovely cream of mushroom soup today, Daisy. It's very good with our special cheese sandwich and tomato aspic."

"Sounds good to me." I didn't like mushrooms but decided they were better than a fuss. I lifted an eyebrow or two at Flossie, who sat with her hands in her lap, staring at the table as if she were two years old and being punished. "Flossie? Is soup and a sandwich all right with you?"

"Fine." Her voice was small and tinny, more of a squeak, really.

"And would you care for tea with your luncheon?"

"Yes, thank you." I didn't bother checking with Flossie since I knew it was tea or water, and I thought a good strong cup of tea might boost her morale some. Although we did need water, come to think of it. "And would you bring a glass of water, please?"

"Right away."

I smiled at Mrs. McKenna, who was ever so nice. "Thanks."

"I'll have your luncheon up in a snap," she said. Casting a puzzled glance at Flossie, she trotted off to fetch our water, which she deposited before me.

I pushed it over to Flossie. "Dump those powders in here and stir it up, Flossie. I know it'll taste bad, but maybe it'll help make you not feel so bad."

Obediently, she withdrew the powder packet from her handbag, tore it open, dumped the contents in the water glass, and stirred. When she drank it down, she grimaced but didn't say a word. Her silence was beginning to worry me a little.

"Do you want to eat something else for lunch, Flossie?" I asked softly. "You don't have to have the special. Maybe the tomato aspic will hurt your lip." Another thing I ought to have thought of before ordering for the both of us. What was the matter with me, anyhow?

Flossie gave a quick shake of her head. A teardrop landed with a tiny splashlet on the back of her hand. "No. It's fine." Lifting her head, she leaned over the table, looked at me in what I can only describe as mortification, and whispered, "I don't belong here, Mrs. Majesty. This place ain't no joint."

It ain't no joint? Whatever in the world did that mean? I glanced around, observing our surroundings, trying to figure out Flossie's enigmatic comment.

She was right. It wasn't a joint. It was a trim, tasteful luncheon room operated by a couple of gentlewomen who'd lost their spouses and were trying to make a living for themselves.

I decided to clue Flossie in. "It's only a lunchroom, Flossie. I know the two ladies who run it. They've both lost their husbands

High Spirits

and are trying to make ends meet the best way they know how. Kind of like us," I added in an effort to make a connection somehow.

And then understanding struck me like a slap upside the head, which is what I deserved. Flossie didn't think she was good enough to eat at the Tea Cup Inn. The Tea Cup Inn, for Pete's sake!

I sat up straight. "Sweet Lord have mercy, Flossie Mosser! If you're going to tell me the Tea Cup *Inn* is too good for you, I might just have to speak to you by hand!" My father used say that to my siblings and me when we were acting up. I thought it was cute, and hoped it might make Flossie smile.

Fat chance. She blinked her purple, swollen eyelids at me and said, "Huh?"

Leaning over the table in my turn, I reached for her hand, whispering hard. "Listen, Flossie, you've got to get over this belief that you don't deserve the decent things in life. This place is just a little tearoom. You're as welcome in it as I am. You deserve for people to be polite to you, to treat you well. Heck, Mrs. McKenna and Mrs. Fincher only—"

"Who?"

"The two ladies who own the Tea Cup Inn. They only want to take your money in return for the food they prepare. Believe me, they don't care who you are. I'm sure that if they knew how awful Jinx was to you, they'd recommend you kick the bum out, but they aren't going to pass judgment on you or anything. They don't even know you!" I didn't, either, for that matter, but I didn't say so. I'd also fibbed. If the two Tea Cup ladies knew about Flossie's relationship with Jinx, they'd have been so shocked and outraged, they'd never have allowed her to pass through their portals again. But that was only because of the illicit nature of Flossie and Jinx's relationship.

Which brings up another point. That sort of thing has never

made sense to me. Sure, I know that if Flossie's character had been stronger, she'd never have become involved with the lousy Jinx Jenkins in the first place, but I didn't think the world should hold her accountable forever for one piece of bad judgment. Providing, of course, that she straightened up and eschewed her unsavory associates from now on. Whether she had the strength of character to do that remained to be seen.

Anyhow, Flossie must have been pretty unhappy in the first place to take up with a guy like Jinx. Heck, I'd never have met a gangster, ever, if not for Stacy Kincaid and her deplorable tendencies. The fact that Flossie had found Jinx even without an intermediary like Mrs. Kincaid or Stacy must mean that her life had been far rougher than mine from the beginning. At least that's my theory.

Nevertheless, my words seemed to make an impression on her. She stared at me as if I'd just told her I was the queen of the world and was going to turn her into a fairy princess. After several moments of stunned silence, she said, "You think?"

"Yes. I do."

"Gee."

Mrs. McKenna brought a tray laden with china teacups, a pot of tea, and cream and sugar. I knew, because the Tea Cup Inn ladies and my family were friendly, that they bought their pretty flowered teacups and pots at estate sales and the Salvation Army Thrift Store on Green Street, but nobody else knew it. Mrs. McKenna and Mrs. Fincher put on a great show of refinement and gentility, and the ladies of Pasadena loved it. The two women figured—and I agreed with them—that nobody had to know they were only trying to make a living, even though that should have been obvious to the thickest-headed of Pasadena's elite. I mean, what did they think? That people operated teashops for their health?

Which made me think of a brilliant suggestion. I hoped it

was brilliant, anyhow. "Say, Flossie, have you ever thought about acting?"

"Acting?" If she hadn't been wearing a veil, I'm sure I would have seen her eyes grow large.

"Yeah. I think it might be a good idea for you to act like you're worth something for a change and see if the behavior won't stick. Jinx is going to kill you one of these days if you don't skedaddle out of that situation."

She lifted her crumpled hankie to her nose, and I saw her shudder. "He's threatened to kill me if I ever leave him."

It was time for my own eyes to bug out. "He *what?*"

She nodded unhappily. "I love him, see, but he's so mean to me, and I'd like to get away from him, but he said he'd kill me if I did."

Good Lord. My mind boggled again. Why in the name of all that's holy would a woman remain in the clutches of a man who not only beat her when she was there, but threatened to kill her if she went away? And how could Flossie stand living the way she did? I didn't understand, which didn't make it the first time an aspect of life had baffled me.

Our lunches arrived and I dug in, not merely because I was hungry, but because I needed to think. I wished there was something I could do for Flossie, but I didn't know what it could be. It was true Flossie might be of help to me in the task Sam had set for me—curse the man—but I judged that relying on her might be perilous. It wasn't so much that I didn't trust her, but she seemed an awfully leaky vessel in which to place my trust. Shoot, if Jinx had threatened to kill *her*, a woman who, one supposed, meant something to him, he'd smash me like a pesky fly if I interfered with him.

I noticed that Flossie wasn't eating. I swallowed some tomato aspic and questioned her. "What's the matter? Does your mouth hurt?"

She shook her head. "Not much." She stuck her spoon into the soup and took a small sip, then bit off a tiny point of her crustless sandwich. After she downed it, she put her spoon down and gazed pleadingly at me.

"Mrs. Majesty?"

My insides sank like a rock in the ocean. "Please," I said, "call me Daisy."

She cocked her head to one side. "I thought you was Desdemona."

"Daisy's short for Desdemona," I lied.

"Oh." Pause. "Well . . . um . . . I wondered . . ."

Uh-oh. I sensed trouble brewing. More trouble, I mean. What I wanted to do was run away and hide, but that option was out. "Yes?" My voice was small. I berated myself as a coward.

"Well . . ." She swallowed hard. "Oh, never mind."

Oh, brother. Attempting a bracing tone, I said, "Nonsense. Something's bothering you. Please tell me what it is. Maybe I can help."

Idiot, idiot, idiot! What I really didn't need at that point in time was to shoulder Flossie's burdens. But I couldn't help myself. I felt *so* sorry for the poor woman, and I knew she needed at least one friend of the female persuasion. Clearly she wasn't getting anything but grief from her beloved.

"Oh, I couldn't ask you to do that," Flossie assured me. Famous last words. "But . . . well . . ."

I hope I suppressed my sigh.

"Well, maybe could you help me look more like you?"

I stared at her over a spoonful of mushroom soup. "Look more like me?"

Now here's the thing. I'm not bad looking. In fact, sometimes when I'm in full spiritualist regalia, with a little help from dark clothing and extremely light powder, I look pretty darned good in an ethereal, wafting-around-like-a-ghost sort of way. But I

High Spirits

couldn't imagine Flossie, whose vividness of dress and makeup were at the opposite spectrum from my demure demeanor, wanting to look like me.

I said, "Um . . ." And my imagination dried up.

She reached across the table, touched my wrist, which had helped the attached hand lay the spoon back on the plate, and instantly withdrew it. The gesture was so spontaneous and so immediately regretted, that my heart twanged. Again. Blast my sensitive innards, anyhow.

"You see, I look like what I am," said Flossie, "and that's no good."

I felt like a priest in a confessional. Not that I've ever been in a confessional, mind you, since I'm an upstanding Methodist, but that's what I felt like anyway. "Oh, Flossie, you don't . . ." But the lie wouldn't come. She *did* look like what she was: a gangster's moll. Oh, dear.

She was shaking her head. "Yes, I do. You know it. I wear these clothes . . ." She made a sweeping gesture with her hand. "And I wear too much makeup, and . . . well, I wish I looked more like you." She sucked in a deep breath and finished lamely, "But I don't know how."

It seemed to me that it would be a simple thing for a lady to wear less makeup and more sober clothing, but perhaps I was wrong. Perhaps, if one were accustomed to putting one face on for the world, it took some courage to change that face.

"Um," I said again. Big help. Taking myself firmly in hand and telling myself I was doing a good deed, not unlike Pudge Wilson, I tried once more. "I'll be happy to help you, Flossie." My head did an instant nose-dive into my shoes. I would.

"Would you?" I could see that she beamed under that silly veil. "Thanks so much." She dipped her spoon into her bowl and took a careful sip of soup.

She seemed so happy, I hated to burst her hopeful bubble,

but a salient point had just reared its big, ugly, and probably lethal, head. "You're welcome. But . . . well . . . um, what will Jinx think of it if you started dressing differently and wearing . . . um, more discreet makeup?"

Her head snapped up. "Jinx? Oh, he'll love it. He's always telling me I look like a—"

She stopped speaking so abruptly that I jerked as if I'd bumped into a brick wall. "Like a what?" I had a sinking feeling that old Jinx was going to spur me on to great heights of helpfulness, blast him.

Bowing her head, Flossie whispered, "He always says I look like a . . . whore."

I barely heard the final word, but it was enough. "Well, he's wrong," I said stoutly. "And I'll help you as much as I can."

Another salient point whacked me between the eyes. "Say, Flossie, do you have a place to stay?" If I had to take her home, I'd bite the bullet and do it, but God alone knew what that would do to my already-tarnished (in my husband's eye) reputation.

She looked up from the sandwich she was about to nibble. "Oh, I gotta go back to Jinx. He'll kill me if I don't."

Mental images of ribbons of machine-gun holes marring the tidy exterior of our home on Marengo Avenue barged into my brain and wouldn't go away. "But . . ."

Again she shook her head. "No. I got to. Honest, it'll be okay. He won't hurt me no more for a while."

He won't hurt me no more for a while? My resolve to help the woman strengthened. I did ask a question of her. I couldn't help myself. "Why did you take up with him in the first place, Flossie? He's obviously a very bad man."

She shrugged. "I didn't have no choice. My old man kicked me out after my ma died. He was on the booze anyways, and life was pretty ugly at home."

Good Lord. I endeavored to keep my mouth from dropping open. "Um . . . where did you grow up?"

"New York."

Aha. Same as Sam Rotondo. I'd always read that New York was a slightly unsavory place—unless, of course, you were rich. But that could be said of everywhere, I guess.

"Hell's Kitchen," she elaborated, then said confidingly, "I don't just call it that. It's what everybody calls it." She hesitated for a moment. "And they're all right. It's hell. At least the part I lived in."

"I'm sorry." I couldn't think of anything else to say.

"Yeah, well, Jinx, he took me outta that place, and it's prettier here. But he's still him."

I knew what she meant. Once more it crossed my mind to ask Flossie to help me with the case Sam had forced me to undertake, but again I didn't. Poor Flossie's heart seemed to be in the right place, but her physical self was definitely vulnerable, and I wasn't altogether certain of her moral character—she was with Jinx Jenkins, wasn't she? Besides, I'm sure I'd crack if somebody tortured me, and I didn't want to be the cause of any more torturing of Flossie on Jinx's part. Not, I'm sure, that he needed a reason to beat up on the poor woman.

"But Jinx says Mr. Maggiori will be setting up another séance, so I'll see you there, right?" She sounded positively happy for the first time since I'd met her.

"Right," said I, wishing it weren't so.

And then Flossie grabbed my hand, burst into tears, and said, "Nobody's never tried to help me before. You're so nice to me!"

Oh, Lord, another weeping woman. Depending on me. I figured that I was not only done for, but that things couldn't get any worse. Boy, was I wrong.

Chapter Seven

Flossie Mosser and I parted soon after that. Because I felt so sorry for her—and because I'm such a sucker—I asked her to meet me at Nash's Department Store the next morning at eleven. I figured we could have an hour to shop and, maybe, tone down her makeup, have lunch, and I could then escape.

Occasionally I ask myself when I'll learn to butt out of other people's business, but I seldom pursue the issue since I'm pretty sure the answer is "never."

At any rate, I offered to drive Flossie somewhere, but she said she'd catch the red car, which ran on tracks down Colorado to, I presume, wherever she was going. In a way I hated to see her go. Not that I wanted to offer her housing or anything. In truth, and I know it sounds mean, but I wished I'd never met her. But I knew she was going back to a vicious man who took out his anger on a helpless woman, and I hated to see her do it. Flossie was an okay kid, for a trollop.

Lest anyone accuse me of denigrating my own sex, let me say that I don't consider females helpless as a rule. It is absolutely true, however, that we have fewer rights than do males, and, therefore, have to maneuver considerably more agilely if we want to make a living. Look at me, if you don't believe me. And there's also no denying that we're generally weaker physically than men, which makes Jinx's predilection for beating up on poor Flossie even more despicable.

It was, therefore, with a heavy heart that I drove the Chevro-

High Spirits

let to our neat little bungalow on Marengo. I noticed Pudge sweeping Mrs. Ballard's sidewalk and guessed he was piling up good deeds so he could take a couple of days off or something. I gave him a jaunty wave, even though I was feeling far from jaunty at that moment. However, it never does to disappoint one's public. Anyhow, I figured the worst of my day was over, and I could relax and enjoy the evening with my family.

Wrong.

As soon as I opened the front door, Spike attacked the brand-new pumps with crossover straps that I'd got at Nash's for a song when they held their annual sale. That wasn't the bad part. I adored Spike and found his enthusiastic greetings always cheered me up when I needed cheering, which I did then.

No. What negated Spike's joyful salutation was the sight of Billy, Pa, and Sam Rotondo sitting at the card table playing gin rummy. They all turned and smiled at me. I suspected Sam's smile of being of a sardonic nature, but perhaps I was projecting my overall sense of abuse onto him. I doubt it.

"Hey, Daisy," said Billy, looking happy for a change. "Aunt Vi's cooking a pork roast for supper."

That, at least, was happy news indeed. "Wonderful," said I, thinking I should really count my blessings instead of dwelling on the unpleasant aspects of my life.

"And she asked me to stay," said Sam, reminding me forcefully of said unpleasant aspects. Nuts.

"Great."

I know my voice conveyed my weariness because Pa said, "Rough day, sweetheart?"

Stooping to pick up Spike, who obligingly licked my chin for me, I said, "You have no idea."

"Well, Vi's dinner will perk you up," Billy said.

Couldn't hurt, I suppose. "Right," I said, and carried Spike through the kitchen, where wonderful aromas floated, and on into the bedroom Billy and I shared. There I flung my hat and handbag on the dresser, plopped Spike on the bed and flopped down next to him, heedless of his little puppy paws on my black-and-white checks. What I wanted to do right then was go to sleep and never wake up. Preferably with Spike in my arms.

Such a happy fate was not to be mine. I knew it even before Vi knocked at the door a half-hour or so later and said, "You asleep in there, Daisy?"

Well, I *had* been, but no matter. "No, Vi. Just resting for a few minutes."

"Can you help me put dinner on the table, Daisy? We've got a guest tonight."

A guest. Right. Sam Rotondo was at our house so often that I sometimes, in my more cynical moments, thought to ask Pa if he'd adopted him. "Sure, Vi. Just have to change clothes, and I'll be right out."

"You haven't changed *yet?*"

Did I detect a censorious note in my aunt's voice, or was it my imagination? Lately I'd been suspecting everything anyone said to me as having more than one meaning. Probably my guilty conscience shading my perspective.

"Almost," I said. "It'll just take me another minute."

"Your mother telephoned from the hotel. She said she might be a little late getting home, but not to wait dinner for her."

And if anything could remind me that I wasn't the only one in the world with problems, it was the mention of my hard-working, selfless mother. "Poor Ma. I'll be right there, Vi."

So, much to Spike's disappointment, not to mention my own, I scrambled out of my nice checked suit and into a faded housedress with once-green flowers adorning it. Thanks to my short, shingled hair, all I had to do was fluff it a little after I rose from the bed, and I was almost ready to face the world when Spike and I exited my sanctuary. I kept telling myself I wasn't the only person who faced distasteful realities on a daily basis, but when I saw Sam Rotondo's broad back hunched over the card table, my internal pep talk fizzled significantly.

"I'll set a place for Ma," I told Vi.

"That's fine. I know she'll be here if those auditors finish up early."

"Glad nobody audits me," I muttered.

Aunt Vi sniffed. "I should say so."

I guess she hadn't forgiven me for upsetting Mrs. Kincaid. Yet one more thing to feel guilty about. If I hadn't already laid out several plates, my sigh might have blown the tablecloth off the table. I was happy to see Ma walk in right before we all sat down to eat.

Dinner was great and went a long way toward soothing my ragged nerves. There's nothing quite as wonderful as Aunt Vi's pork roast, which she serves with roasted potatoes, green beans, and Harvard beets. To top it all off, we had one of Vi's delectable apple pies, with which she served vanilla ice cream. After I'd eaten far more than I should have, I decided the world might be worth living in for one more day, if not even a little bit longer.

And then, as if he couldn't allow me even one evening of peace, Sam asked if he could speak to me outdoors for a minute or two. I glanced at Billy, who nodded his approval. He would.

Nevertheless, I stepped out onto the front porch with Sam. It was cold out there, and I'd forgotten to put on a sweater, so I hugged myself and said snappishly, "Make it fast. I'm cold."

"Want to go get a wrap?"

Oh, brother. If there was one thing I didn't need, it was a solicitous Sam Rotondo. "No!" I sounded positively waspish that time. "What I want is for you to leave me alone."

He frowned down at me. "We made a deal, Daisy."

I muttered, "Some deal. For the benefit of not getting arrested, I run the risk of getting myself killed and leaving my family bereft. And Billy with only his pension to support him. And I was only trying to do a good deed!" Can you tell I felt very abused and mistreated?

"Oh, for God's sake," he snarled. "You're not going to get killed. Just listen to me."

"I'm listening. Hurry up." Sullen. Very sullen.

"We got word today that Maggiori is setting up shop in Lamanda Park."

Lamanda Park was a nice little area east of Pasadena that had just been annexed and was now a part of the city. I was kind of surprised since Maggiori's last place of operation was outside the city limits, in the County of Los Angeles. "Really? Boy, that was fast."

"Yeah. Now listen up. We want you to set up another of those séances as soon as you can."

"I can't just call him up on the telephone and ask him if he'd like me to conduct another séance for him!" I protested hotly. "For one thing, I don't have his number. And for another thing, he'd probably think it was really odd."

"Don't worry." There was a sneer in his voice, although it was too dark by that time to see the sneer on his face. "According to my sources, he's keen on getting you back again. He really wants to get in touch with that dead criminal uncle of his."

"Oh, joy. Oh, rapture," I said, paraphrasing the Gilbert and Sullivan operetta Billy, Ma, Pa, Vi and I had seen last year at the Pasadena Presbyterian Church. Those Presbyterians have a lot of fun.

"Yeah," Sam snarled. "Both of those things. When they *do* call, I want you to tell us exactly when and where the séance will be held. Do you understand?"

"Of course, I understand. For Pete's sake, Sam, I'm not an idiot."

He said, "Huh," in a tone that let me know he disagreed with my assessment of myself.

So that capped my evening. At least dinner had been good.

The next morning before I left the house to meet Flossie, a trip I wasn't exactly looking forward to, I suggested that Billy and I take Spike for a walk. In truth, this meant that I'd hold onto Spike's leash while Billy tried to remain upright at my side, using my arm and shoulder as a prop. These outings were rather painful for both of us, although Spike loved them. He'd have loved them more, of course, if I'd allowed him to dash around off the leash. However, I didn't want him to get smashed by the occasional motor vehicle that tootled down Marengo, and I *really* didn't want him to poop on any of our neighbors' lawns. Most of our neighbors were swell folks, but I didn't want to push it, if you know what I mean.

It was slow going. I knew Billy had taken his morphine, but I also knew the drug didn't kill all the pain in his legs. And then there was the problem with his lungs, which were never going to recover from that blasted mustard gas. And whoever invented *that* noxious stuff ought to be forced to enter a room full of it and then sent straight to hell where he belongs. Taking the Kaiser with him. If ever a totally evil weapon was made, that cursed mustard gas was it.

On that particular February morning, the air was nippy, and it worried me a bit. "Are you sure you want to do this, Billy? It's cold out there."

"Aw, hell, Daisy, every year has cold days and hot days. If I don't learn how to live through them all, I might as well not live at all."

I *really* hated to hear him say things like that. Rather than take him to task or attempt to buck him up, which never worked and generally ended up with a snarling Billy and a weeping me,

I said, "Okey-dokey, let me roll your chair down the ramp, and then you can stand up." I didn't want him to attempt to negotiate the porch steps.

So, with a frolicking Spike's leash over my arm, I maneuvered Billy's chair down the ramp, and stood with a then-leaping Spike while Billy struggled out of his chair. I didn't help him because he hated it when I did that.

It was during those times, when Billy tried *so* hard to regain even a fraction of the strength he'd had before he went to war, that I pitied him the most. And if Billy knew that, he'd resent me even more than he already did. He didn't want to be pitied. He wanted to be whole. And I wanted him to be whole so much. But he never *would* be whole. And I felt like crying.

Naturally, since I'd been blessed with a strong character, no matter what Sam Rotondo thinks, and since I loved my husband even if he wasn't the man I'd married, I only smiled and let Spike romp until Billy had managed to catch what little breath he could and had stopped panting.

"All set," he rasped, and I knew the chilly air was bothering him already.

With a suppressed sigh and a bright smile, I went to him, he draped an arm over my shoulder, and we set off down the street.

Oh, here's another thing I suppose I might explain here. Pudge Wilson, who lived next door to us on the north, was a zealous Junior Cub Scout. He'd have positively loved to help Billy walk—all darned day, if he could. I'd had to take him aside one day several months ago and explain to him that, while Pudge's heart was in the right place, it wouldn't be a good idea to offer his services. Poor Billy had enough to deal with without a ten-year-old kid helping him walk. Pudge had understood, I guess, although I'm not sure. Whether he understood or not, he never offered to assist Billy, and I was grateful for it. In fact, I sometimes wondered if Pudge's self-restraint might count as one of his good deeds, but I never pursued the matter.

That morning, we headed south on Marengo. We lived on a hill, although it's more of a slope than anything, but even that much of an angle could play havoc with Billy's legs and lungs. We got as far as the Matthews' house to the south before Billy hacked out, "Better turn around now. I'm about done in."

For approximately the billionth time since Billy came home from that damned war, I suppressed my tears. "Right-o." Spike nearly pulled my arm out of its socket when he spotted Mrs. Killebrew's cat, but through the grace of God and my very strong shoulder muscles, I somehow managed not to joggle Billy. I did roar, "Spike!" which did about as much good as it ever did.

After barking hysterically for a few seconds, Spike decided he'd done his dogly duty and came to heel, his tail held high, his ears perky, and with, I swear, a grin on his face.

I think Billy would have laughed if he'd had strength enough. As for me, I expected to have an achy arm for a few days to go with my football-player's shoulders. Stupid dog.

Anyhow, when we got back to the house, Billy pretty much collapsed into his wheelchair. I felt awful for him—but I always did, so that was nothing new.

After I'd rolled him into the house, he said, "What are you going to do today, Daisy?"

"I'm meeting a friend for shopping and then we're going to take lunch, probably at the Tea Cup Inn." Although Billy hated it when I left him for work, he hated it even more when I left him for play. One more thing to feel guilty about.

He frowned. "Who're you meeting?"

"A girl named Florence Mosser."

"Never heard of her."

And I prayed he'd never hear of her again. Almost wishing I'd lied and said I was meeting an old chum from school, I tried to explain. "I met her through Mrs. Kincaid." Which was true, in a way. "The poor kid's had a rough life, and I thought it wouldn't hurt to hang out with her a little bit and try to cheer her up."

Billy said, "Huh," and I knew he was thinking it was my duty to try to cheer *him* up, and I should forget the lonely women of the world.

Naturally, I couldn't tell him the truth, but I really did try not to lie to him—most of the time. Feeling browbeaten, I said, "Honest, Billy, she really needs a friend right now. She's been through a very hard time."

"Yeah," he said, sneering, "there's a lot of that going around."

I knew what he meant. "At least you have a family. Flos—Florence doesn't have any family at all, and she's alone in Pasadena." Almost true.

His eyes narrowed, and I knew he'd spotted my blunder. Billy was definitely not stupid. "Wait a darned minute. Are you meeting this kid called Flossie? Is *that* who you're deserting me for?"

Nuts. I gave up. "Yes! Yes, that's exactly who I'm *deserting* you for, Billy Majesty! If you could meet her, you'd understand. She grew up in the very worst part of New York City, and she's with a goon who beats her up for fun, and she has nowhere to turn! She showed up at our door yesterday morning, battered and bruised, and I felt sorry for her! I didn't want to upset you, so I didn't let her in the house, but darn it, I'm trying to be a friend to her. Maybe even help her! Is that so wrong?"

His eyes were extremely narrow, and his mouth was set into a grim line. "She showed up at our door?"

"Yes." Uh-oh. I sensed I'd created another trap for myself and fallen right, smack into it.

"How'd you meet her?"

I sighed deeply. "Through Stacy Kincaid."

That made his eyes open up. "*Stacy?*"

"Yes. Flossie is one of the people Mrs. Kincaid is so afraid is going to influence Stacy for the bad."

"I doubt it's possible to make that girl any worse."

"You and me both. I think it's the other way around, actually."

"How'd she know where you live?"

I was *really* trying not to lie. "Through Pudge Wilson. I guess somehow she knew approximately where I lived, and she asked Pudge. It was Pudge who led her to our door."

And then, to my utter astonishment, Billy said, "Well, then, no. I guess it's not so wrong for you to try to help her."

I'm sure my eyes bulged. "It's not?"

"Naw. Go on. You're right. She probably does need a friend, and Stacy Kincaid isn't the kind of friend she needs." And then, darned if he didn't positively dumbfound me by trying to laugh. It came out more like a hack, and I winced. "Hell, why don't you introduce her to Johnny Buckingham?"

My bulging eyes stopped popping and widened like soup plates, I'm sure. "Johnny Buckingham?"

"Why not? Isn't he a captain in the Salvation Army? And aren't they always trying to save lost souls? This Flossie kid sounds pretty lost to me."

I stared at my husband in awe. "Billy," I said after a moment or two of pure wonder, "if you're not the most magnificent man in the whole world, I don't know who is." And I bent and kissed him, hard, on the mouth.

He was still grinning when I left the house.

I saw Flossie before I parked the Chevrolet in front of Nash's Department Store on the corner of Colorado and Fair Oaks. Couldn't miss her. If her improbably blond hair didn't draw the eye, her bright yellow polka-dotted dress might have done the trick. But the real clue was the bright yellow hat with the black veil. I'm pretty sure I sighed.

I truly appreciated Flossie's problems, and I honestly hoped (I'd even prayed about her the night before, which goes to show I'm not a totally selfish person) that she'd learn to get along in the world without bums like Jinx making her life miserable, but I also honestly didn't much want to be seen with her. Anyone looking at us would know that she and I came from different worlds. And if any of my customers saw us, I was in big trouble because my business depended on folks considering my behavior above reproach.

Silently cursing Sam Rotondo, I parked the motor, got out, sucked in a deep breath of still-chilly air, and moved toward Flossie, who was staring off in the other direction. When gently I touched her arm, she jumped like a spooked cat and let out a muffled shriek. I was glad for the muffled part, although I know I sighed again.

"It's only me," I said ungrammatically. I was pretty certain Flossie wouldn't mind.

"Oh, my," she said, slamming a hand over her heart. "I didn't see ya coming."

I think she was going to say more, but she didn't. She only looked at me. "Oh, you look swell," she whispered in an awed-sounding voice.

Glancing down at myself, I said stupidly, "I do?"

"Oh, yeah." The hand she'd slammed over her heart now clutched its partner over her breast. "I want to look like that."

"Um . . . like what?"

"Like that." She swept one of said hands in an arc meant, I suppose, to encompass my overall self.

"Oh. Well, I'm sure we can do something about that." I attempted a bracing tone.

Really, I suppose the poor woman had a point. I always made

sure I looked like a well-bred, well-dressed Pasadena matron. Mind you, I could never pass for one of the fabulously wealthy ones, but I was always neat and trim and wearing my best, most fashionable duds when in public.

That day I had on a suit I'd made myself—I couldn't afford to dress well if I didn't sew—of blue-gray worsted with an unfitted jacket, decorated around the collar and hip-level pockets with black braid. The sleeves were three-quarter length, and the skirt ended at a modest mid-calf, which—my calves, I mean, along with the rest of my legs—were sheathed in black stockings. My hat, which I'd also created myself, matched the gray-blue of the suit, and was decorated with the same black braid. Under the suit jacket, I wore a white shirt and a little narrow tie. Before I'd left the house, I'd actually thought myself that I looked pretty swell.

However, that's not the point. The point was that I always did my best to look subdued and natty, and I was sure I'd be able to help Flossie achieve a reasonable facsimile of the same idea. We could tackle her poorly dyed hair once we got her clothing under control, and her bruises would fade with time.

"Did you have anything special in mind?" I asked, taking her arm and guiding her through the front door of the best department store in Pasadena.

"Only that I wanna look like you do. You know, classy."

Classy, eh? Well, we'd see. "Very well. Come along." A thought occurred to me. "Um, do you have any money?" I sure didn't bring any cash with which to dress Flossie Mosser. Heck, I didn't even buy ready-made stuff for myself. I definitely couldn't afford to clothe a strumpet.

I didn't mean that. It was unkind of me, and I'm sorry.

However, I truly *couldn't* afford to buy anything for poor Flossie.

"Oh, yeah. Jinx give me some money. He's always sorry after

he roughs me up. He's real generous."

Generous, was he? How kind of him.

"All right, then," I said, opting not to comment on Jinx's magnanimity, "why don't we go to the ladies' wear section."

"Is that where you get your dresses and stuff?"

"Good Lord, no. I make my clothes. Couldn't afford to dress like I do if I had to buy everything."

"Honest?"

I realized she'd stopped walking when I felt a tug on my arm and turned to discover her rooted to the spot. Another sigh tried to force its way out, but I firmly held it inside. "What's the matter?"

"You mean that?"

"What?"

"You make all your clothes?"

"Sure. Why not?"

"Didja make that?" She nodded in my direction, and I presumed she meant the suit I had on.

"Sure. Sewing's about the only thing I'm any good at." With a little laugh, I confessed, "At Christmas time I made matching shirts for the whole family. Including the dog. My husband thought it was stupid, but I thought we all looked swell."

I stopped babbling when I saw Flossie start to shake her head.

"What's the matter?" I wasn't sure I wanted to know.

"I prolly ought to go home now."

"What?" My tone, I confess, was rather sharp. Darn it, she'd come to my *door*, for pity's sake. If she didn't want my help, why'd she ask for it?

"I-I mean, I shouldn't ought to be bothering you. I knew it yesterday. You got better things to do than waste time on me. I'll just go along now." She pulled her arm from mine, turned around, and began to hotfoot it toward Nash's front door.

Naturally, guilt took a big bite out of my heart. "Wait!" cried I, hurrying after her. I caught her arm again and another wallop of guilt smacked me when she yelped in pain. I'd forgotten about her bruises. "I'm really sorry, Flossie."

"It's nothing." She wouldn't look at me, which led me to believe she was probably crying.

Blast me! What's the matter with me?

Very well, this wasn't actually a job I faced with much enthusiasm, but I'd still more or less volunteered to help the woman, and I truly didn't mean to make her feel worse than she already did. Never mind that I didn't know how I'd managed to do it; I knew I had.

"Please, Flossie, what's the matter? I thought we were going to have some fun shopping for new clothes for you. Don't you want to do that?"

I heard a fairly loud sniffle and glanced around to see if any sales clerks were watching. Luckily for us, we hadn't hit the ladies' wear department yet. That was upstairs. But I knew a couple of the clerks who worked there, not to mention one of the elevator operators because we'd all gone to school together. I really didn't want to lead a weeping woman around a fairly grand department store.

Another sniffle. "Naw. You don't have to do that for me. I was just being silly. You have better things to do."

"I do not!" My stout declaration might not have been especially heartfelt, but I didn't want Flossie to know that. "I set aside this whole morning so we could have a nice time shopping and having lunch and stuff."

She finally turned around. I was right. She was crying. I let her arm go so she could dig in her handbag for a hankie. As she mopped her face under her veil, she said thickly, "You sure?"

"I'm sure."

I don't think she believed me, but at last she said, "Okay,

then. Thanks, Mrs. Majesty."

"Daisy," I said, trying not to grit my teeth. Flossie Mosser genuinely did need some friends. Jinx had her believing she wasn't even worth a morning out with the girls, for heaven's sake! Well, a morning out with me, which amounted to the same thing.

"Daisy," she said, coming across as a dutiful student.

"Good." Relief flooded me.

"But sewing's not the only thing you're good at. You're a good person," she said, still sounding a trifle thick. "And you're pretty, and you dress good, and you can talk to dead people, and all that stuff. You're . . . you're . . . you're the best."

Oh, brother. "Thanks. But I'm far from the best."

"You are, too."

We'd made it to the elevators, and I pressed the button. Deciding not to argue my merits with Flossie—she should talk to Billy for a minute or two, and she'd change her mind in a hurry—I said, "Do you need mainly day wear, stuff to wear around the house, or evening wear?"

The elevator stopped, and for once I was grateful for Flossie's veil. Vivian Blake, one of my least favorite people, was womanning the elevator that day. Not that there was anything really wrong with Vivian, but I'd known her since first grade as one of the biggest tattlers and storytellers in Pasadena. I didn't want her to get a glimpse of Flossie's black eyes, or she'd surely tell the tale all day long to anybody who got on her elevator.

I smiled charmingly. I was an expert at that. "Good morning, Vivian."

" 'Lo, Daisy." Vivian eyed Flossie's remarkable costume with an avid eye.

I decided the best thing to do under the circumstances was pretend to ignore her. Speaking to Flossie in a confidential manner, as if we were the closest of good buddies, I said, "I'm sure we can find something perfect for you at Nash's. I know your clothes are the height of fashion in Paris, but we're a little more subdued here in Pasadena." I gave a light-hearted laugh and prayed Vivian would spread a story about Daisy Gumm (which is who I was in the first grade when I met her) bringing a rich friend—or possibly a client—all the way from Paris, France, to shop at Nash's.

I don't think God will get me for that one. Vivian was truly a confirmed gossip. And Flossie, as we've already discussed, needed help.

Chapter Eight

Flossie and I left Nash's a couple of hours later, having spent a good deal of Jinx's money. More power to us, I say!

"You're sure Jinx won't mind you spending so much?" I asked for about the fiftieth time.

"Naw. He'll be happy."

From what I could see through her veil, Flossie wore a dazed sort of expression on her battered face. I don't think she'd ever had so much fun shopping before. I had, but that's only because I had lots of good friends and none of Flossie's problems.

"You want to go out to lunch now?"

"Sure. Thanks."

"Quit thanking me, Flossie. I've been enjoying myself." That was true for the most part. After the first half-hour or so, anyhow.

It actually had been kind of nice to be able to buy whatever struck my—well, Flossie's—fancy. And really, since Flossie deferred to me at every turning, it actually *was* my fancy being called into play. I'd never been able to do that before.

When we were through, though, Flossie was set—from the inside out. We didn't shirk our responsibility when it came to undergarments, stockings, shoes, and hats. No longer was Flossie to wear rolled-down flesh-colored silk stockings. No, sirree. Granted, one of the pairs of cotton hose we purchased was flesh colored, but they were thicker than silk and went better with the new and subdued image she strove to achieve. For the outer woman, we'd bought a lovely shepherd-check suit in brown and cream with long sleeves and a matching belt (in case she decided to visit town or ride a train somewhere during the day) and a serge and cotton number in black with a long, braid-trimmed collar that continued below the belt onto the small peplums. If it weren't for her bruises and her yellow hair, Flossie would look positively normal! We'd also bought three (three, for heaven's sake, but she said it was all right) housedresses for indoor wear, in case she decided to dust the furniture or anything like that.

When we exited Nash's, not loaded down with parcels since we'd had the foresight to have them sent to Flossie's address which I still didn't know since she didn't seem to want to tell me, Flossie was clad in her shepherd-check suit and cream-colored hose, discreet and sensible walking shoes and a broad-brimmed brown hat that went splendidly with the suit, along with a brown handbag to match. She'd slung some veiling over the hat so people wouldn't stare at her black eyes, but I figured that was only fair. She'd eaten up my advice on how the well-dressed, modest young woman should look. And darned if she didn't look like a well-dressed, modern young woman now! I was proud of myself. And Flossie, too, of course.

"Do I really look all right?" she whispered when we sailed out into the February gloom. Sometimes—often, in fact—Pasadena can get warm in February, but that day the sky was overcast and it looked as though it might actually rain, which didn't happen much in our fair city.

"You look wonderful," I assured her, glad to be speaking nothing but the truth. She did look great.

"I can't thank you enough, Daisy."

"You've already thanked me quite enough, Flossie." I said it with a laugh, but I meant it. Her overwhelming gratitude was getting me down. "You want to visit the Tea Cup Inn again? Or would you rather have luncheon closer to where we are?"

"Gee, I dunno. I'm not too familiar with Pasadena."

"Well, let me see."

We stood on the corner of Colorado and Fair Oaks, watching the cars zip past while I thought. I'd have liked to visit the library again to see if there were any new thrillers, but I doubted that Flossie would enjoy that. Besides, I didn't want her to have to walk a lot. As she'd tried on clothing, I was privy to several more of her bruises, and I knew she must hurt.

As far as I was concerned, Jinx Jenkins could roast slowly over a hot pit and still not reap sufficient punishment for what he'd done to Flossie Mosser.

Just as I was about to open my big mouth to suggest we walk down to Pico—provided Flossie was up to the jaunt—and dine at a Mexican restaurant called Mijare's that Billy and I loved, the musical strains of a street band smote my ear.

It was fate! It *had* to be fate!

Forsaking Mijare's, I bethought me of a vegetarian lunchroom near the corner of Colorado and Marengo Avenue and grabbed Flossie's arm. Gently, of course.

"Let's go down here. There's a little place where we can get a pretty good salad and sandwich." If I had a choice, I wouldn't eat vegetarian stuff, but that music meant only one thing: the Salvation Army band was out and about! And where the Salvation Army band was, Johnny Buckingham was sure to be nearby. This wasn't because he was a captain in the Salvation Army, although he was, but because he played the cornet. He'd played the cornet with the John Muir High School marching band, and he'd adapted his expertise now that he served in the army of Christ, or whatever they called themselves.

"Sure," said Flossie, ever obliging.

For only a second I dared wish that the rest of the world could be so accommodating, but that didn't last long. If the rest of the world followed my example, its citizens would all be

High Spirits

languishing in jails somewhere. Or consorting with gangsters' molls.

But I didn't want to think about that.

Our progress was kind of slow, due to Flossie's injuries, not to mention her new shoes, and I prayed the whole way that the band wouldn't abandon that corner for another one before we got there.

I needn't have worried. They'd attracted quite a crowd by the time Flossie and I drew near. Some folks were listening happily, some were even joining in when they knew the hymns being played, and a couple of the listeners were looking kind of guilty. I wondered if Johnny's flock would grow.

As we drew closer, Flossie's footsteps began to drag a little. At first I chalked this slowness up to sore feet, but when I glanced at her to see how she was holding up, I realized there was another cause for her hesitation. She didn't think she was good enough for the Salvation Army. The Salvation Army, for crumb's sake! Gee whiz.

The Army took in everyone. That's what they were there for. They took in all the folks who didn't fit anywhere else, and as far as I'm concerned, their operating principle was much more Christian than that of lots of regular churches, the congregations of which would flinch with horror if someone like Flossie crossed their sacred thresholds.

Heck, Jesus consorted with the lowest of the low as well as the highest of the high, didn't He? So there you go.

It occurred to me that it was His consorting with the low that got him into all that trouble, but I banished the thought and reminded myself that I was doing a good deed.

Anyhow, Johnny Buckingham had always been a sterling character. He and my cousin Paul were the tops when it came to moral fiber and character and stuff like that. But war does evil things to people (remember Billy?) and Johnny wasn't the only former soldier to hit the skids when he was shipped back home. Don't ask me why this is because I don't know. I understand Billy's physical injuries, but there are other, inner, soul-deep injuries that I'll never comprehend, ones that woke him up screaming sometimes in the night. I've never been exposed to battle and bloodshed, and I've never seen my friends shot dead or blown to bits. While I can imagine how horrid that might be, I don't *know* what it's like.

Anyhow, I knew for a certified fact, that the Salvation Army would love to get its hands on Flossie Mosser, and I aimed to introduce Flossie to Johnny then and there if I could.

Flossie's self-confidence was truly a fragile reed, but if she could find a good influence—Johnny Buckingham, for example—to replace the bad one—Jinx Jenkins, may he rot in hell—she might just survive her wretched beginnings and demeaning early adulthood and become a worthwhile woman. Maybe. Hey, a girl can always hope, can't she?

And there, as if he'd been sent by God Himself, stood Johnny Buckingham, playing "When the Roll is Called up Yonder, I'll Be there" with all the enthusiasm in him. I offered up a silent but sincere prayer of thanks.

"Um, I don't know if I wanna stand around and listen to a band, Daisy," Flossie said, whispering, although there was no need. What with the cornets and the trombones and the tambourines, nobody could hear anything she said.

"Sure you do," I said heartily. "And I'll introduce you to a friend of mine, too."

Johnny spotted me and lifted an eyebrow in greeting. I could tell he smiled, too, because his cheeks went all funny. Johnny was a great guy. I knew he'd be kind to Flossie.

She tugged on my arm a little. "Oh, no, Daisy, please don't do that!"

The poor girl sounded panic-stricken.

I tried to brace her up. "Nonsense. This is the Salvation Army. See that guy there?" I pointed to Johnny, who winked at us. "He and my cousin Paul were best of friends. They even went off to war together, but only Johnny came back. Paul was killed."

"Oh." Even over the band's lively rendition of the hymn, I heard Flossie gulp. "I'm sorry. That stinks."

"It sure does. Johnny was pretty much of a wreck for a while after he got home. But he found his own redemption in the Salvation Army, and he's been helping war veterans ever since." I stumbled a bit over the last part of that sentence because I'd been going to add *and other lost souls* after the *war veterans* part but thought that wouldn't be tactful. Flossie already knew she was about as low as a person could get. She didn't need me rubbing her nose into her abasement.

She said, "Oh," again and stopped trying to escape. I'm not sure if she decided she was interested or if she just didn't want to be seen fleeing from me, but she stood there beside me, docile as a kitten, and listened.

So did I. And I also surveyed Johnny Buckingham, wondering if I was doing the right thing. Johnny was a handsome guy, and he was a good man. But did he need Flossie Mosser and her problems in his life?

Then I chided myself for being stupid. I wasn't going to ask the fellow to marry her! I was only going to introduce them and hope Flossie might be moved to change her way of life. Clearly, she needed a change. And if there was anyone who could understand and assist in that endeavor, it was Johnny Buckingham. And the rest of the Salvation Army, too. For all I knew the Army was crammed full of former Flossies.

After the band finished that hymn, there was lots of applause from its listeners, and I heard money chunking into the tambourine being offered to the crowd by a pretty girl in a private's uniform. She smiled shyly at Flossie and me, and I dropped a dime into her tambourine. To my utter astonishment, Flossie, looking nervous, threw a wadded bill into the make-do offering plate. I wasn't sure, but I think I saw the number five on that bill. The girl must have seen it, too, because she flashed Flossie a lovely and gratified smile before she moved on to collect other offerings.

I'd just began to ponder how I was going to get Johnny and Flossie together, when darned if he didn't appear right smack in front of us.

"Hey, Daisy, good to see you." Johnny's twinkling baby blues hadn't missed Flossie. He was a shrewd cookie, and I'm pretty sure he'd taken in her bruises, in spite of the veil.

"Johnny, I'm so glad to meet you today. I was actually hoping I would. I want to introduce you to a new friend of mine." Turning to Flossie, whose cheeks were pink under the black and blue, I said, "Flossie Mosser, please allow me to introduce you to Captain Johnny Buckingham."

Johnny swept his captain's hat from his head, took the limp hand Flossie extended, and bowed over it. "Very happy to meet you Miss Mosser."

"Pleased to meetcha, too, Mr. Buckingham."

So. The introductions were over. Now what?

I said, "Um . . ." and ran out of inspiration.

Thank God for gentlemen like Johnny. He said, "How's Billy doing, Daisy? I keep meaning to go up and visit, but my days are kind of full. Still, that's no excuse. I'll make a point of visiting him tomorrow."

"That would be nice of you, Johnny. I know he gets lonely." Although, it must be said, he wasn't nearly as lonely as he'd been before the advent of Sam Rotondo. At least Sam was good for something, I guess.

"You still have that fierce guard dog?" Johnny said with a laugh.

"Sure do. Spike will bite the ankles of anyone who tries to sneak into the house."

Flossie turned to me, puzzled. "Their ankles? Why's he bite their ankles?"

"I was joking, although it's true that Spike would defend us with his dying breath. But he's really short, you see, so he'd have a hard time reaching higher than anyone's ankles. You met him, remember?"

"Oh. Yeah. I guess I didn't notice because you were holding him." For the first time since I couldn't remember when—since I'd met her?—Flossie smiled.

"Say, Daisy, we're dedicating a new chapel on Sunday, and I'd sure love it if you and your friend and Billy and the rest of your family could come and help us celebrate. The ladies are serving a covered-dish lunch after the service."

Go to the Salvation Army Church for a Sunday service? Would my Methodist God strike me dead if I did that?

"Er . . ."

"It's only for one Sunday." Johnny smiled his charming smile.

I glanced at Flossie and darned if she wasn't staring at me with hope on her face. Well, nuts. Daring reproof from my family and condemnation from my church, I said, "Sounds like a good idea, Johnny. I'll have to ask Billy and Ma and Aunt Vi, but I'm sure they won't mind. I mean, I'm sure they'd love it." Oh, brother. I could say the stupidest things sometimes.

Good old Johnny laughed out loud. "I think you had it right the first time, Daisy. But if they really wouldn't mind, I'd love to see you there." He turned to Flossie. "And you, too, Miss Mosser."

"Gee, thanks," said Flossie, again flushing around the blue and green bruises on her face.

"Here, let me give you a card with our address. We're really easy to find. We're right downtown here in Pasadena."

If there was a bad area in Pasadena in those days, and from what I've read about other places—New York City springs to mind—there really weren't, the Salvation Army had plunked itself right down in the middle of it. To me that pointed out the fact that the Salvation Army was a good place for Flossie to start rescuing herself.

"Thanks," said Flossie, tucking the card into her handbag.

"Thank *you*, and I hope to see the both of you—and Billy, Daisy—on Sunday." He gave us a wave with his cornet and went back to his fellow band members.

We watched as the band marched down the street where they paused on another corner and started playing "Onward Christian Soldiers," which, I guess, was their theme song. I'd suggested we sing that hymn in church one time the year before, and the choir director nearly had a fit, although I don't know why. I like the tune, and the words are positively stirring.

Lunch at the vegetarian restaurant wasn't half bad. They fixed us sandwiches with some sort of filling made with creamed cheese mixed with chopped walnuts and olives, and it was quite tasty. I thought I'd tell Aunt Vi about it. She'd probably scoff, but I decided I'd maybe just pop into the restaurant again one of these days.

Flossie and I parted after lunch, and I made my way back to Nash's, picked up the Chevrolet, and drove home.

You'd have thought I'd suggested we all go to the top of Mount Wilson and fling ourselves off when I asked Billy if we might attend the Salvation Army church on Sunday.

"The Salvation Army?" Billy squinted at me, and I detected suspicion in his expression.

"Yes. You suggested I introduce Flossie to Johnny Buckingham, and I did. You ought to be happy."

"Yeah, I suppose so. But why do we need to go to the church?"

High Spirits

"Johnny asked us. He said they're dedicating a new chapel or something, and Sunday's a special service. They're serving lunch afterwards, prepared by the Salvation Army ladies."

"Oh, yeah?"

I definitely detected a sneer that time. My heart plummeted, and I braced myself. "Yeah. What's the matter, Billy? Johnny asked specifically after you, and he said he'd be coming to visit you."

"Hmm."

Ma walked into the house just then, so I decided to try her. "Say, Ma, I ran into Johnny Buckingham today, and—"

"Oh, how is the poor boy?" Ma removed her hat, and I'm sorry to say she looked really tired.

"He's all right. Very happy now that he's off the bottle and into the Army."

Ma sighed and sank into an armchair. "Yes, I've heard the Salvation Army does wonders for people who have gone astray."

Gone astray. I liked that wording. It sounded so much better than *succumbed to sin* or *fell into degradation* and some of the other expressions I've heard. The way Ma said it, it sounded as if Johnny had merely taken a wrong turning in the road of life and managed to find his way back onto the right one.

"Absolutely," I said stoutly, thanking my Maker for my family. As bad as things were for me, they could have been *so* much worse if I didn't have my wonderful family around me.

Ma shook her head. "He and Paul used to be such cut-ups. It's such a shame about Paul. I don't think your aunt Vi will ever fully recover from that blow."

"I can't imagine how anyone could recover from losing a child," I said, beginning to feel a trifle melancholy, what with Billy scowling at me from behind and Ma sagging wearily in front of me. Giving myself an internal smack and a short lecture, I forged onward. "Say, Ma, Johnny asked if we'd mind going to the Salvation Army church this coming Sunday. They're dedicating a new chapel—at least I think it's a new chapel—and he asked us especially."

"He asked us?" Ma looked at me with a puzzled expression on her face. My mother isn't awfully imaginative, which can be good and can be bad. On the one hand, she can't think of a lot of alternatives to various problems and situations. On the other hand, she's easily led by someone who *does* have a good imagination.

I had one, and it struck then. "Yes. I think he misses Paul, too, and would like Paul's family to be there at the dedication. You know, I really think Johnny considers the Salvation Army as the organization that saved his sanity, if not his life."

That might have been laying it on pretty thick, but Ma's wasn't a suspicious nature.

Billy's, however, was. I heard him snort softly and prayed he wouldn't start a nasty row in front of my mother. I should have known better. Billy loved my family almost as much as he'd loved his own until they all died.

Lordy, that sounds terrible, even though it's true. His folks were both done in by the huge influenza epidemic that ravaged the country—I guess it ravaged the entire world—a few years earlier. At any rate, he'd never do anything on purpose to distress my mother or father. Therefore, that soft snort was the only indication of his less-than-rapturous approval of the Salvation Army idea.

"Oh, my," said Ma. "If that isn't the sweetest thing. He truly is a special young man, isn't he?"

"Yes, indeedy," I said, bracing myself for Billy's next sardonic snort. Again, I underestimated my husband. He said nothing at all.

"I'm sure Vi will be pleased." Ma struggled to rise.

Naturally, I felt guilty. Those days, I *always* felt guilty, even when I had no real reason to, which I didn't then. Shoot, my main purpose in herding all of us to the Salvation Army was to save the skin, if not the soul, of a poor, abused woman named Florence Mosser. I didn't see how even Billy could object to that, especially since he'd suggested it in the first place.

I found out how he could object when we both retired to our room to get ready for supper.

"It's Johnny, isn't it?"

I'd removed my suit and was hanging it in the wardrobe. Looking over my shoulder, I discovered Billy sitting in his chair, looking unhappy. "I beg your pardon?"

"It's Johnny, isn't it?"

His repeating the question didn't enlighten me any more the second time. Grabbing my good old once-green housedress and sliding it over my head, I said, "What's Johnny?"

"You're seeing Johnny Buckingham, aren't you?"

"I saw him today. I introduced him to Flossie. Is that what you—" My mouth dropped open and the words fell out of it, unspoken. If words had weight, they'd have clanked on the floor. "Wait a minute. Billy Majesty, are you accusing me of stepping out with Johnny Buckingham? Johnny *Buckingham?*" I couldn't believe he meant that. I stared at him, and incredulous doesn't begin to describe what I was feeling.

Billy had rolled his chair over to the window and was looking out into our backyard. The orange trees were bare, and the grass was brown, and the scene was as wintry as my soul at that moment. "I can't blame you, Daisy. You know I think you deserve a whole man."

Suddenly I felt almost too exhausted to support my weight—which wasn't a whole lot, in spite of Aunt Vi's delicious meals. Suppressing a mad urge to climb into bed and burrow under the covers and hide there for the rest of my life, I instead sat on the bed and stared at my husband. The husband I loved. The husband who frustrated me more than any human being ought to frustrate another human being, but whom I couldn't fault because of his own tremendous sufferings.

"Billy Majesty, are you crazy?"

He turned and gave me a sad smile. It was all I could do not to burst into tears. "I don't blame you, Daisy. I'm only kind of surprised at Johnny."

"You're surprised at *Johnny?*" I whispered.

"Yeah. Kind of." He lifted an eyebrow. "Although I can't really blame the guy. You're real pretty, Daisy."

"What about *me?*"

He lifted another eyebrow. "What do you mean?"

"You're telling me that you find it difficult to believe that Johnny Buckingham might have an affair with a married lady. But you wouldn't find it hard to believe that *I* might have an affair with another man?"

Billy shook his head, looking about as miserable as I felt. "I didn't mean that, Daisy."

I stood again and, hands on hips, I stared at my poor husband, whom I pitied and loved and resented all at the same time. "That's what it sounded like to me."

Another weary head shake. "Let's just skip it."

"Skip it? After you accuse me of running around with another man?"

"Aw, hell, Daisy."

"Don't you 'Aw, hell, Daisy' me, Billy Majesty. For your information, you're the only man I've ever loved. You're the only man I ever *will* love. And I'd never, *ever* cheat on you."

"I guess I know that."

"You *guess?*"

"I mean . . . oh, hell, I don't know what I mean. I mean you deserve a whole man, dammit, and I'm not one."

I kneeled at his side. The blasted wheelchair prevented me

from taking him in my arms. "Billy, when we got married, we promised each other it would be for better or for worse. I meant it."

"Yeah, I know, but I also know you didn't know that the worse part would be this bad."

"Oh, Billy."

When I finally crawled into bed that night, I had a vicious headache, a melancholy that weighed a ton and a half, and the no-doubt mad wish that I'd just die in the night and not have to face another day.

Chapter Nine

Naturally, such a benevolent fate was not to be mine. Billy and I hadn't even finished breakfast before Mrs. Kincaid called. She was, of course, in a tizzy.

"Oh, Daisy!" she wailed after I'd shooed Mrs. Barrow off the party line. "Stacy keeps talking about that Jinx creature, and she won't stop seeing him!"

The more fool she, thought I. I didn't say it. "I'm sorry, Mrs. Kincaid." Which was the truth. If Stacy would only straighten up and be a decent human being, my own life would be much brighter because I wouldn't have to accept these constant, irritating telephone calls from Stacy's mother. Not to mention having to consort with vicious, murdering bootleggers.

Looking at Billy and rolling my eyes, I mouthed, *Stacy Kincaid.* He grinned sympathetically, which was a whole lot better than accusing me of having an affair with Johnny Buckingham.

After consoling Mrs. Kincaid as best I could and promising to visit her that morning with my tarot deck—and don't ask me why she kept asking me to do that. I mean, if you're future's your future, it isn't going to change on a daily basis, is it, no matter what a deck of cards, however special, told you?—I hadn't even sat down to finish my toast when Spike forsook his place at our feet in his constant pursuit of crumbs and darted to the front door, barking his silly head off.

The headache I'd had the night before still lingered around the edges of my brain, although I'd taken a powder for it the night before and another one that morning, and I dashed after him, hoping to pick him up and clamp my hand over his muzzle. He had a deep, not unmanly bark, but it was too darned early in the day for that much racket with the remnants of a headache waiting to be jolted to life.

With said hand in said place, I opened the door with my other hand and suffered my next great blow of the day. Sam Rotondo.

He didn't even ask if he could come in, but barged right on in past me. I didn't slam the door, although I wanted to. "And good morning to you, too, Detective Rotondo."

He turned on me and frowned. *He* frowned at *me*, for crumb's sake! I glared back, wanting him to know how much I didn't want him there.

I got the feeling he knew. "I have news for you."

"What is it?"

Not a word of hello or a "how are you today?" or anything like that. All business, Sam and me that morning.

"Maggiori's place is going to open next Monday."

Instantly, I got a stomachache to go along with my headache. I stared at Sam over Spike's wriggling body.

"Have you set up another séance?"

I set Spike down and hoped he'd piddle on Sam's shoe again. He didn't. Rather, the indiscriminate hound jumped up onto Sam's leg, wagging his tail and yipping merrily, happy as a lark to see a friend. Huh. Some friend. Sam bent and petted him. And he hadn't even said good day to me.

"How can I set up another séance, curse you?" I spat at him. "And lower your voice. Billy doesn't know about this, you know."

"Yeah, I know. But you've got to get into the place. We *have* to find out where the leak is."

"I know, I know."

Defeated—and it wasn't even eight o'clock in the morning

yet—I slumped back to the kitchen, Sam at my feet, Spike bounding rapturously after Sam.

Billy looked up from the *Star News* and smiled at Sam. " 'Morning, Sam. What brings you here so early?"

"I'm headed up to Altadena to the sheriff's station. We're trying to get a line on some bootleggers operating in the area, and I thought I'd drop by and see if you wanted to play rummy tonight."

"Sounds great. And Joe's always up for a game."

"Where is Joe?" Sam looked around as if he expected to see my father hiding in a kitchen cupboard or under the sink.

"He always takes a walk after breakfast," I said. "Generally he takes Spike, but we were eating breakfast when Pa left, and Spike wanted to see if he could cadge some crumbs. He'd rather eat than walk."

"Can't say as I blame him."

"Have you had breakfast, Sam? I'm sure Daisy can fix you some toast or something." Billy glanced doubtfully at me.

I didn't appreciate that glance. True, I wasn't the world's best cook. And true, too, that I'd been known to burn the occasional piece of toast. But that was before we got our new electric toaster—with money *I'd* earned, mind you—and it was harder to burn toast in that than when you held the bread over the fire on a fork.

After a glance at the stove and another at me, Sam said, "No, thanks. I already ate."

As his stomach rumbled at that moment, I do believe he'd just lied to us. I didn't care, even if his lie was provoked by mistrust of my ability to fix toast. I didn't want to feed him anything except maybe my fist. Well, I didn't want to feed him *my* fist. I wanted some big bruiser to punch him.

Alas, such was not to be. Sam left a couple of minutes later, gesturing surreptitiously for me to accompany him to the door.

I went, but I didn't want to.

"Listen, Daisy, somehow or other, you have to set up another séance with those people."

I rolled my eyes so far back in my head, I'm surprised they didn't get stuck there. "How in the name of sweet mercy can I do that? *I* don't know where those miserable maggots live. *I* don't have any contacts with them at all, except through Stacy Kincaid."

As soon as that pernicious name left my lips, I knew I'd erred. Sam brightened instantly. "Say, that's right. The Kincaid kid will probably be able to get you access to Maggiori and his crew."

"Stacy and I don't speak," I muttered unhappily, thanking my lucky stars I hadn't mentioned Flossie Mosser. "I work for her mother. That's it. Stacy hates me, and I hate Stacy."

"Yeah, yeah. Do it anyway."

And he slapped his hat on his head and departed, stumping out of the house as if it were my fault I wasn't intimately acquainted with Vicenzo Maggiori and his company of criminals and cutthroats. Nuts.

I left for Mrs. Kincaid's house as soon as I'd cleaned up the kitchen and taken a leisurely bath. I don't generally take leisurely baths, but that morning I needed one. What's more, I put bubbles in the tub. If I hadn't started feeling really guilty, I might still be there, my body long since turned to prune. In truth, if I'd been asked which I'd rather do, conduct another séance for a bunch of hoodlums or beard Mrs. Kincaid in her den, I honestly don't know which I'd choose as the lesser of two evils.

Since I had no choice, I eventually dragged myself out of the tub and put on my most severely tailored and comfortable spiritualist outfit, a black suit with an unfitted jacket with a long waist, completely free from adornment. I wore it with a black cloche hat and handbag and black pumps with black hose.

"You look like you're going to a funeral," Billy commented as I made to leave the house. He'd rolled his chair into the living room and was sitting in the fireplace inglenook, glancing through the latest issue of *National Geographic*. He loved that magazine, probably because it took him to all sorts of far-away places he'd never get to visit. Even if a bucket of money descended upon us from heaven, his health wouldn't permit him to travel.

"I feel like it," I said, adjusting my hat in the mirror. "I'm not looking forward to this meeting with Mrs. Kincaid. She was in full wail when she called."

Shaking his head, Billy said, "I don't know how you do it."

At least he hadn't asked *why* I did it for once. I think he still felt a little ashamed of himself for accusing me of having an affair with Johnny Buckingham. Besides, he knew good and well *why* I did it, no matter that he kept asking the question. I did it because I had to. There was no way on God's green earth that we'd be able to afford our comfortable little bungalow on Marengo Avenue in Pasadena, California, if I didn't make more money as a spiritualist medium than I could at an ordinary job. That fact of life generally didn't dissuade him from carping at me, but, as I said, I think he was feeling a trifle abashed that morning.

"Sometimes I don't, either," I said gloomily as I exited the house via the side entrance, where our new Chevrolet stood waiting for me, bless it. The Chevrolet never scolded me or asked me why I did things. I loved that car. It was ever so much easier to drive than the old 1909 Model T that had to be cranked to life every morning, even on mornings when I felt about as much like cranking as I did like flying to the moon. Or visiting a distressed Mrs. Kincaid.

Oh, well. A woman's got to do what a woman has to do.

Jackson opened the gate for me, a big smile on his face. It still bothered me that his son played in a band for a crook like Maggiori, but I had enough problems of my own. Jackson's family was his own lookout.

I parked the Chevrolet on the big turnaround in front of the massive porch and slumped to the marble stairs. I glared back at the two plaster lions staring at me and plopped the brass knocker without enthusiasm. As if he'd been awaiting my knock, Featherstone whipped the door open and bowed his head at me.

Stepping into the elaborate hall, I mumbled, " 'Lo, Featherstone."

"Good morning, Mrs. Majesty."

"Is it? I have my doubts."

Featherstone never responded to my little comments, whether I spoke in jest, as I sometimes did, or when I spoke out of misery, as I did that day. What a guy. If he were any more professional, I expect he'd be working for a queen somewhere.

I followed Featherstone down the hallway to the living room—I beg your pardon. The *drawing* room—where Mrs. Kincaid must have been sitting on the edge of her seat, waiting for me to arrive. She leaped forward and ran at me like a rather pudgy, but small, Pamplona bull. I almost flinched and stepped aside, but my sense of survival took over at the last minute, and I braced myself instead. "There, there," I said as I held the silly woman in my arms. "There, there."

"Oh, Daisy!" she cried, wailing like a banshee at a Scottish moor. Or are banshees Irish? Oh, who cares? "Stacy hasn't been home *all night long!* I don't know what to do!"

My suggestion would have been to lock the door so she couldn't get back in, except that saying so might jeopardize my career. However, I couldn't bring myself to say nothing at all about Stacy's bad behavior. "I'm so sorry, Mrs. Kincaid. But the cards did say that something might happen, you know."

She let out a wail that topped any other wail I'd ever heard from her. "Oh, Daisy! I know! I know!"

"There, there," I repeated helplessly, praying Aunt Vi hadn't heard that screech in the kitchen. "Would you like me to get you a posset?" I think I had a death wish that morning or something. After the last time I had to get the woman a posset, I never wanted to face Aunt Vi with such a request again.

Thank God Mrs. Kincaid had other plans for me. She stepped back, wiped her streaming eyes with an already-sodden handkerchief, and said, "No, no. I must have you read the cards, Daisy. I *must* know what's going to happen!"

Oh, brother. For the sake of common sense, I said meekly, "I doubt they'll say anything they haven't said before."

Fortunately, her wail wasn't so loud this time. "Oh, Daisy, that's what I'm afraid of."

People continually amaze me. I guess plain old poor folks like me would be just as nutty as Mrs. Kincaid if we had money to burn, but I'm not so sure. I guess if you're born with it and have never had to think or scrape or do anything but wake up in the morning in order to live in the lap of luxury, this dependence on tarot cards and Ouija boards might make a little bit of sense. But not much. Those of us who have to work for a living know what's what. You work, you get paid. You don't work, you starve. At least that's my theory.

However, that's neither here nor there. I led the trembling Mrs. Kincaid to the sofa, where I tenderly lowered her and plumped a pillow at her back. Then I drew up one of those lovely dark red medallion-back chairs over to the table before the sofa, sat on it, pulled out the pretty little embroidered bag I'd made especially for the cards, and began to shuffle.

Because I felt compelled to do so, I gave Mrs. Kincaid a

High Spirits

gentle lecture as I shuffled the deck. "You know, Mrs. Kincaid, the cards can only tell you what *may* happen. They aren't absolute, and sometimes they're downright wrong. The best way to make sure your life is pleasant is to ensure that your surroundings are pleasant."

She nodded unhappily.

Sucking in a huge breath for courage, I then went farther than I'd gone so far in the Stacy Kincaid debacle. "If your daughter is causing you trouble—and I know she is—because of her inappropriate behavior, you might be well advised to take a firm hand with her. Sometimes firmness goes a long way toward straightening out a twisted path." I used the *twisted path* reference because spiritualists are supposed to say stuff like that.

I didn't know this for a fact, of course, because I didn't have any children of my own. However, I vividly recollect some of the lessons in discipline I got as a child and how much of an impression they made on me. Or on my behind, which amounts to pretty much the same thing. Not that I expected Mrs. Kincaid to throw Stacy across her knee and paddle her bottom, but a stern word here and there, or even a threat to withhold money, might help. If it wasn't already too late, which was what I feared. Somehow or other, I didn't think Stacy Kincaid would take well to discipline delivered so late in her life. And the brat was only my age, for Pete's sake!

Mrs. Kincaid sniffled miserably and mopped up more tears. "I know. I know. It's all my fault. I should have left her father earlier. I should have been more forceful with her."

I had a hard time envisioning Mrs. Kincaid ever being forceful.

"But Harold isn't like Stacy! Or his father! *He* turned out quite well!"

He did, indeed. He was one of my dearest friends, in fact. "I don't know the answer," I admitted. "But someone needs to take Stacy in hand."

Yeah, but who? Oh, well, she wasn't my problem. Thank God! The particular piece of reality brightened my mood considerably, believe it or not.

Therefore, without further ado or lectures, I told the cards—you've got to do things like that when you're pretending to be a spiritualist—that we wanted them to tell us anything they could about the future of Stacy Kincaid. Then I dealt out a Celtic cross pattern and read the results thereof. Mrs. Kincaid was in tears again at the end of my reading. But, darn it, that wasn't my fault! The cards fell where they fell, and I didn't have anything to do with it. Nor did fate. Heck, cards are cards. They can't think or predict or anything like that, no matter what people think.

I must say, however, that I felt a certain degree of satisfaction that their so-called prediction seemed so dire if Stacy Kincaid didn't straighten up.

Poor Mrs. Kincaid took no satisfaction whatsoever from the reading, although she thanked me lavishly, even pressing money into my palm. Because I felt guilty (my most pervasive emotion at that time in my life), I actually dared to put my arms around her and give her a hug. She evidently didn't mind because she hugged me back so hard, she darned near suffocated me.

She even led me to the door, usurping Featherstone's prerogative as butler. Sniffling all the while, she said, "Oh, Daisy, I can't thank you enough for coming here today. I know I shouldn't burden you with my problems, but you're *such* a comfort to me."

I was, was I? Perhaps that's why she was still crying, thought I to myself. Stifling my sigh, I lied outright. "You're never a burden, Mrs. Kincaid. I only wish I could offer some sort of advice to help you in your hour of need. Alas, the only thing I can do is consult the Other Side." What hogwash.

High Spirits

Anyhow, my conscience was somewhat assuaged by the knowledge that I actually *had* offered the woman some sound advice. She could either take it and discipline her daughter, or she could ignore it and allow Stacy to slide farther into the world of gangsters, booze, and illegality. It didn't really matter either way to me. The more Stacy misbehaved, the more Mrs. Kincaid would call on me. And, while sometimes her calls were inconvenient, they always resulted in lots of money. I had no reason to complain.

Until I encountered Stacy Kincaid tootling up the long driveway as I drove down it. She looked as if she were just returning from another night's debauch. When I saw her, my temper erupted just like photographs Billy had shown me of Mount Kilauea doing in the *National Geographic*. I think I honestly saw red for a minute.

Bringing the Chevrolet to a screeching halt in the middle of the drive so that Stacy couldn't pass, I rolled down my window and waved to the wretched female. She looked at me with the sneer she reserved especially for me. But she stopped and rolled her window down, too.

"Are you just getting home?" I demanded.

"What's it to you?"

"It means a lot to me, because it means a lot to your mother. I suppose you were consorting with those bums Maggiori and Jenkins, too."

"So what if I was?"

It's undoubtedly good that she seemed to be suffering from last night's overindulgence, or she'd probably have ripped right on past me and gone to bed, even if it meant sheering the door handle from the family's lovely new Chevrolet. But her eyes were puffy and red, and she looked as if she were suffering from a zinger of a headache. Her face had a kind of greenish tinge to it.

I was so mad by that time, I actually opened the door, got out of the car, and stomped over to the driver's side of her car, a glossy, wildly expensive Wills Sainte Claire Roadster.

"You miserable brat! Don't you know that you're killing your mother with your irresponsible, not to mention criminal, behavior? Don't you realize that your mother endures agony every time you act up and pretend to be something out of a Fitzgerald novel? Don't you understand that you're totally unprepared to deal with the kinds of people you're running around with now?"

"What do you know about it?" she asked sulkily.

"I know a heck of a lot more than you do, evidently! Do you know that Jinx Jenkins, that fellow you're so fond of, beats his women black and blue for fun?"

Her bloodshot eyes popped wide, and her mouth opened, but I stomped flat any words she'd been planning on saying.

"And don't you realize that Vicenzo Maggiori is a vicious hoodlum who'd have no more compunction to fill you full of Tommy-gun holes than he would stomp a bug? Have you see Flossie Mosser lately?"

"No. She hasn't been around."

"And do you know why that is?"

"I don't care." Boy, was she sulky now.

"You'd care if you could see her. Your precious Jinx blackened both her eyes and nearly broke her ribs the other day, and all because he got mad about that raid you and I were picked up in. And I was only there because your mother was hoping I could help keep you out of trouble."

"But—"

"But nothing! I'm through with that. *Nothing* can keep *you* out of trouble. You're just a moth drawn to a flame, aren't you? You won't be satisfied until you're killed in a raid, or beaten to death by your precious Jinx and your mother's prostrated with grief, will you? Well, I think that stinks! I think *you* stink!"

And with that last, not-very-professional sally, I turned on my somber black heel, marched back to the Chevrolet, pressed the starter button, pulled to the right of the drive, and high-tailed it out of there. I shot a glance at Jackson as I sped past the gate, and he was smiling broadly at me and giving me a thumbs-up gesture. I guess he'd heard my diatribe.

That probably should have made me feel better, but it didn't. I knew I'd behaved in a most unprofessional and wildly ill-considered manner, and I only hoped word wouldn't get around to my other clients. Or to Mrs. Kincaid. She might despair of her daughter, but I'm sure she didn't want idiots like yours truly yelling at Stacy in her mother's own driveway.

I went home after that and prayed nobody would call me about anything at all. I almost got my wish. Mrs. Bissell, from whom I'd received Spike as a gift after ridding her home of a ghost (it wasn't really a ghost), called and asked if I could work as a palm-reader during a party she aimed to hold in April, which was fine by me. I always picked up lots of clients when I worked parties. Billy only looked at me.

"Want to go for a walk?" I asked because that look of his made me edgy. "It's not as cold today as it was yesterday."

Naturally, since Spike was a smart dog, he started going wild as soon as he heard the word "walk." I should have spelled it, although it wouldn't have surprised me if Spike learned to spell next. He could already sneeze when I said gesundheit, a trick I taught him one morning at the breakfast table, profiting from a sneezing attack on his part.

"Sure."

So we walked. We got a little farther that day, probably because the weather cooperated with us and no cats crossed our path. We got all the way to the end of the block, where Marengo met Bellefontaine, before turning around and heading home.

"That wasn't so bad," said Billy, and my heart soared, although my arms ached like crazy.

"You're getting stronger every day, Billy," I said, and even as I spoke the words, I wasn't sure if they were true or if hope colored them.

"We'll see," said he. Billy always was more practical than I.

Nevertheless, I felt jollier for the rest of the day, especially after Johnny Buckingham came to call, and he and Billy had a grand old time chatting about the good old days, when they'd played baseball and football on the high school team, and life was bright and unbothered by Kaisers, mustard gas, gangsters, or the problem of making a living.

Amendment time. I felt better until after supper. That's when Sam Rotondo showed up to cast a blight on my evening. Not that Sam did anything, mind you. He was just there, a great, big physical reminder of the trouble I was in.

Chapter Ten

Billy, Pa, and Sam were having a grand time playing gin rummy, Ma was reading *An American Tragedy,* Aunt Vi was flipping through a cookbook, and I was playing the piano, softly so as not to disturb anyone, when a knock came at the door.

"Who in the world can that be?" Ma asked, looking up over the rims of her reading spectacles.

I popped up as if I'd been yanked by a puppet master, saying brightly, "I'll see!"

My heart pounded like crazy, and I prayed it wasn't Flossie Mosser or anyone else from the Maggiori clan, or . . . Good God! Could it be Stacy Kincaid, come to shoot me? Or Mrs. Kincaid, here to tell me never to darken her door again?

All those possibilities and more flashed through my brain, although I altered the one about Mrs. Kincaid. She'd call on the telephone and wail at me.

When I scooped up a hysterical Spike and opened the door, enlightenment didn't dawn. Utter bewilderment prevailed. I stood there, puzzled, staring at a large man in a dark suit and overcoat with its collar lifted in back and with a dark hat pulled down over his eyes.

"Mrs. Majesty?" His voice was an ebony rumble and reminded me of jagged, velvet-covered rocks and stuff like that.

"Yes?" I said, still puzzled.

"Mr. Maggiori says youse is supposed to come with me."

"M-Mr. Maggiori?" I stammered, feeling my knees getting

weak and my heart sink. I cast a panicky look at the gin-rummy table. Sam nodded at me. The miserable rat! I narrowed my eyes and glared at him, but he only nodded again. Pa and Billy were studying their cards.

"Yeah," said the man. "Mr. Maggiori's in the car. Waiting."

Oh, Lord. Oh, Lord. Oh, Lord. This time when I glanced at Sam, I gritted my teeth and hissed at him, *"Sam!"* He only nodded again. Darn it!

However, there seemed no salvation for me unless I wanted Maggiori's goon to toss a bomb into my beloved home, thereby killing my beloved family, so I reluctantly told the man to wait on the porch while I got my coat and hat and handbag. I shot a hateful look at Sam when I put Spike on the floor at Billy's feet. Sam only smiled benignly.

I ripped my housedress over my head and scrambled into a sober suit, quickly donned stockings and black shoes, pinned a black hat to my head, grabbed my black handbag and coat, and hurried to the front door. Turning and saying, "Be right back," in as chipper a voice as I could manage, I then scrammed it out of there before anyone could ask me anything.

A long, black car that went darned well with my outfit was parked at the curb in front of our house, and it felt as though I were headed directly to my doom as the big man and I approached it. The big man opened the back door politely, and said, "Mrs. Majesty, Mr. Maggiori." And, with one last glance back at the house I figured I'd never see again, I slid into the car. Vicenzo Maggiori sat on the other side of the back seat, smiling at me.

That's when I knew for certain I was done for. I'd figured all along that Sam Rotondo would be the death of me, and it looked as if this was the night. I was one unarmed female in a car full of three murdering hoodlums, and nobody'd probably ever see any part of me again.

High Spirits

Perhaps, if they shot me and took me out into the Mojave Desert to dispose of me by allowing vultures to clean my carcass, a coyote might run across my mouldering corpse and carry a thighbone to a nearby ranger's station or something, but I doubt that anyone would know it was *my* thighbone.

Or maybe, if they took me to the end of the Santa Monica pier and threw me into the drink wearing cement overshoes, my bones might wash up on the beach someday, but again, would anyone recognize them as *my* bones? Certainly not.

I was truly depressed in spirits as that big black motor rumbled away from my cozy abode on Marengo.

Mr. Maggiori's voice, horning in as it did on my melancholy thoughts, surprised me so much, I must have jumped a foot. "It was very kind of you to join me this evening, Mrs. Majesty."

I gulped. "Sure." My voice was barely a squeak, and it annoyed me. Darn it, it wasn't my fault I'd become involved with these blackguards! Stiffening my jellied spine, I said, "Certainly," much more forcefully.

"I want you to see the new place. We'll be opening up on Monday, and it would be swell if you could do a séance and get in touch with my godfather. He needs to know how we're carrying on the business."

The business, eh? Hmm. Still, it didn't look as if Maggiori was going to direct his henchmen to dispose of me. Yet. "I'll be happy to hold another séance for you, Mr. Maggiori," lied I, "but you didn't have to come in person. You could have telephoned."

"Naw. I like the personal touch." He pronounced it *da poisonal touch*. "Besides, I want you to see the joint. That way you can tell me where's the best place for you to do the deed."

Do the deed? Or, rather, *do dah deed*. Reminded me of the Camptown Racetrack. However, that's neither here nor there. "Very well," I said, striving to recapture my spiritualist serenity.

"I shall be happy to."

I can't remember a single other time in my life when I'd said so many lies in so short a period of time. Well, unless you count all the séances I've held and tarot cards I've read and Ouija boards I've manipulated. Oh, all right, I guess I'm a fairly accomplished liar—but only in business situations.

"Good. That's good." He rubbed his gloved hands together, and I instantly envisioned those hands tightening around my throat. Oh, boy, this was bad. Sometimes I wish I were as unimaginative as my mother.

However, we all got to Lamanda Park in one piece, and the machine stopped behind what looked like a perfectly respectable house surrounded by orange groves. There were a lot of orange groves in Pasadena at that time. In April, you could positively swoon from the fragrance if you drove near some of those orchards. It was heavenly. Which made the existence of Maggiori's speakeasy amongst those innocent trees even more of a blasphemy than the one in the sycamore grove had been, in my opinion, not that anyone cares about that.

Maggiori's goon was Johnny-on-the spot when it came to opening doors and stuff. He leaped from the front seat of that automobile and had my door opened before I had caught my breath. Then he rushed to Maggiori's side of the car and opened the door for him. At least he'd opened mine first.

"Right this way, Mrs. Majesty," said Maggiori, taking my arm and guiding me gently through the back door. Although I felt like yanking my arm from his grasp, I didn't, thereby demonstrating that I can occasionally control myself.

The same goon who'd met Harold Kincaid and me at the door of the former speakeasy, met Maggiori, his henchman, and me at the door of this one. He must have been watching through the peephole because he had the door open before we'd reached it. Boy, were these guys organized! The Pasadena city government might want to take lessons.

"Right this way, Mrs. Majesty."

"Thank you," I mumbled as, feet dragging, I reluctantly crossed the threshold. Wasn't there something in *Dracula* about a person not being vulnerable to the vampire's fangs until she or he had walked into the count's castle of her or his own accord? I think so, and I felt kind of like Jonathan Harker must have felt when he'd entered Dracula's castle on that long-ago night. Except that Jonathan Harker didn't have a clue that the count was an evil so-and-so, and I *knew* these guys were. The more fool me, I reckon.

"Let me show you around." Maggiori, like Count Dracula, sounded perfectly at ease. "Would you like to take off your hat and coat first?"

How polite. "Um . . . no, thanks. I really can't stay long." Even if I had to walk the seven or eight miles home in the pitch-black of a cold February evening.

"Right. Well, I'll just show you around a bit then."

"Thank you."

My heart thundered like mad as he led me through that place. Yet there was nothing remarkable about it, really. It looked as if it might have been a farmhouse once upon a time. Probably the people who'd planted the orange groves had lived there. It looked to me as if a couple of walls had been knocked out to create what would probably be a dance floor on Monday night, and a long shiny bar ran along one wall of that room. They must have pinched it from the old place after the police had left. Another few rooms were, I suppose, where people could gather, drink, and chat if they felt like it because several round tables resided in them, all of which had chairs upended on them.

"And this here is my office," Maggiori said, and he opened a door.

I'd just peeked inside, when I heard a delighted shriek that nearly gave me a heart attack. Slamming a hand over my cheek, I prayed my heart wasn't weak like Pa's.

"Daisy!"

And darned if Flossie Mosser wasn't dashing up to me. She stopped short right in front of me, apparently realized her behavior might not be approved of by all present, and cast a frightened glance at Maggiori. "I'm sorry, Mr. Maggiori. I'm just so . . . happy to see Mrs. Majesty again."

Thank the good Lord, Maggiori was feeling benevolent that evening. Rather than telling the goon to haul Flossie out to the orange grove and shoot her, he only chuckled. The sound he made reminded me of rough pebbles rolling around in a velvet-lined box. A black, velvet-lined box.

In order to spare Flossie any possible repercussions of her happy outburst, I pasted a huge smile on my face and reached out to her. "Flossie! How nice to see you again!" I'd already lost count of the lies I'd told that night. And really, in the overall scheme of things, that wasn't a big lie. I was happier to see Flossie than anyone else present.

She threw her arms around me and gave me a big hug. I hugged her back, resigned to my fate. When I glanced over her shoulder, I saw Jinx Jenkins scowling at the both of us, so I put more enthusiasm into my own hug.

"How are you, Flossie?"

"I'm swell, thanks."

She didn't look swell, although her bruises were more yellow and green than black and blue now, and the puffiness around her black eyes had gone down. With another glance over her shoulder, I saw Jinx still scowling malevolently, and whispered, "You probably need to get back to him now." I jerked my head so she'd know to whom I was referring.

Poor Flossie. She wasn't the brightest candle in the box, as I

High Spirits

may have mentioned. It took her a few seconds to figure out what I was trying to tell her, and it wasn't until the despicable Jinx hollered, "Floss! Get your butt over here," that she jumped like a frightened hare and scurried back to her man. Huh. Some man.

To my horror, I looked at Maggiori and discovered him scowling, too. When he said, "Watch your manners, Jinx. There's ladies present," I almost fainted with relief.

A telephone jangled somewhere in the distance, but I didn't pay much attention until another of Maggiori's underlings sidled up to him and said, "It's him, boss."

Giving a minuscule nod, Maggiori said, "I'll take it in the 'phone room." He turned to me. "You just look around, Mrs. Majesty. I was thinking this room would be best for the séance 'cause it's got soundproof walls, but you know better than me."

Maybe. We'd see.

So Maggiori sloped off with his minion and I, deciding I was doomed anyway, decided to snoop around a little bit on my own. Heck, the big boss had given me permission, hadn't he? And since there was no other way to know who "him" was who'd called, it might be a good idea, if not a wise one, to see if I could overhear something of Maggiori's conversation.

Therefore, I pretended to be fascinated by the lush decorations in the various rooms while trailing several feet behind Maggiori. The telephone room proved to be a nook reserved for the magical invention located just underneath the staircase leading to the upper rooms. Nobody'd said anything about what went on upstairs, but I figured no one would mind if I examined the staircase a little. I didn't hear much of the conversation.

"Maggiori here."
Silence.
"Yeah. Monday."
Silence.

145

"Right. You know what to do when you hear about another raid."

Silence.

"You'll get paid, dammit. Quit whining."

Silence.

"I don't give a good God damn if you lose your job on the force. I'm paying better than the damned *law-enforcement* people do, and don't you forget it." He said the words *law enforcement* as if he thought they represented a lousy joke.

A law-enforcement person? Was the guy on the other end of the wire a *policeman?* Mercy sakes. I guess that would explain why the police always found Maggiori more or less ready any time a raid was planned, wouldn't it?

But who could the culprit be?

I wandered away from the 'phone room, figuring I'd better not press my luck, my mind spinning in circles like a whirlwind.

Maybe the rat wasn't a policeman. It could be a deputy sheriff, I suppose. Or perhaps it was someone who merely worked for the police or sheriff's department. A clerk or a secretary or a switchboard operator—someone like that.

Would a clerk or a secretary or a switchboard operator have inside information like when the cops planned a raid? What the heck did I know about that sort of thing?

Bother.

Well, at least I had something to tell Sam Rotondo, providing I got home in one piece. It looked as though I would because right after I made it back to the room where Flossie and Jinx still sat, Maggiori joined us, rubbing his hands in a satisfied manner, and smiling a smile that might have looked friendly on somebody else.

"Well, that's taken care of." I presumed he was talking about the telephone call. "You wanna see anything else, Mrs. Majesty?"

"Um . . . I don't think so. Thanks."

"Sure you won't have a drink?"

Good Lord, no! "No, thank you. I need to get home."

"Good. Then I'll take ya."

I prayed he meant it.

Before Maggiori could escort me back to my family's precious little bungalow on South Marengo Avenue, Flossie, eluding Jinx once more, cornered me.

"It's so good to see you again, Daisy."

"You, too, Flossie. Say, are you going to the Salvation Army church on Sunday?" I hoped so. And I hoped she'd see the error of her ways, join the Army, and leave Jinx, too. Hey, without hope, the world would be a pretty dismal place.

Shooting a quick glance over her shoulder, she said, "I guess so. I'd really like to." She focused on me again. "Are you going?"

"My whole family's going," I declared, although nothing had been decided yet. My family still thought I was nuts for asking, actually.

"Say, Daisy." Flossie looked down and began toeing the thick rug at our feet. "Um, you wouldn't want to get together again for lunch or something, would you?" As if she anticipated a negative response, she hurried to say, "I know you probably don't want to, but I just thought—"

"I'd love to," I lied nobly, breaking into her apology since I just couldn't bear it. The poor woman *really* needed an infusion of self-respect.

And then, by golly, Mr. Maggiori, his goon, and his chauffeur drove me home. Maggiori and I discussed the séance, and I told him that his office would be fine for the setting of same. He seemed pleased, thank God. The goon escorted me to my front door, where Spike, who has the sharpest ears in the universe, madly barked on the other side.

Turning to the goon, I said, "Thanks."

"It's nothin'," he said. I think he meant it.

He waited until I'd opened the door, eluded Spike, and stepped inside before he turned and retreated to Maggiori's motor.

I bent down to pet Spike and tell him what a good doggy he was to announce all visitors in so forthright and audible a manner. When I stood up again, it looked as if the entire masculine contingent of my family was ranged against me. Plus Sam. I think I staggered back a step. I know I gasped.

Billy and Pa were frowning at me. Sam was looking neutral, but he was so big and so . . . oh, I don't know . . . there, that he might have been a monster out of a fairy tale come to strike me dead.

"What?" I asked nervously. "Why are you all staring at me like that?"

Billy spoke first. "Who the devil was that?"

"Um . . . you mean that guy at the door?"

Stupid question. I shot a frantic glance at Sam, who appeared at that moment to have turned into some kind of immovable object. A block of granite, for instance.

"Daisy," Pa said softly, in his most reasonable voice—instantly, my eyes teared up. "Do you think it's wise to get into automobiles with other men at night? It doesn't look good, you know. It looks as if you're not respecting your marriage vows."

Billy stared at me, as grim-faced as ever I'd seen him.

Tears spilled over and ran down my face. Turning again to Sam, I cried, "*Curse* you, Sam Rotondo! This is all your fault!"

"Daisy!" Pa was shocked.

Billy's eyebrows lowered into a fierce V, and he looked first at me and then at Sam. "What's Sam got to do with it?"

Furious, ashamed, bitter, and miserable, I said the first thing that popped into my addled brain. "Oh, Lord, Billy, you're not going to accuse me of having an affair with *Sam* now, are you?"

I could have shot myself as soon as the words hit the air. Unfortunately, all of the guns and ammunition Billy had brought back from the so-called Great War were locked up.

"Daisy!" Pa was even *more* shocked.

"Darn it!" I wailed. "This isn't fair!"

At last, after far too many minutes during which he stood still and did nothing, Sam stepped forward. "Calm down, Billy and Joe. I think I can explain this. But you have to promise not to say a word to anyone. This is top-secret business."

I turned on Sam like a cyclone. "You're going to *tell* them? Why couldn't *I* have told them days ago and saved myself all this agony, Sam Rotondo? You miserable . . ." I couldn't think of a word bad enough to describe him.

"It wasn't a good idea. It's still not," said the stoic Sam. "But we're going to have to let the cat out of the bag now, or your husband and your father will never trust you again."

With a wretched, *"Ohhhhhh!"* I flung myself down on the couch. *Damn* Sam Rotondo, whose words were worth less than the breath it took to say them. He was going to tell them everything, and then both Billy and Pa would forever afterwards look at me as if I were evil personified. And I'd only tried to do a good deed for Mrs. Kincaid! Life was *so* unfair, although this was, I suppose, merely a drop of goo compared to the avalanche of mud life's unfairness had mired me in so far.

Thank God Spike jumped up on the sofa. I grabbed him, hauled him onto my lap, and sobbed into his shiny black coat. At least dogs were fair and reasonable people.

"You see, it's like this. We've got a new, but serious, problem with bootleggers in the city."

Pa and Billy grunted. They read the newspapers; they knew that already. I braced myself, thinking *here it comes.*

"And Daisy has an in with a lot of folks that we on the force can't get to."

"Like who?" asked Billy. His voice was hard, as if he wasn't buying anything yet.

"Like Stacy Kincaid and her mother," said Sam, sounding quite matter-of-fact. "The Kincaid girl has got herself mixed up with a bunch of thugs, one of whom, Vicenzo Maggiori, runs a mobile speakeasy. What's more, there's a rat in the works who warns Maggiori whenever we plan a raid."

"What's all that got to do with my daughter?" asked Pa reasonably.

"Daisy knows the Kincaid brat. And she's good friends with Stacy's brother. I asked her if she could help the police shut down Maggiori's outfit. She agreed."

I lifted my head from where it had been buried in Spike's fur and gaped at Sam. I couldn't believe it. He hadn't ratted me out. Yet. Wiping my eyes, I listened.

"Yeah?" Billy said. He pursed his mouth as if he were considering this bit of information but still withholding judgment. "But why Daisy? Couldn't you get somebody else to help you?"

Sam shook his head. "Not nearly as well as Daisy can. Maggiori's got a bee in his head about wanting to communicate with his dead godfather, a gangster who was gunned down in New York City a year or so ago. Daisy's the only person I know of who does séances."

Comprehension dawned on Pa and Billy's faces.

Pa said, "Ah."

Billy said, "I see," as if it almost made sense to him now.

"So," Sam said, "I approached her about doing a séance for Maggiori. She didn't want to do it."

I finally spoke, although my voice was thick with tears. "*That's the truth!*"

"But she finally agreed to help us. I had to warn her not to tell anybody, though, because the more people there are who

High Spirits

know about it, the more apt word is to get back to Maggiori. That wouldn't be safe for Daisy."

I nodded vigorously, thinking it was about time Sam agreed this was a dangerous assignment he'd given me. Not that I'd had any choice about accepting the deal at the time it was thrust upon me.

Billy was frowning again. "I don't know, Sam. It sounds as if Daisy might be in a world of trouble if any of those hoodlums figure out she's working with you."

I *knew* there was a reason I loved my husband!

"They can't find out. How can they?"

"I don't know, but it sounds dangerous to me."

"Me, too," I said, sniffling.

"Nuts. All she has to do is try to find out the name of the leak. There's no way in the world Maggiori or any of his men will ever know who passed the information along."

"Was that guy one of Maggiori's goons?" Billy asked, hooking his thumb toward the front door.

I answered him. "Yes! Yes, he was, and I was scared to death the whole time I was with them. They're terrible men! They're murderers! They beat their women! They're . . . they're . . ." I ran out of words, dumped Spike on the sofa, and rushed over to Billy, where I fell on my knees, threw my arms around him and cried on his lap.

Poor guy. But Billy was good about it. He only stroked my head and said, "I'm sorry, Daisy. You should have told me."

"I c c-couldn't," I said through my tears. "S-Sam wouldn't let me."

"It's true, Billy. We need to have a cloak of secrecy around this operation. Those guys aren't dumb." If anyone had told me that Sam Rotondo would come to my rescue like a knight in shining armor, I'd have laughed myself silly. But he did it that night. Even if it was his fault I was in this fix in the first place.

Oh, very well, it wasn't *all* Sam's fault. I guess I could have stood my ground and not bowed to Mrs. Kincaid's wishes that I perform the first stupid séance.

"Anyhow," said Sam, who was beginning to sound as if he wanted to go away, "Daisy is performing a good deed for the citizens of Pasadena, and she's been of great help to the department. There might even be a commendation from the mayor in it for her."

If I survived. Anyhow, what did I care about stupid commendations?

"That's my girl," said Pa, smiling at last.

"Yeah," said Billy. I could hear the smile in his voice.

I still wanted to die.

Chapter Eleven

Before Sam left that night, I told him I had some information for him, but I wasn't going to impart it to him then. I'd developed a massive headache, was totally exhausted, and only wanted to go to sleep.

"Meet me at the library tomorrow morning," I said, sounding much more authoritative than usual. I guess that's what being dog-tired and scared to death, not to mention, worried almost beyond endurance does to a person.

"What time?"

No argument. No counter-offer. Nothing. I stared at Sam through puffy eyelids, waiting for the other shoe to drop. It didn't. Good heavens, perhaps he actually *did* appreciate my help in this matter.

"How about ten-thirty? I don't think I'll be up to much before then. Anyhow, I have to meet Flossie for lunch at noon."

"Flossie? Flossie Mosser? Good God, now you're friends with *Flossie?*"

"Don't you say another single word, Sam Rotondo. Florence Mosser is a nice girl who fell for the wrong man."

"I'll say."

"I said stop talking! I'm trying to help her. Anyhow, if it weren't for *you*, I'd never have met her in the first place."

He rolled his eyes, but he took my advice and didn't say another word, thank God.

I very nearly yielded to my headache, melancholy, and fatigue that night and swiped some of Billy's morphine syrup, but I got hold of myself before I could succumb to the urge. I only took a powder and crawled between the sheets. Once more I wished I'd die before I awoke, but the old prayer didn't work that night any more than it had the night before or the night before that. Figures. I don't have any luck at all, unless you count the bad variety.

At any rate, I felt as if I'd been left to soak overnight in a bucket full of lye soap, rinsed roughly, and then thrown over a rusty clothesline to dry when I awoke the next morning. My eyelids were swollen, my eyes felt as if somebody had thrown sand in them, my headache still hovered, and if I'd felt any more sluggish, I could have gone out into the garden and joined the snails. In short, I felt like heck.

Too bad, Daisy Majesty, I said to myself. *You got yourself into this fix, and now you have to see it through.* Every now and then, I wished my mother and father hadn't instilled such strict Methodist principles into me when I was young.

My lousy mood wasn't improved any when I caught sight of Billy stuffing a bottle into his bedside stand. And here I hadn't even thought to look *there*. Which was silly. I knew darned well that the poor guy took more morphine than I thought was good for him.

Before my mind could start rushing around in unending circles of what was better for Billy, addiction or pain, I put a firm clamp on my thoughts.

Except for my meeting with Sam at the library and Flossie on the corner of Fair Oaks and Colorado at noonish, I didn't have a single other thing to do that day. I could almost relax for once in a blue moon. Well, except for trying to talk my family into attending the Salvation Army church the next day.

And then, all of a sudden, as if a bolt of lightning had struck me, it occurred to me that my entire family *didn't* have to go to church with me! I could jolly well tell them that I was going to meet Flossie Mosser at the Salvation Army church, and they could all go to the Methodist church as usual if they wanted to. I'm not that independent as a rule, but even *I'm* entitled to a day off every once in a while.

I think my chin must have had a defiant lift to it that morning because when I more or less staggered into the kitchen, Pa said, "What's the matter, Daisy?"

"Just tired," I said, not fibbing. I really was tired. Worn to a nub was more like it.

Fortunately for me, Pa dropped the subject. "Your aunt Vi left something she called a breakfast casserole on the warming plate for you and Billy."

God bless my aunt. "Great. I've gotta go check the bathroom mirror first, though. I think I need help."

When I got a good look at my frazzled features, I realized how true those words were. I'd already realized my eyes were puffy. That always happened after I'd been crying. But I hadn't realized how bloodshot they were, or how haggard I looked. Oh, boy.

Fortunately, my blessed mother always had a supply of boric acid on hand, and a little eyecup. After I'd rinsed my poor, abused eyes, they didn't look quite so bad. They'd look better if I could lie down with a couple of cucumber slices covering my closed lids, but I'd do that after breakfast.

I was starving to death. Not literally, of course. In actual fact, I was far from the idealized boyish figure of a woman depicted in the fashion magazines I read religiously in order to gather ideas for my spiritualist wardrobe. I had curves, by gum, no matter how hard I tried to hide them. That's what comes of living in a household with Aunt Vi. But I'd rather live with Aunt Vi and be a little rounder than was the fashion than live without her and not even have good food to cheer me up.

And cheer up I did, if only nominally, when I dished out a plate of Aunt Vi's breakfast "casserole," whatever that was, and set it before Billy with a sliced orange. He sniffed at his plate and looked up at me quizzically.

"What's this?"

"New dish. Aunt Vi must have found it in a magazine or something. It smells good."

"What's in it?"

I sat down with my own plate and studied the food thereon. "Looks to me like eggs, sausage and potatoes with cheese on top. It looks as if the potatoes serve as a kind of crust."

"Hmm. Just like breakfast, in fact," Billy mumbled.

Pa, who was still at the kitchen table reading his newspaper, laughed. "It's *exactly* like breakfast. Try it. You'll like it."

He was right. I'm not sure why Vi decided to mix everything together the way she did, but the end result was heavenly. If I could cook, I'd make it a lot. Thank God I don't have to worry about breakfasts. Or lunches or dinners, either, for that matter.

"Whatcha doing today, Daisy?" Billy asked as he sipped his coffee. He'd sighed as deeply as he was able when he'd finished his breakfast, a sure sign that he'd enjoyed it.

I'd enjoyed it too, but Billy's question brought reality crashing in on me with a vengeance. Shooting a quick glance at the clock—it was only eight o'clock, which meant I had about an hour and a half to get myself ready—I sighed, too, although not with pleasure.

"I have to meet Sam at the library to tell him what I learned last night." Frowning, I added, "For what it's worth. I didn't hear much."

"Oh?" Billy's eyebrows quirked up with interest.

Pa laid his paper beside his empty plate. "Oh?"

With another sigh, I said, "Yeah. I heard Mr. Maggiori talking to somebody on the telephone last night. I have to tell Sam what I think the conversation meant."

"You're being mighty cagey, Daisy," said Billy with a hint of disapproval.

If I sighed any more, I'd pass out from hyperventilation. "I know. But . . . darn it, these guys are killers. I don't want my family involved with them."

"We're already involved with them," growled Billy.

In an effort to divert us from this tangent, Pa asked, "How can we be involved with them if you only tell us what you heard?"

"I don't know," I admitted sorrowfully, "but I'd rather you didn't know anything. I wish *I* didn't know anything. I wish I'd said no when Sam asked me to do this." Of course, I'd be in jail if I had, but Pa and Billy didn't need to know that.

"You're really scared of these folks, aren't you, sweetie?" Pa asked.

I loved my family *so* much. "Yes. I am. And I'm scared they might come after you if you know anything."

"How about you tell us all about it after it's all over," Pa suggested. He glanced at Billy. "That all right with you, son?"

Billy hesitated for a second, then nodded. "Yeah. I guess that's fair."

"Thanks. I appreciate it. I really hate this."

And with that, I cleared the table and washed the dishes. I managed a half-hour in a bubble bath with cucumber slices over my closed eyes, but I was afraid if I stayed that way very long, I'd go to sleep, drown, and miss my two appointments. While that didn't sound like a half-bad idea, I knew I'd have to pay later if I failed to meet Sam, and I'd have sorely disappointed Flossie, who didn't need any more disappointments in her life.

Therefore, I was at the library at precisely ten-thirty. Sam and I hadn't set up a specific place to meet, so I stayed in the courtyard, pacing, waiting for him to show up. He was late, which irked me, as the Pasadena Police Station was pretty much right across the street from the library. All right, so he had to walk around the block and down the street a bit. So what? I'd had to drive from way down the street. Truth to tell, the library, on the corner of Walnut Street and Fair Oaks Avenue, was relatively close to both of our places of origination. Therefore, it was stupid for either of us to be late, and I wasn't, so Sam was the only stupid one of us that morning.

Not that it mattered, since he held all the cards in this particular deck.

Nevertheless, I frowned when I saw him lumber up the steps to the library. I met him under the center arch with a crisp, "You're late."

He glanced at me and grunted. It figures.

"So what do you have to tell me?" he asked when we were both in the courtyard.

"Not here. Come to the periodical room."

I know he rolled his eyes, although I couldn't see him do so because I turned on my smart brown heel and led the way into the library, across the main floor, and down the stairs to the periodical room. I'd chosen this room because it wasn't generally occupied until school let out and all the kids came here to do research for their next term papers.

Sam followed me into the archives, muttering under his breath. I didn't care.

When we got to the stack holding old issues of *Vanity Fair*, which was toward the back of the room, I turned, grabbed Sam by his coat sleeve, and tugged him into the aisle. He was scowling hideously by that time.

"It's somebody in the police department."

His scowl got even more hideous. "What the devil are you talking about?"

"The snitch you wanted me to discover for you, darn it!" We were both whispering, which limited the amount of rancor I could put into my voice, but I tried really hard. "The bad guy works for the police."

Sam paused for a second before whispering, "How the devil do you know that?"

In order not to holler at him, I sucked in a huge breath and held it for several seconds. It tasted like old paper. After I was pretty sure I wouldn't throw a tantrum, I growled, "Because Maggiori told whoever it was that he paid better than the law-enforcement people did."

Sam was silent while he mulled over my revelation. "That doesn't mean the police department. It could be the sheriff. Or a private firm."

It was my turn to roll my eyes. "Of course, it doesn't mean the police department, but it gives you somewhere to start, doesn't it?"

"What else did you hear?" he asked, not bothering to answer my question.

"Only that Maggiori told whoever it was that he was opening up on Monday night, and that he'd pay big-time if the guy—or girl—" I modified, in an effort to achieve impartiality, "told him when the next raid would be."

"You didn't get a name?" He sounded as if he thought I'd shirked my duty.

Through pinched lips, I said, "No."

"Huh."

I'd had it. "What do you mean 'huh'?" I snapped. "Darn it, Sam Rotondo, I'm putting my life in danger to tell you this stuff, and all you can say is 'huh'?"

"Your life's not in danger," muttered Sam.

"Oh? I'm having to consort with a pack of gangsters and bootleggers, and I'm frightened to death the whole time, darn it! And it's all because I'm trying to help you."

His eyebrows were pretty formidable when they were drawn down into a V the way they were when he glared at me then. "The only reason you're trying to help the force is because otherwise you'd have been arrested."

"Maybe." I was feeling mighty sullen by that time. "But that's only because I was trying to help a friend, and you guys raided the joint."

He said, "Huh," again, clapped his hat onto his head, wheeled around, and started to march off. When he got to the end of the aisle, he turned. "Thank you."

Good Lord. I said, "You're *ever* so welcome," in a voice so caustic, I'm surprised my mouth didn't wither.

The morning got better after that. Miss Petrie, my friend in the cataloguing department, had saved three new books for me. I decided that, since the last two days and this morning had been so horrid so far, I'd jolly well sit in the reading room and begin one of them. It was great: *The Devil's Paw*, by E. Phillips Oppenheim. It had come out a year or so before, but Mr. Oppenheim was from England, and I guess it took a while for books to get across the ocean. Anyhow, I hadn't read it yet. I was disappointed when time came for me to meet Flossie on Colorado and Fair Oaks, and not merely because I was sick of hanging out with gangsters and their various outriders.

However, kindness beckoned, so I did my Christian duty and left off reading right smack in the middle of a thrilling chapter. I'd planned to walk to the corner of Fair Oaks and Colorado, so I visited the Chevrolet on Walnut in front of the library, shoved the books into the backseat, and made my way south on Fair Oaks.

I heard the Salvation Army band before I saw them. They were on Colorado, and when I turned east on that street, I not only saw the band, but Flossie Mosser, too. She stood there gazing with rapture at Johnny Buckingham, who was playing his cornet for all he was worth in a rousing rendition of "When the Saints Come Rolling In," *not* a hymn we Methodists sing as a rule, but a lively one. I like it, anyway.

Which reminded me that I needed to telephone Mr. Floy Hostetter, our choir director, and tell him I wouldn't be in the choir the next day. He'd not throw a fit. I mean, I'm a fairly good alto, and I am sometimes selected to sing duets with a soprano, but I fear I'm not indispensable.

Flossie, I was pleased to see, was demurely clad that day. What's more, the outfit, a dark green suit with black shoes and hat, wasn't one that we'd bought at Nash's, so evidently she'd taken my lesson to heart and had actually picked out a tasteful costume on her own. I felt like a fond grandmother, or something.

She didn't notice me until I touched her arm. Then she started like a frightened faun and whirled around. When she saw me, she slapped a hand over her heart and let out a gusty breath. "Daisy! I'm so glad it's you."

"Whom did you expect?" I asked out of curiosity.

"I was afraid Jinx might've followed me."

I doubted Jinx had that much interest in the poor woman except as a punching bag, although I didn't say so. I only smiled and said, "Nope. It's only me." I also doubted that Flossie knew much about grammar.

The last crescendo sounded, and Johnny Buckingham, panting slightly, joined us on the corner while one of his lieutenants or privates, or whatever she was, handed around the tambourine for donations. I plunked in two bits, and Flossie, looking embarrassed, deposited a rolled-up bill.

"How are you two lovely ladies today?" Johnny asked. He seemed to have eyes only for Flossie.

"I'm fine," I said, thinking things were moving along smoothly for once. Well, unless Jinx got a hint of the attraction between these two. Then God alone knew what might happen.

"Me, too," said Flossie shyly.

"Will you be joining us for church tomorrow?" Johnny finally tore his gaze from Flossie and aimed it at me. "It would be great to see you and Billy in the congregation."

"You'll see me, anyhow," I told him. "I'm not sure about the rest of my family."

"Well, I hope you can all come."

I had a sudden inspiration. That happens sometimes. "Say, Johnny, if you're not doing anything for lunch, want to join Flossie and me? We're going to have a bite at . . ." My voice trailed out, since we hadn't decided on a place.

"Sure," he said with marked enthusiasm. "How about we grab a bite at the Crown."

"What a wonderful idea!" I'd forgotten all about the Crown Chop Suey Palace on Fair Oaks, which was silly of me since I adored Chinese food. Well . . . I adored pretty much all food, actually. "Do you like Chinese, Flossie?"

She looked at me blankly, as if nobody'd ever before bothered to ask her what she liked, then nodded. "Sure."

"Great. Be right back."

So Flossie and I waited while Johnny stowed his cornet in its case, spoke briefly with some of his minions, and rejoined us on the corner. "It's only a block or so away." And we all walked to the restaurant.

Lunch was swell. I especially liked the cashew chicken. My sense of duty did not desert me, though, even there and then. As we munched happily, Flossie blushing shyly every time Johnny addressed a comment or question to her, I thought. Thinking occasionally hurts my cranium, but I do it anyway.

While I was fairly sure by this time of Flossie's overall, or perhaps that should be underlying, character, I still didn't think

High Spirits

it would be a good idea to entrust her with the nature of my—or rather, the police's—interest in Maggiori. Not, as I said before, because I thought she was a bad person, but because she clearly wasn't tops in the decision-making department. She remained a weak vessel and, while I had great hopes for her if she stuck with Johnny Buckingham and Co., I wasn't ready to trust her with my life. So to speak.

That being the case, I still might be able to get some information from her. And, as Johnny Buckingham was perhaps the only person in the world whom I'd trust with a secret—well, besides Harold Kincaid—I figured I might be able to do it as we dined.

"Say, Johnny, did you know that I was doing a séance in a speakeasy when the joint was raided a couple of weeks ago?"

Johnny almost choked to death on his noodles. Then he laughed so hard, he had to wipe his eyes. I tried not to resent this reaction from an old friend.

"Oh, my Lord, Daisy, does Billy know about this?"

I sighed. Johnny knew me too well. "No, not really. He only knows that—" Sweet heaven, I was about to say *he only knows I'm working with the police.* Sometimes I think I need to be locked away in a safe place and only let out on a short leash. Like Spike. "He only knows that I conducted a séance for Mrs. Kincaid. He doesn't know where I did it or what happened there."

Johnny shook his head, although he looked more amused than censorious. I guess when you've been down as low as Johnny was after the war, you become tolerant of your fellow human beings' foibles. "You're really something, Daisy."

Flossie broke in. "She's swell."

I appreciated this accolade and decided to take the plunge. "Say, Flossie, I overheard Mr. Maggiori talking on the telephone to someone last night. It sounded as if it was somebody who gives him tips about police raids. No wonder the police have trouble shutting his operation down completely."

"Oh, sure," she said happily. "That's Pete Frye. He's one of Mr. Maggiori's tame coppers."

I almost dropped my teeth.

Flossie misunderstood my reaction. "I know. It's a shame that some coppers are dirty, but they are."

"Um . . . I see." I drank some tea, thinking I could have saved myself a whole lot of heartache and worry if I'd only asked Flossie the name of the rat earlier in the game.

Chapter Twelve

"*What?*"

I hadn't expected Sam Rotondo to be overjoyed at my request, but he didn't have to bellow into my eardrum.

"I said get over here right now."

"Why?"

"You know why." Curse it! Why was the man so darned dense?

"Cripes," he said.

"It's one of your very own."

"I don't believe you."

"It's not *me* you don't believe, curse you, Sam Rotondo. I'm only relaying information." I think I really hated him at that moment in time. "It's one of your very own people," I repeated stiffly into the receiver. I didn't dare be more specific, since the telephone wire wasn't a secure way to relay information.

Silence.

Well, to heck with that. "His name—"

"Stop!" bellowed Sam.

If I went deaf after this telephone conversation, I was going to sue the Pasadena Police Department. I said nothing.

"We've got to meet somewhere. I don't want this to go over the telephone wires."

"You can jolly come here, then," I told him.

"Well . . ."

"I'm not stepping foot out of this house one more time today, Sam Rotondo."

More silence.

"Well?" I said crisply.

"I don't want to do it there, either."

I assumed "there" in this instance was my home. He probably didn't want to be seen entering our nice little bungalow in the middle of the day instead of merely in the evening, as he did all the time for card games. And a fine time it was for him to begin thinking about the safety of my family, thought I.

"Well?" I said again.

"You going to church tomorrow."

"I always go to church." My voice was as cold as Sam's temper was hot.

"I'll see you there and talk to you after the ceremony."

"Service," I corrected.

"Whatever it is, I'll talk to you then."

"Not if you go to the First Methodist Church, you won't." He'd surprised me there one Sunday morning about a year earlier. I'd been singing a duet with Lucille Spinks and nearly fainted when I'd seen him looming in the congregation.

"Huh? What do you mean?"

"I mean I'm going to the Salvation Army church tomorrow. A friend of ours is a captain in the Salvation Army, and he invited us to the dedication of a new chapel. So we're going there." In that instance, I guess I was using the so-called "Royal Us," as I still hadn't confirmed with the rest of my family that they'd join me.

"Yeah, well, I'll talk to you there. We'll probably be able to get a minute alone."

"Probably." I was none to happy about it, either.

"What was that all about?" Billy asked when I hung up the receiver.

Sighing heavily, I turned to him and slumped into a chair at the table. Our telephone was in the kitchen, so I didn't have far

High Spirits

to go in order to accomplish my slump. "I found out the name of the person who's tipping Mr. Maggiori about police raids. He's a policeman."

Billy whistled softly. "Whoo boy, Sam's not going to like that."

"He already doesn't like it. I don't like it, either." After briefly burying my head in my hands, I said piteously, "I'll be *so* glad when this whole thing is over."

"I bet." Billy sipped from a fresh cup of tea I'd brewed for us right before I telephoned the police station.

I added milk and sugar to my own tea and took an appreciative swig. For some reason, and I don't know why, I find tea with milk and sugar very comforting.

"I wish I'd never agreed to do this in the first place. I knew Maggiori and his gang were criminals, but I didn't realize how scared I'd be whenever I was with them."

"Well, you're doing your duty as a citizen, I guess," Billy said doubtfully.

Equally doubtfully, I said, "I guess."

Billy squinted at me across the table. "So you're going to the Salvation Army tomorrow?"

"Yeah. I introduced Flossie Mosser to Johnny, just as you suggested, and there seems to be a spark of interest there." I heaved another largish sigh. "I guess that's encouraging, anyway. Maybe Johnny can get her to leave that beast who beats her up."

To my great relief, Billy grinned at me. "I'll go with you. I want to see this Flossie character."

My heart leapt up as I beheld my husband, not in the sky, but in a supportive position across from me at the kitchen table. How often did *that* happen? I can tell you: not often. I reached for his hand and squeezed it. "Thank you, Billy." A tear dripped from my eye, and I swiped at it with my other hand. "You don't know how happy that makes me. I really didn't want to go alone."

"You won't be alone," said my marvelous husband stoutly. "We'll get the whole family to go. Then, when you have to talk to Sam, you can kind of sneak off to a corner." He grinned again.

"Thanks, Billy. You're the tops."

His grin soured. "Yeah?"

I didn't want him to sink into one of his despondent moods, so I chirped, "Yes, you are. And I'm afraid you won't be able to understand the full glory of Flossie's transformation. She's toned down her overall appearance, except that she still has that brassy bottle-blond hair. She's really quite pretty." When I spoke the words, I realized they were not merely true, but that they surprised me.

When I'd got my first glimpse of Flossie Mosser amongst that crowd of criminals and flaming youth types in the speakeasy, she'd seemed sort of like a gaudy ornament. It had been difficult to think of her as an actual person. But now that she'd adopted tasteful garb and softened her makeup, and I'd become slightly better acquainted with her, I realized she was not merely an actual person, but a good-looking one with feelings, dreams, and ambitions, if only to lift herself out of her present life.

Billy was as good as his word. He talked the entire family, including Aunt Vi, who didn't hold with any church but the Methodist variety, into attending the Salvation Army the next morning. I called Mr. Hostetter to tell him I'd be absent from the choir. As luck would have it, he wasn't home, so I spoke to his wife, who was a very nice lady. She didn't even shriek or anything when I told her why my family planned to defect for the day.

"The Army does valuable work in the community," she said,

which amazed me, since Mr. Hostetter had almost fainted at the suggestion the choir sing "Onward Christian Soldiers."

Aunt Vi fixed us a delicious dinner, as usual, and when I finally got to bed that night, I actually slept well, and without a headache for the first time in days.

As soon as my family piled out of the Chevrolet—it was always a struggle to get Billy anywhere, since we couldn't very well stash his wheelchair in the motor, and he couldn't walk far—a woman rushed up to us. I thought perhaps she'd been assigned by the Army to greet strangers, although she was clad in a nice blue suit instead of a uniform, and I smiled at her.

It wasn't until she cried, "Oh, Daisy, I'm so glad to see youse guys!" that I realized the woman was none other than Flossie Mosser! Looking absolutely *normal!* She must have gone to a hair salon and had her hair dyed, because it was a nice light brown color, and all the marcelled waves were gone. She now wore it in a short, but tasteful, bob. I was flabbergasted.

"Flossie! Your hair!"

That was a stupid thing to say since it only made her uncomfortable. She stopped short and began madly patting away at her hair. I grabbed her other hand.

"You look wonderful, Flossie. I honestly didn't recognize you at first."

"You didn't?"

"No. I hadn't expected your hair to be so . . . lovely." I didn't want to tell her she'd looked like a gaudy doll before and prayed that she'd take my words as praise. "You look truly beautiful." Only a tiny fib, and I expected God would forgive me for it.

"You think so?" she asked in a small voice, clearly unsure of herself.

"Absolutely!"

When I introduced her to the rest of the family, they all

seemed pleased to meet her, although Billy appeared slightly disappointed. I know he was hoping to see the traces of her dissipated former life. Or present life, if Jinx was still in the picture. I wasn't able to ask her about that, but figured I'd learn soon enough, when I performed my séance on Tuesday. The notion made me shudder. Not of seeing Flossie, but of being with that gang of thugs again.

However, I must say that the Salvation Army puts on a rousing service. Not only was there a lot of music and singing, but people from the congregation stood and told their stories before the sermon. Some of them were even more dismal than Johnny Buckingham's. One man evidently had begun a life of crime as a child and continued along the same path until he'd been saved by a Salvation Army chaplain who'd visited the jail in which he resided at the time. It was really an interesting—dare I say entertaining? I don't know if that's allowed in church—service.

Well, except that Sam was there, glowering at everything from a back pew. His arms were crossed over his chest, and he couldn't have looked much more sour if he'd sucked on a lemon immediately prior to entering the sanctuary—which, by the by, was quite nice. The Army didn't go in for frills. I reckon they spent their money on other things, but the place had nice white walls and a serviceable, if plain, platform up front where the general (or whoever he was) delivered a most inspirational sermon. He reminded all of us in the congregation that Jesus hadn't limited His works to the gentry but had included everyone in his message of salvation. His sermon was full of joy and God's forgiveness of sins, which was a heck of a lot better than the hellfire and damnation some churches preached (or so I've been told. I'm a Methodist, and we're fairly tame as far as the brimstone stuff is concerned). All in all, the entire service was quite uplifting.

High Spirits

It was during the sermon that I realized Flossie had started crying. Poor thing. She was sitting in between Billy and me, and I took her hand and squeezed it. She squeezed back but kept sniffling. Poor Flossie. I sensed that her life was about to make a huge turn in a different direction, and I hoped it would be a better one for her. It was while I was trying to offer Flossie comfort that I spied someone in the congregation that, I swear, looked exactly like Stacy Kincaid. After blinking several times, I squinted again at the apparition I thought I'd seen, but whoever it was—it couldn't possibly have been Stacy—was hidden behind some lady's big hat. Well, it didn't matter.

After the service, we all took a side trip to the new chapel, where the minister prayed over it and blessed it. That was nice, too, and the chapel was quite pretty.

And then we were all invited to dine. Ma and Aunt Vi didn't say anything as the congregation surged toward the place where they were serving the covered-dish lunch. I walked with Flossie since I couldn't very well desert her to find out what my mother and aunt had thought of the service, but my curiosity ran rampant. I thought it had been swell, and exactly what I'd have liked to hear if I were down and out (which I prayed would never happen).

Thank God for Sam Rotondo.

Boy, I never thought I'd ever say *those* words. But while the rest of the throng was making a beeline for the food, Sam made a beeline for Billy. He and Pa assisted Billy—they really sort of carried him but tried to make it look as though he was walking on his own between them—to the room where the covered dishes, salads, vegetables, rolls and butter, and cakes and pies had been set out. I guess the Army folks call it a fellowship hall, just like we Methodists do.

Except for the threat of a private conversation with Sam, I actually enjoyed the lunch and the company. Those Army folks are mighty friendly, and they can cook, too. Flossie sat with us, and Johnny Buckingham joined us beside her at a long table. I guess he was a big gun at that church because nearly every person there that day came over to talk to him, and he introduced every single one of them to us and Flossie. They all seemed to be particularly gracious to Flossie, who seemed to blossom under the uncritical attention. It occurred to me that now that her bruises had faded and her hair color and dress had been toned down, she probably didn't feel so alien in that group. They welcomed her with what appeared to be unfeigned joy, which probably helped as well. It's nice to fit in.

Only two sour points marred that morning. The first was Sam, even though I appreciated his assistance with Billy. I couldn't help dreading our pending conversation, although I knew it had to be done. Not only that, but it might well signal the end of what I'd begun to think of as the Maggiori problem.

I was happily munching away on a delicious fried-chicken thigh when Sam bumped my shoulder. Turning my head, I saw him looming at my back. I swallowed my chicken, glanced at Billy who nodded, I sighed deeply and rose from my seat.

"Save my seat," I told Billy.

"Of course," Billy said with a grin and a wink at Sam. "I won't even eat your potato salad." Huh. It looked as if they were both against me that day.

However, I knew I had to do this, so I followed Sam back into the sanctuary, where we had the place to ourselves. Even the ushers had cleaned up the pews and were probably enjoying the meal *I'd* been enjoying until now.

Sam started things on a disagreeable note. "Well?"

That's it. No, "Thanks for doing this for us, Daisy," or, "Will you please tell me what you've discovered." Nope. Just "Well?" in that bass rumble of his. Phooey.

If that's the way he wanted to play the game, so be it. "The rat is Peter Frye, and according to Flossie, he's a policeman. So the leak *is* one of your own." I'd have taken more satisfaction out of delivering this piece of information if I weren't so troubled about having learned that one couldn't even trust the police in this day of gang wars and illicit booze. I mean, if you couldn't trust the cops, whom *could* you trust?

And then Sam truly shocked me.

He said, "Shit."

And in a *church!* On *Sunday!* Even as forgiving a church as the Salvation Army undoubtedly didn't want people saying words like that in their sanctuary, for heaven's sake.

"Really!" I said, miffed.

At least he had the grace to say, "Sorry."

"Do you know this Frye character?"

Sam heaved an aggrieved sigh. "Yeah, I know him. He's pretty new in the department."

"Evidently he's a rotten apple."

"Yeah. Evidently." He squinted at me in what was by that time a very dark room since the sanctuary lights had been turned out. "You sure about this?"

"All I know is that I heard Maggiori talking to somebody on the 'phone, and it sounded as if the person he was talking to had connections with law enforcement. Then yesterday, when I was having lunch with Flossie, she said the snitch's name is Peter Frye, and he's a policeman."

"Hell."

There he went again.

I snapped, "Sam!"

He didn't apologize that time but only grunted again and turned to go back to the covered dishes. I followed him, feeling crabby. Sam could take one of my good moods and turn it on its head faster than any other person I'd ever met. Well, except for Billy, but Billy's circumstances were exceptional, and I gave him a lot of leeway. At least I tried to.

The dear man had not only saved my place at his table but had managed to get someone to refill my plate by the time Sam and I got back to my family. Billy scooted a little farther toward me to make room for Sam, for whom he'd somehow acquired a plate, too. Billy wasn't able to stand in a line, so he must have talked someone else into doing Sam and me this service. What a guy my husband was. Every time his old sweetness resurfaced, I cursed the Kaiser and his deadly gas another few times. On Sunday. In a church. And I didn't feel the least bit guilty about it, either.

I kept a close eye on Flossie during the rest of the festivities. She'd been quite animated at first, but as the meal progressed, she began to withdraw into herself. I considered this a bad sign. Could it be that, while she'd welcomed the congregation's greetings at first, she was getting tired of them? I gave her a measuring glance. Or could it be that she appreciated everyone's friendliness but didn't believe that she deserved to be among these people in the long run? I glanced measuringly some more. It was difficult to tell, although her symptoms pointed to the latter theory.

Her head was bowed, her chin quivered slightly and, while she tried to smile when Johnny addressed comments to her, she looked to me as if she were trying not to cry. She was merely toying with her food, which was a shame. Not only did she need proper nutrition, but the meal was really delicious. Poor Flossie. I resolved then and there to find Johnny Buckingham on a street corner tomorrow and have a good long chat with him about Flossie. If anyone could help her, I sensed it was Johnny and his Army of earthly saints.

The second sour note (Remember? There were two of them) occurred when I caught sight of the woman I'd thought looked like Stacy Kincaid in the fellowship hall and discovered that she actually, really and truly, *was* Stacy Kincaid. I dropped my fork. Billy looked at me. "What's the matter, Daisy?"

My state of shock was so absolute, I couldn't speak. I only shook my head for a few seconds before stammering out, "I-I can't believe it."

Billy seemed puzzled. For good reason. "What can't you believe?"

"That-that . . . *person.*" Against etiquette, I pointed a trembling finger.

Billy glanced over to see what I was pointing at, but again the mob had swallowed Stacy up. Or, rather, it had swallowed up the woman whom I believed to be Stacy, although, when I thought about it, I realized that was patently impossible. Stacy Kincaid might frequent speakeasies and horrible people and think it was fun to smoke and drink and drive her mother into an early grave, but she'd *never* visit a church. Especially not a Salvation Army church. My mind was playing tricks on me.

I shook my head. "I-I . . ." I shook my head *again,* hoping to rattle my brain back into place. "I must be wrong."

Still bewildered, Billy asked, "About what?"

"Oh, nothing." Then I laughed, seeing the humor in my wild surmises. "I thought I saw Stacy Kincaid!"

The notion was so utterly ridiculous that Billy laughed too. His laugh turned into a coughing spasm that had me wishing I'd kept my fat mouth shut.

Anyhow, after lunch we thanked Johnny for inviting us and asked Flossie if we could drive her home. Johnny was gracious and seemed genuinely appreciative that we'd come.

"I'll visit you again, Billy. Take care of yourself."

"I'll try," said Billy, with a trace of his customary bleakness.

"You can do it." Johnny patted Billy on the back, but when he looked at me, I knew *he* knew what kind of torment Billy lived with every day. Still, for some reason, when Johnny talked to Billy he never made it sound as though he pitied him. I considered that one of Johnny's most telling personality points.

He also didn't say what lots of church people say: "I'll pray for you." Billy and I both knew—and I could tell Johnny did, too—that prayers, while nice and kindly meant, weren't going to do Billy any good. His body was all shot up and his lungs were damaged beyond repair. When I realized Johnny knew exactly what I was thinking because he'd been through the hell and aftermath of that miserable war, too, I darned near started blubbering on the spot. Thank God I controlled myself.

I did grab his hand, look him in the eyes—mine were full of unshed tears—and say, "Thank you, Johnny."

He squeezed my hand. "It'll all work out, Daisy. God's got a plan for Billy and you, too."

I wished I believed that. I could tell Johnny knew what I was thinking because he grinned at me, winked, and bent to kiss my cheek. As he did so, he whispered in my ear, "You know, Daisy, once you're here on earth, there's only one way out. Only one person I know about ever cheated the grave—and He didn't do that either, come to think of it."

Nodding my understanding and closer than ever to tears, I said, "Thanks, Johnny." He understood. He didn't sugar coat the benefits of religion or the realities of life, and I honored him for it.

Flossie declined our invitation. She said she had transportation but thanked us. Her shoulders were slightly bowed, and she looked the picture of despair when she walked away from our group—and Sam, blast him. I wanted to call her back, but there were too many members of my own family to think about that morning, so I didn't.

The rest of the day was pleasant. We didn't do much. I think we all took a nap (I know I did), then Aunt Vi fixed us a nice supper of beef stew and biscuits.

High Spirits

Billy didn't eat much. When I asked him if he was all right, he looked at me as if I was crazy and said, "I'm fine."

But he wasn't.

By the time morning came, he had a raging fever and his lungs were so congested, he could scarcely breathe.

In a panic, I telephoned Dr. Benjamin at his home. He came to call at our house not long after I'd called him. He was such a wonderful man. He was also the one who'd told me so often that Billy's undoubted morphine addiction was surely better for him than living with constant pain.

He doctored Billy as best he could, bringing with him a jar of Vick's VapoRub and a couple of mustard plasters. "Don't use 'em too much because they'll burn the hell out of his chest."

I promised I wouldn't.

He also recommended that we keep a steaming pot of water near his bed. He gave us some eucalyptus pods to put in the water, telling us the merits of eucalyptus as an aid to better breathing. He also said that if they ran out, I should dump some VapoRub into the pot. Then he and I propped Billy up with pillows so his lungs would be less likely to fill and smother him.

"Keep cool compresses on his forehead when his fever is high and wipe him down," he advised me as he was leaving. "Give him salicylic powders every four hours, and don't worry about the morphine. He needs to rest as free from pain as possible."

My chin quivered and my words shook when I said, "Thanks, Dr. Benjamin."

And then he did something that would have shocked me if I hadn't been so frazzled. He hugged me and whispered, "You know, Daisy, one of these days something like this is going to take him away from you. It might be influenza, or it might be a cold, or it might be pneumonia, but one of these days, one of those traitors will get him. Damned mustard gas."

I broke down and wept on his shoulder. It wasn't the first time I'd wept in front of Doc Benjamin, but this time I sobbed like a baby. It was *such* a relief to be able to do so that day. My stiff upper lip needed a break every now and then, and Dr. Benjamin provided it.

After crying for I don't know how long, I pulled away, sniffled pathetically, made a futile swipe of my streaming face, and said, "Thanks, Doc."

"You know I'm available to take care of Billy—and you and the rest of your family—any time, Daisy. I've been doctoring you all for years now, and I'm not going to quit on you or Billy, either one."

I said thanks approximately thirty more times, wiped my eyes as well as I could, prayed that this present problem wouldn't be the illness that separated Billy from me for all eternity, and returned to our room, where Pa had been holding a damp cloth to Billy's head.

Pa and I looked at each other, Pa smiled, I tried to do likewise, and I resumed my nursing duties.

Chapter Thirteen

Billy hovered on the brink between life and death for almost two weeks. I scarcely thought about my other obligations as I nursed him. I think Ma called a few of my clients to tell them I'd be unable to keep appointments, but I'm not even sure about that.

I'm also not sure who or how, but someone let Maggiori know why I wasn't conducting his séance. I know that because we received several lovely bouquets from him. I probably should have thrown them all out, seeing as how they'd come from a murdering gangster, but I didn't. It was nice to have fresh flowers in the house in February, and I let them stay.

It seemed to me that this would be a great time for the police to raid the joint—when I wasn't in it, I mean—but they didn't.

When Sam came to visit Billy, which he did practically every day, I asked him about that.

"No. We're going to wait until your séance."

"But *why?*" I whined. "Why don't you do it now?"

"We don't dare. We want you to be a distraction. If we raid the place while Maggiori and all his goons are on the alert, it might get messier than if he's sitting in the dark in a back room somewhere and occupied with ghosts when we bust in."

"It didn't help the last time," I reminded him, feeling quite bitter.

"Yeah, yeah, but that's because Frye called just before we got there, and he isn't going to be able to call the next time."

"How do you know that?"

"Because we've got Frye in our sights now. There's no way he'll be able to tip those sons of . . . um, dogs about another raid."

"Hmm. I still don't understand why you can't raid the place now."

"Well, we can't. Stop whining."

"I'm not whining! Curse you, Sam Rotondo, I hate those people, and they scare me!"

"Don't worry. When the time comes, the raid will go like clockwork."

"Great." Just what I wanted to hear. I was a distraction, and everything would go like clockwork, and they couldn't raid the joint now because . . . well, because. Nuts. I know I sighed, but that was nothing unusual.

Flossie Mosser and Johnny Buckingham came to pay their respects, too. Flossie actually telephoned a couple of days after we'd all attended church together. She wanted to know if I could meet her for lunch again, and she sounded extremely tentative and as if she didn't think she ought to be bothering me. Unfortunately, under the circumstances, I didn't think so either, but I tried to let her down gently.

She gasped when I told her about Billy's illness.

"Oh, my gar," she said. "I'm so sorry. Can I do anything to help?"

I wiped my forehead and wished people would stop asking me that. *I* didn't know what to tell them. However, I really did want to assist Flossie in her attempt to reclaim herself. So I said, "Um, yes. Could you drop by the drug store and get some more salicylic powders? I'm almost out, and Billy needs to take them every four hours. That way, I won't have to leave his side." In reality, we had tons of the powders and if I'd thought for a few more minutes, I might have come up with something useful for her to do, but I hadn't had much sleep for several days, was exhausted and worried, and my brain wasn't working very fast.

"Sure. I'll get some now and bring 'em right over."

"Thanks, Flossie."

With a sigh, I went back to my nursing duties.

When Johnny Buckingham came to visit, I was worn to a frazzle and decided I'd just jolly well tell him about Flossie Mosser then since I hadn't had the opportunity to do so earlier, and ask him to help her. So, even though it wasn't my story to tell, I snitched on Flossie, from her miserable beginnings to her unfortunate adolescence. I was about to launch into her disreputable connection to Jinx Jenkins and Vicenzo Maggiori when Johnny placed a hand on my arm. "I already know all that, Daisy."

I'm sure I blinked up at him dumbly. "You do?"

"Sure. I know all about Maggiori and his gang. I know about Miss Mosser and that Jinx character."

"Oh."

He chuckled. "Daisy, don't you understand yet that the very people who frequent speakeasies and drink illegal booze and gamble and break the law are often the very ones we at the Salvation Army see every week. They're exactly the sorts of people we strive to help into a life that works without all those crutches people use to escape their problems. I learned a long time ago that those kinds of escapes only become problems themselves."

"Oh."

He gave me a peck on the cheek, and laughed. "Daisy, you're a peach. Don't worry about Miss Mosser. We'll take care of her."

"Oh." Sometimes it took me a while to assimilate stuff that should have been right under my nose the whole time. When I looked at it Johnny's way, I realized that what he'd just said was the very reason I'd wanted to get Flossie into the Salvation Army church to begin with. It was exactly why Billy had—jokingly, to be sure, but only just—suggested I introduce Flossie to Johnny.

Boy, am I thick at times!

Dr. Benjamin visited at least once a day. I think it was on the fifth day, when Billy's fever seemed to be dropping, that he told me it looked as if my husband would pull through this one. I bowed my head and thanked both him and God. In the next heartbeat, I damned the Kaiser to hell for all eternity. I'm only human, you know.

"You'll get through this, Daisy," Dr. Benjamin said in a low voice. "Life isn't fair, and you and Billy have been hit with more than your share of burdens pretty early into the game, but you'll get through them."

"Thanks, Doc," I whispered, knowing he was correct but not feeling it at that moment.

And, as I said, Sam visited. I acquit him of trying to drive me crazy, but he did a good job of it anyway. Every day, right before he plopped his hat on his head and opened the front door to leave, he'd ask, "When do you think Billy will be well enough for you to do the séance?"

Because there was an extremely sick invalid in the house, I never once screeched at him. I only said, "I don't know, Sam," every time he asked the same stupid question, all the while wishing he'd go away and fall off a mountain somewhere.

But he never did.

Then there were the huge bouquets from Mrs. Kincaid. She called once or twice and sounded unhappy and panicky, but she was sensible enough (what a surprise!) not to push me to visit her while Billy remained in crisis.

"I'm so sorry you have to go through this, my dear," said she.

So am I, thought I. However, I said, "Thank you, Mrs. Kin-

High Spirits

caid. It's Billy who's suffering, not I." Liar, liar. "It's not in us to understand God's will for our lives." That was the pure-D truth, and it irked me a whole lot, but I never once wavered from my silky spiritualist voice when talking to the idiot woman. "The spirits are with us to guide us through these travails." And what a load of garbage *that* was. I had yet to have assistance from any but living human beings during my lifetime. Of course, I was young, but I doubted I was going to be dancing with spirits any time soon.

"As soon as he's better, I need for you to visit me, Daisy. There's no rush, of course."

I didn't believe her. She sounded desperate. But, darn it, she was *always* desperate, and Billy was sick, and I wasn't about to leave his side to read tarot cards or palms or a rounded hunk of crystal for a silly woman with more money than sense.

The neighbors were swell, too. Mrs. Killebrew across the street brought a lovely cake. "For the family, dear. You all must be so worried and harried at the moment."

We were, and we all appreciated her cake, which was an apple-walnut one and which we ate for breakfast. Whenever we needed supplies, Pa would drive out and get them. He also helped me take care of Billy during the day.

Flossie visited one day about a week into Billy's illness. I was beginning to believe that he was going to pull through—this time—and had just gone to the sofa in the living room to lie down for a few minutes, when the knock came at the door.

Spike, who didn't like it that the household was in an uproar and things no longer happened on the schedule he deemed appropriate, naturally went crazy. He ripped out of the bedroom where Billy lay, raced through the kitchen and dining room, and attacked the front door as if it had knocked on itself.

With a sigh, I got up and trudged to the door, scooping the wriggling dog up as I grasped the doorknob. When I opened the door, Flossie thrust a big bouquet of roses at me.

"Here, Daisy. I brung you guys some flowers."

I know I sighed, but I hope Flossie didn't notice. My face was hidden behind the hysterical body of my dog. He wasn't hysterical in a bad way. He liked Flossie and wanted to lick her. "Thanks, Flossie. Come on inside." What the heck. I wasn't going to rest much anyway.

"I don't want to bother you," she said, hesitating at the door.

I wanted to screech, *Why are you here, then?* at her, but naturally, I controlled myself. It seemed as if I was always controlling myself. Was controlling oneself what made one human? Was it only beasts that gave in to their initial impulses in various situations? How did one explain people like Jinx Jenkins if that was true?

Nuts. I was too tired to philosophize just then. "Don't be silly. I'm happy you came. Come on in."

At last she entered the house, and I could put Spike down and take her flowers. They were truly lovely. Spike instantly began leaping on Flossie. Fortunately, she didn't seem to mind.

I said halfheartedly, "Spike, stop that." He didn't, of course.

"Oh, I don't mind him," said Flossie, bless her. "I love dogs. Wish I could have one."

"Doesn't Jinx like dogs?" I asked, faintly curious.

"He don't like anything," Flossie said grimly. "But I'm not with Jinx no more."

This statement surprised me so much, my exhaustion fled for a couple of seconds. "You're not?"

"Naw. I moved out."

I wanted to hug her, but I had my hands full of roses. "I'm so glad, Flossie!"

Then she equivocated. "Well . . . I'm not really *out* yet, but I will be as soon as I find a place to live. Someplace that Jinx won't find me."

Oh. Well, so much for that faint hope. I decided not to comment on her situation. My own was enough for me to handle at the moment. "Come on into the kitchen, and I'll find a vase to put these in."

"I was gonna bring a vase, too, but I couldn't carry everything."

"That's okay. We have lots of pots and things."

So we went to the kitchen. The bedroom where Billy lay with Pa at his side led off of the kitchen, and Flossie could see into the sickroom. She whispered, "How's your husband?"

After heaving a huge sigh, I said, "It looks as if he's getting better. The doctor said he'll . . ." I broke off. I had been going to say that Doc Benjamin had told me Billy would survive this particular round of illness but stopped myself in time. Flossie had her own problems. She didn't need to worry about ours.

Evidently Flossie didn't read anything into my aborted comment. "Good. I'm glad. You don't need no more worries."

Boy, *that* was the truth! I rummaged through the cupboard where we kept vases and so forth, and found a white one that would serve well as a container for Flossie's roses.

"It was so nice of you to bring these, Flossie."

"Oh, shoot, it wasn't nothing."

I entertained the caustic thought that she was correct there. These roses weren't nothing. They were something, indeed. "Well, they're really pretty."

"Thanks. I got 'em at the Farmer's Market."

The Farmer's Market on Colorado and Walnut was a great place, where you could get just about anything you wanted, from Christmas turkeys and geese to fresh flowers, as Flossie had just demonstrated.

"There," I said, standing back from the bouquet. I wasn't very adept at flower arranging, but the roses looked pretty in spite of me. "I think I'll take these in to Billy."

I didn't have to. At that moment, Pa emerged from the sickroom. He winked at Flossie. "How-do, Miss Mosser. Did you bring those beautiful flowers?"

Flossie, by-gum, blushed! "Yes, Mr. Gumm. I brought 'em for Daisy and Billy."

"Well, that's just swell. Thank you." Pa, who was one of the nicest men in the world, then turned to me. "Say, Daisy, why don't you take a break from your nursing duties and go out to lunch with Miss Mosser here." Reaching into his trouser pocket, he handed me two dollars. "Here. You need a rest. Why don't the two of you go down to the Tea Cup Inn or over to the Crown and have a nice little sandwich or something."

"Oh, Pa, thank you!" I threw my arms around him and gave him a big squeeze. I *did* need a break.

"Gee, thanks, Mr. Gumm," said Flossie. "Are you sure you can spare the time, Daisy?"

"I'll watch the patient," said Pa, patting me on the back.

"We won't be gone long," I promised him. Turning to Flossie, I said, "It'll just take me a minute to change."

And I was as good as my word. Tiptoeing so as not to startle Billy, who, thank God, was sleeping, I whipped off my housedress, pulled a one-piece gray woolen dress over my head, put on black shoes, grabbed my black hat, snatched up my black bag and black coat, and was ready to go in not much more than sixty seconds.

"We won't be gone long, Pa," I said to my marvelous father, kissing him on the cheek.

"Take your time, sweetheart," he told me. "I'll just trot this beautiful bouquet in to Billy."

If I didn't have my family, life wouldn't be worth living.

Flossie and I didn't go to the Tea Cup Inn or to the Crown. Instead, we went to the Rexall Drug Store near Colorado and

Marengo. It was only a drugstore with a luncheon counter, but it was on the main east-west street in Pasadena, and I had a not-so-faint hope that we'd see Johnny Buckingham and company somewhere in the vicinity. After all, in those days you couldn't turn around without seeing or hearing a Salvation Army band on some street corner or other. We didn't find him before we settled ourselves onto stools at the lunch counter, but I brought Johnny into the conversation anyway.

"Did you enjoy the church service at the Salvation Army, Flossie?" Not very delicate, but I was too worn out to practice subtlety. Anyhow, Flossie wasn't apt to understand anything that wasn't set plainly before her.

"Yeah," she said, but I noticed her head was bowed and appeared kind of unhappy.

Reaching across the counter, I took her hand. The gesture surprised me more than it did Flossie, I think. "What's the matter, Flossie?"

She sighed deeply. "Oh, nothing. It's just that . . ."

I waited, but she didn't continue. "It's just that what?" I withdrew my hand, wondering what had possessed me to grab it in the first place.

She hesitated some more, then burst out with her whispered confession, the nature of which didn't surprise me since I'd already surmised she was a victim of what the magazines call low self-esteem. "It's just that I'm not good enough for them people."

"Nonsense. You're every bit as good as any of them, Flossie Mosser. Why, Johnny Buckingham himself had all sorts of troubles after the war. He was there in the trenches in France, just like Billy. But while Billy got shot and gassed during the war, Johnny started having problems afterwards. He got so low, he even tried to kill himself." I'd just then remembered that part of Johnny's sordid saga, and I'm glad I did because it jarred Flossie.

"No!"

"Yes. In fact, Johnny was about as low as a person can get. I'm telling you this because Johnny's story is pretty common. I mean, he's not the only one who was shell-shocked and had terrible problems after that wretched war, and it's a darned shame. Johnny took to drink, Flossie."

Her mouth fell open. "No!"

"Yes. In fact, he himself says that he was a dipsomaniac, and the booze would have killed him if not for the Salvation Army. That's the reason he loves it so much. The Army doesn't turn people away just because they have problems. They accept everyone and try to help them with their troubles." Inspiration, which had a hard time struggling to the surface of my sleep-deprived brain, finally poked its head out. "Not only that, but I think Johnny really likes you."

Darned if Flossie didn't blush again. "Naw. He couldn't."

"Why not?" I demanded. "Look at you! Why, you're a lovely young woman, Flossie Mosser, and you're sweet and kind and . . ." And easily led astray and currently involved with a vicious hoodlum. But I didn't want to bring those distasteful facts up that day. "And you have good, kindly instincts." Okay, the ending was feeble, but the rest of the speech was pretty good.

Flossie blinked several times. She'd have spoken if the waitress hadn't delivered our lunches: tuna salad sandwich for me and corned beef for Flossie, along with green river floats, which were exclusive to that counter, as far as I know. I don't know what was in them, but they were green, and they were good.

After taking a bite of my sandwich, which was served with potato chips, I leaned toward Flossie. "I know Johnny is taken with you, Flossie. Don't you think you could care for him, too?"

I hoped I wasn't wrong about Johnny's interest in her, but I didn't think I was. In actual fact, I was kind of afraid Johnny was seeing things in sweet Flossie that weren't really there but that he was hoping were. Although, come to think of it, Flossie was so eager to please, and Johnny was such an overall good guy, she'd probably blossom into whatever he thought she was. If you know what I mean.

Flossie didn't respond for the longest time. I was about to prod her, when she whispered, "I do care for him. I think I love him."

Thank God! I didn't say that out loud. I said, "Well, then, that's good."

"Huh."

I glanced sharply at her. "What do you mean, 'huh'? What does that mean?"

She put down her sandwich and took a sip of her Green River. "I gotta get away from Jinx first."

"I'll bet Johnny can help with that."

She turned so precipitately, I darned near fell off my counter stool. "No! Oh, no, Daisy, I don't want Johnny nowhere near Jinx. Jinx is bad. He might hurt Johnny."

I have to admit that possibility hadn't occurred to me. "Hmm. Well, I think we should talk to Johnny about that. I'm pretty sure he could help you."

After a huge pause, during which I finished my sandwich and munched my chips and Flossie did nothing but stare blankly into space—I darned near grabbed half of her corned beef, but restrained myself—she finally said, "Well . . . maybe."

I guess it was better than a flat *never,* but I still wanted to hit her. I think that was because I'd been under a lot of strain lately.

Flossie was spared a taste of my uneven temper, however, by the appearance of none other than Johnny Buckingham! He was in his uniform, so I guess he and his army band had been out and about on Colorado Boulevard, but he was alone in Rexall Drugs when I spotted him.

Leaping from my stool, I hollered, "Johnny! Over here!" He'd been heading toward the side of the store where they carried bandages and foot plasters and stuff like that. I guess marching along Colorado Boulevard all day every day makes your feet ache. He—along with nearly everyone else in the store—turned and spotted me. A huge smile spread over his face, and he waved and began making his way to the lunch counter. I was *so* glad to see him. And not only because I wanted him to rescue Flossie, either. I'd started feeling guilty about abandoning my sick husband.

"Well, fancy seeing you two here," he said as he took a stool next to Flossie. "How's Billy, Daisy?"

"He's getting better, thank God."

"Thank God," said Johnny, and I knew that for him the expression wasn't merely what everyone says when they're glad about something.

"In fact," said I, thinking as fast as my sluggish noggin could think, "I really need to get back to him. Say, Johnny, are you here for lunch? Flossie hasn't finished hers yet, and if you could sit with her while you eat your own, I could get back to Billy." Sneaky little devil, aren't I?

"That sounds like a great idea to me," said Johnny, grinning like an imp.

"Oh, but . . ." Flossie looked scared.

"Nuts," I said. "You need to finish your lunch, and I need to get back to Billy. I'll see you both later." I tossed the money Pa had given me on the counter. "Pay the lady out of this, will you please? I think there's enough for you, too, Johnny."

It was definitely enough for three lunches, and Johnny smiled gratefully. "Thanks, Daisy. That's real nice of you."

"It's nothing." It was nothing to me, at any rate, and I figured Pa wouldn't mind.

And with that, I abandoned Flossie and hurried back to my formerly abandoned husband. Sometimes life just works out. Not, unfortunately, very often.

Chapter Fourteen

By the end of the second week of Billy's illness, he was able to get out of bed and get around the house in his wheelchair. It looked to me as though the days of helping him learn to walk again were over, at least for a good long while. Even maneuvering himself around in his chair exhausted him.

"Wish I weren't such a burden to you, Daisy," he mumbled one day when we both sat on the front porch.

March had limped in, and the weather had turned almost balmy. The gentle breezes brought leftover scents from the rainstorm we'd had the night before. Pretty soon the orange trees would begin to blossom, and then the air would be fragrant enough to make a sensitive person faint dead away from ecstasy. I'm not that sensitive, but I still love the aroma of orange blossoms. They always reminded me of my wedding, memories of which almost always made me cry.

Crumb.

"Stop it, Billy. You're not a burden. Anyhow, if our situations were reversed, you'd take care of me, wouldn't you?"

"You bet I would," he said, taking my hand. "I can't imagine my life without you, Daisy."

To keep from bursting into tears and ruining the moment, I chuckled weakly. "Yeah, we've known each other for a long time, haven't we?"

He chuckled, too, although not for long. I held my breath for the duration, praying that he wouldn't start coughing. "I'll never forget how you used to chase after me when we were kids."

"I loved you then, too." It was true. I'd had a "pash" for Billy ever since he was in fourth grade and I was in second. He was just the perfect guy in those days. And he still was—or he would have been if his health hadn't been ruined.

"Yeah?" He grinned at me.

"Yeah." I grinned back.

And wouldn't you know it? At that very sensitive moment, who should pull up in his big ugly Hudson motorcar but Sam Rotondo. I muttered something indelicate under my breath.

Billy raised a hand and waved. He'd have hollered out a "Hey, Sam," but he didn't have the breath.

As he walked jauntily up the front walkway, Sam removed his hat and smiled broadly at my husband. "Good to see you up and about, Billy!"

"Up, anyway," said Billy with a grin.

Sam plopped himself on the porch rail. Then he frowned at me. He would. "I'm afraid we're going to have to get that séance set up pretty quick, Daisy."

I groaned inside. Since I didn't want to upset Billy, I didn't let my groan loose into the world. "Yeah?"

"I don't like Daisy being involved with those guys, Sam."

"Me, neither," I muttered, knowing that to protest would be useless. It was play with the crooks or go to jail. Sam had made that perfectly clear to me already.

"I don't like it either, Billy, but she's about the only in we have with those guys."

"I don't see why," I said in spite of knowing it would do no good. "You know where they are and what they're doing. Why don't you just raid the place?"

Sam sighed as if he'd already gone over this issue with me already and didn't want to have to do it again. "We need to know that all the big shots will be there. Usually only Maggiori's employees are at the speak. They'll *all* be there for the séance."

"Oh." I hated to admit it, but that made sense even to me. "I guess so."

Billy still didn't like it. I could tell by his stony face.

"So let me know as soon as you set up the séance. All right?"

"Yeah," I said. "I guess."

"Hey, I brought you guys something," Sam said, his mood lightening. He reached into his coat and withdrew an advertising brochure. "We talk about these things all the time, and I just picked this up downtown."

I almost could have thanked Sam for removing the expression of severe disapproval from my husband's face. When Billy took a gander at the brochure, he lit up like a firecracker. "Oh, boy, Daisy, look at this! It's all about radio signal receiving sets."

If there was anything less interesting to me than radio signal receiving sets, I can't imagine what it might be, although I feigned joy for Billy's sake. "My goodness!"

"Look at this," said Sam, bending over and pointing at what looked like a bundle of wires and a strange-looking box. "It says here that if you set these things up right, you can get signals from all over the country. All over the world, someday, they say."

"Wow." Billy stared at the strange drawing, entranced.

I couldn't see the point myself. Not that I wanted to rain on anybody's parade or anything. Still, I said, "Um, what will you hear if you pick up signals?" Just curious. That's me.

Billy glanced at me as if he couldn't believe I'd asked such a stupid question. "What can you *hear?* Why, eventually, you'll be able to hear everything!"

I still didn't get it. "Like what? I mean, what will you hear all over the world? Or the country? Or wherever?"

Sam looked at me as if he couldn't believe I'd said such a stupid thing, either, but wanted to humor me for Billy's sake. "Music. Baseball games. Things like that."

I glanced from him to the drawing once more. It still looked like a box and wires to me. Still, I was willing to give it a chance. "You mean that with that thing, you'll be able to hear an orchestra play in . . . in New York City?"

"Sure," said Billy, wide-eyed and happy. I was glad of that, anyhow.

"Yeah," said Sam. "And maybe someday, you'll be able to hear plays and stuff like that, too."

Puzzled but game, I said, "Um . . . and will you be able to hear anybody anywhere? Just because you have one of these things?"

I think Sam was beginning to understand my befuddlement. "Well, not unless the orchestra or whatever is set up to send a signal."

"Oh." I was still confused but didn't feel like talking about that sort of thing any longer. Besides, I heard the telephone ringing in the kitchen. With a sigh, I got up, fearing what that ring foretold. "I'll let you two talk about this stuff. I've got to get the wire."

My premonition of disaster (we spiritualists are good at these types of things) proved to be correct. On the other end of the wire was Mrs. Kincaid, hysterical as usual.

"Oh, Daisy!"

I rolled my eyes. "Good morning, Mrs. Kincaid."

"Oh, it's not! It's not! I'm just beside myself!"

Beside herself, was she? Did that mean there were now two of her? Heaven forfend! At least she wasn't beside me.

"I'm very sorry, Mrs. Kincaid. Perhaps if you sat very still and let your mind go blank"—*which shouldn't be too darned hard for you,* thought I nastily—"then the spirits will be able to soothe you and offer you guidance."

You'll notice that I didn't instantly volunteer to rush over there with my various bags of tricks (tarot cards, crystal ball, Ouija board, Rolly). I was tired after two weeks of worry over whether or not my husband would survive his latest illness, and the silliness of Mrs. Kincaid and her ilk didn't sit well with me just then. Not, of course, that I was going to tell *her* that. I still needed to earn a living, after all.

"I've tried, Daisy," she said piteously. "I've tried *so* hard. But something has happened that terrifies me!"

Egad. This sounded serious, although I wasn't going to take anything Mrs. Kincaid said as fact without checking it out first. "The spirits haven't helped you?" What a shock. "Are you sure you've emptied your mind and meditated on them?" It shouldn't be too difficult for her to empty her mind since there was so little in it.

"Yes, yes!" she sobbed.

Knowing the reason for her present state of alarm, but faintly hoping, I asked, "Is it Stacy?"

A wail that nearly split my eardrums preceded her, "Yes! Yes! Oh, Daisy I don't know what to *do!*"

I'd already thought of a whole bunch of things she could do to Stacy, but I'd never once mentioned them to Stacy's mother, and I didn't plan to begin now. When you looked at it one way, Stacy Kincaid provided me with a whole lot of my income. Therefore, I bit the bullet, sighing inside. I never let my sighs be heard by my clients. "Do you need me to come over, Mrs. Kincaid?"

"Oh, yes! But I know you're taking care of your husband, Daisy, and I'd *never* ask you to desert him in his hour of need."

Sure she wouldn't.

Oh, very well, I was feeling particularly surly that day, probably because I was bone weary and Sam Rotondo was lurking right outside on my front porch. I tried to snap myself out of it, but snapping didn't help. Therefore, I pretended. We spiritualists are good at that, too. "It would be no burden, Mrs. Kincaid. Billy is no longer in danger." Or, to put it another way, the spirits, whoever *they* were, hadn't snatched him away from me yet.

She sent a pathetic sniffle across the telephone wires, and it occurred to me that I hadn't shooed any of the party-liners off the wire. Oh, well. I don't suppose they'd mind this bit of human drama. Heck, it might make them feel better about their own lives to know that an incredibly wealthy woman was so idiotic.

"Are you sure, dear?"

"Yes, Mrs. Kincaid."

"Are you *positive?*"

Why do people do that? Of course I was sure, or I wouldn't have offered. Would leaving Billy so soon after his brush with death bother me? Of course, it would. Would I do it anyway? You bet. It was the Mrs. Kincaids of this world who kept the Daisy Gumm Majestys of this world out of the poor house. Did I like it? No. So what? So nothing.

"It would be no bother at all, Mrs. Kincaid. I'll be there in . . ." I hesitated, trying to think of how soon I could get myself ready and drag myself out of the house. It took almost no time to powder my nose, brush my hair and slip into one of my spiritualist costumes, but I had to prepare myself mentally for the upcoming ordeal as well, and that would take some time. ". . . Um, I'll be there in two hours. Will that be all right with you?"

She sobbed loudly. "Oh, *thank* you, Daisy! You'll never know how much this means to me."

I would if she gave me a big tip, which I expected she would. Therefore, I only said kindly, "Try not to worry too much, Mrs.

Kincaid. Help is at hand."

All right, so I lied. I made my living lying, as Billy so often pointed out. Nevertheless, it was a fine living, I was good at it, and, therefore, I would continue doing it until I didn't have to any longer.

I put the receiver back, sighed deeply, looked at the kitchen clock—it was only nine in the morning—and shuffled back out to the porch, where I found Billy and Sam still engrossed in their radio signal receiving set. Pa and Spike had joined them by this time, and even Spike seemed interested. I guess it was something men liked. I couldn't quite make myself care about radio signal receiving sets.

Billy looked up from the brochure. He saw my face, lifted his eyebrows, and said, "Mrs. Kincaid?"

"You can tell by looking?"

With a grin, he said, "Yeah. You look as if you've just agreed to attend a hanging."

With yet another sigh, I sat on the porch railing. Pa had taken my chair, and Sam was kneeling next to Billy. "That's what I feel like. She's hysterical again, but she wouldn't tell me why."

"But it's Stacy." Billy was well versed in the Kincaid saga.

Sam looked up from the brochure, his heavy eyebrows drawn down into a V over his eyes. "What's she up to now?"

"I have no idea. I'm going to take my cards and board and Rolly over to Mrs. Kincaid's. Told her I'd be there in a couple of hours."

"Who's Rolly?" Sam asked.

Pa, Billy, and I all looked at each other. This time it was Pa who grinned. I stood, waved a hand at them all, and said, "Have Pa or Billy tell you. I have to prepare myself."

And I did so, first by taking a nice hot bath—I pitied people who didn't have hot and cold running water, even though we'd only owned this nifty bungalow with same for a couple of years—and washing my hair. Fortunately, said hair was thick, short and easily maneuvered, and it dried as I dressed.

Because the weather had turned warmish, I donned a lightweight, russet-colored suit. Because I didn't feel like fussing, I used the same black shoes, stockings, handbag and hat I usually wore. Then I gathered up my spiritualist accouterments, looked in the mirror, despaired of the dark circles under my eyes, powdered my face—as a spiritualist, I strove to appear pale and interesting—and set forth into the world as a knight of old might have gone off to battle. Or as a squirrel might climb a tree looking for nuts. I figure we humans aren't alone in needing to scramble for our sustenance.

I nearly fell over dead when Sam Rotondo, watching me emerge through the front door of our very modest castle, said, "You look nice."

Would wonders never cease? I eyed him for signs of sarcasm, observed none, and said, "Thanks."

"That's my girl," said Pa. "Pretty as a picture."

Bless the man for a saint.

Billy said, "You look too good for *that* family, for sure."

Bless him, too, because he made me laugh.

"Thanks, fellows. I'm good at my job. I even dress the part." And, with a waggle of my eyebrows, a pat for Spike, and a peck on the cheek for Billy, I hied myself off to earn the money with which to bring home the bacon. Or, if we were especially lucky, a leg of lamb, one of Aunt Vi's particular specialties.

Mrs. Kincaid belonged to the Episcopal Church. I know that sounds irrelevant, but it's as good an introduction as anything as to why Father Frederick, the Episcopal priest of St. Mark's, met me at the door. I must admit to being somewhat surprised, since Mrs. Kincaid's butler Featherstone generally greets callers.

"Father Frederick!" said I, amply demonstrating said state of surprise.

He had a wonderful smile, and he leveled it at me then. "Come in, come in, Mrs. Majesty. I'm afraid Mrs. Kincaid is laid rather low at the moment."

"Is that why Featherstone isn't answering the door?"

"Indeed it is." And darned if he didn't wink at me.

A roly-poly man, Father Frederick didn't fit my mental image of what an Episcopalian churchman should look like. Ma and Aunt Vi always sniffed when speaking about Episcopalians, and I vividly recall them whispering about people being too big for their britches and thinking they were better than everyone else when discussing the Episcopalians they knew. The only Episcopalians I knew were Mrs. Kincaid, who was terminally silly, Stacy Kincaid, who was probably evil, and Father Frederick, who could pass for Father Christmas in a pinch and whom I liked a whole lot. Therefore, I held none of my mother's prejudices and figured Episcopalians were just like everybody else, although many of them had lots more money than most of us.

I adored Father Frederick, mainly because he never disparaged the way I made my living, but that's not the only reason. In his own way, he reminded me of Dr. Benjamin and Johnny Buckingham in that he seemed to accept people as they were. Mind you, he wasn't above the occasional little sermon, but his sermons didn't seem designed to make people feel worthless or useless, as some did. Come to think of it, it isn't only preachers who do that.

But that's not the point. Father Frederick answered the door, and I asked him what was up.

"I'm afraid Stacy has really done it this time," he said, although he smiled as he did so.

"Oh, dear. What's she done now?"

"I think you'd best let Madeline tell you that. It's not my place to tell tales."

Phooey. But I guess he was doing his duty according to his calling in life. Sort of like me.

When Father Frederick and I made it to the living room (called a "drawing room" by the wealthy Mrs. Kincaid), I discovered why Featherstone had not answered the door. He was otherwise occupied. And it didn't look as if he cared for it much.

Mrs. Kincaid lay prostrate on the sofa, a fancy number with deep red velvet upholstery that went well with the medallion-back chairs. Mr. Algernon Pinkerton (called Algie by Mrs. Kincaid), kneeling at her head, waved vinaigrette under her nose, while Featherstone stood behind the sofa, stoic in his bearing, holding a polished silver tray with stuff on it. I presumed the tray held things that would be used for Mrs. Kincaid's revival should the smelling salts fail.

I said, "Oh, dear."

Mr. Pinkerton turned and glanced over his shoulder. "Oh, Mrs. Majesty! I'm so glad you're here. Poor Madeline is beside herself!"

She'd told me that much already. I drew closer. "What struck her down?" I asked in my mystically modulated spiritualist's voice.

Mr. Pinkerton creaked to his feet, setting the vinaigrette on Featherstone's tray. Featherstone averted his nose, and I don't blame him. With a glance down at Mrs. Kincaid, Mr. Pinkerton whispered, "It's that wretched daughter of hers."

Ha! So I wasn't the only one who disliked Stacy Kincaid! Not that I'd believed I was, but it was nice to get confirmation. And from Mrs. Kincaid's special gentleman friend, too. I suspected they would marry one of these days, and I approved. Of course, they didn't need my approval, but Mrs. Kincaid's first husband had been a true louse, and she deserved a nice man in her life. Mr. Pinkerton was a very nice man, if almost as flighty as Mrs. K. herself.

I murmured, "Oh, dear," again, mainly because I couldn't think of anything more pertinent to say.

"Madeline has been dying to see you," went on Mr. Pinkerton, in what I hoped was an exaggeration. "She's so worried, you see."

"I see." And, indeed, I did. Whatever Stacy had done this time had clearly knocked her poor mother for a loop. Also, however much I joke about Mrs. Kincaid and her silliness, I liked the woman and didn't appreciate Stacy being such an overall poop. If frequenting speakeasies, drinking liquor, and smoking cigarettes wasn't enough to send Mrs. Kincaid to the sofa with a vinaigrette, I almost didn't want to know what Stacy had done this time.

No. I'm lying. I detested Stacy, and I wanted all the ammunition I could get to fuel my dislike.

Mrs. Kincaid started moaning softly, so I guessed my services would be called for soon. Wafting nearer to the sofa, I said in my most melodious voice, "Dear Mrs. Kincaid, what can I do to help you?"

"Daisy?" she whispered, her eyes still shut. "Daisy? Is that you?"

"Yes," I said. "I am here to be of service to you."

Her eyelids quivered for a moment and then, shoving Algie Pinkerton aside, which I thought was kind of rude, Mrs. Kincaid heaved herself to a sitting position. I acquitted her of selfishness when she realized what she'd done, grasped Mr. Pinkerton's arm and said in a trembling voice, "Oh, Algie, I'm so sorry. Please forgive me."

Mr. Pinkerton, gentleman to the core, patted her hand and said stoutly, "There's nothing to forgive, my dear. You've suffered a severe blow."

After giving a most unspiritualistic start of horror, I realized the blow he spoke of was of a mental nature and not a physical one delivered by Stacy. I hoped no one saw my jerk. To maintain my image, I stood there, head bowed, my Ouija board and red silk tarot bag clutched to my unfortunately well-rounded bosom. Even though I bound my breasts, I couldn't achieve the boyish silhouette fashionable then. Anyhow, in that pose and with luck, I'd look as if I were either praying or gathering my aura around me in order to perform feats of arcane wonder.

"Thank you, Algie. I don't know what I'd do without you."

By gum, Mr. Pinkerton blushed! He was really kind of cute. A good deal leaner than Mrs. Kincaid, he was also on the short side and balding, was always impeccably groomed, and was as rich as Croesus, whoever he was. Some fabulously wealthy Greek, I think. From what Harold Kincaid had told me, he came from what they call "old money," and had moved out to California for his health, which didn't cotton to the cold winters of New York. I think he was about Mrs. Kincaid's age, which I reckoned hovered in the early fifties. She seemed older than my parents to me, but I think that was because my parents were hard workers and vigorous, even Pa with his weak heart. Mrs. Kincaid had been relaxing all her life, and she seemed elderly and soft to me.

However, that's not the point. I stood there, waiting to be called upon. And, after apologies and forgiveness had been exchanged, I was.

"Oh, Daisy, thank you so much for coming. And at such a trying time in your life, too."

She had that right. "Please, Mrs. Kincaid, think nothing of it. A gift like mine is only worthwhile when it is shared."

Sniffling, she whispered, "Oh, thank you, my dear. Is that your board I see?"

"It is."

"And do you think Rolly will forgive me for asking him to appear in that dreadful place a few weeks ago?"

"He has already done so," I told her, which was the truth. I figured poor old Rolly was a victim of my own lousy judgment. Mind you, my judgment was usually better than Mrs. Kincaid's, but, that being the case, I should have had more sense than to bow to her entreaties that I perform that first cursed séance for Mr. Maggiori.

She burst into sobs. I sighed internally. I hated these scenes. We poor folk didn't have time to wallow in our various grievances and melancholy because we were too busy earning a living. It kind of irked me that Mrs. Kincaid, who had so much money and so much time, could afford to spend so much of both on one lousy daughter. Mind you, Stacy was a particularly grim burden to bear, but at least she hadn't been shot all to heck and had her lungs burnt out by mustard gas.

There I go again. Please forgive me.

After a minute or so, Mrs. Kincaid got herself under control. "Thank you, Daisy. Please. Take a chair." She glanced around and saw no chair.

Mr. Pinkerton jumped to help us. He was *such* a nice man. I noticed Father Frederick sitting on an overstuffed armchair in a corner, an amused expression on his face, but I decided it would be better not to pay too much attention to him. It would be awful to break out laughing when I was fiddling with the Ouija board. Mrs. Kincaid took this stuff *so* seriously. She'd be stung if I demonstrated such a lack of mediumistic sensibility. And so would I be stung when she fired me.

Anyway, Algie Pinkerton fetched one of the pretty medallion-backed chairs from a corner and plunked it on the other side of the coffee table situated before the sofa, and I sat upon it waftingly. We spiritualists are superb wafters.

High Spirits

The thing about the Ouija board is that, even though I *know* this spiritualist stuff is all bunkum, it still doesn't feel as if I'm manipulating the planchet when I use the board most of the time. And honestly, it doesn't move for some people at all. One time I talked Billy into playing the Ouija board with me, and the silly planchet sat there like a piece of wood, which it was, and didn't budge. Even when I exerted some pressure, the stupid thing only moved as far as I pushed it and didn't travel any farther. You figure it out; it's beyond me.

That day, however, that silly little block of wood zipped and zoomed over that board on its three little peg legs. I still didn't know what Stacy had done to cause so much trouble, but it didn't seem to matter a whole lot. I'd be really sorry for Mrs. Kincaid if Stacy had turned from booze to opium or cocaine, both of which were very much in fashion among the so-called bright young things of the day. I thought they were merely stupid, but that's because I can't afford vices. Well, except for clothes, which I guess might be considered a vice, but at least I made them myself.

"Would you like to ask Rolly a question, Mrs. Kincaid?" I said after we'd established the presence of sweet Rolly, a process I won't go in to now.

"Yes, please." Her voice still quivered like a blade of grass in a strong wind.

"Very well. Rolly awaits."

Mrs. Kincaid swallowed hard, and then said, "Rolly, is this latest crazy of Stacy's going to be permanent?"

Rolly seemed to hesitate. Like Mrs. Kincaid's voice, the planchet quivered. Then, instead of moving to the "yes" or the "no" painted on the board, darned if it didn't start spelling out words. I watched in fascination, even though I *knew* in my bones that Rolly was a figment of my imagination and that pieces of wood aren't intelligent and can't answer questions.

However, that day, Rolly, the planchet, or I spelled out, "I don't know."

Mrs. Kincaid collapsed in a weeping heap. When I told her how sorry I was that Rolly didn't give her the news she wanted to hear, she moaned out, "No. No, it's all my fault. You and Rolly have nothing to do with this. I'm reaping the consequences of my folly. I should have sent Stacy away to that school run by nuns in Switzerland when Father Frederick suggested it years ago."

Goodness. I lifted an inquiring eyebrow at Father Frederick, who looked up from the *Saturday Evening Post* he'd been leafing through, caught my questioning glance, and nodded.

"Rolly *did* say that he couldn't fully and accurately interpret the future in this instance," I said in an effort to ease her sorrow.

Sitting up and groping for her handkerchief, which lay in a sopping heap at her side, Mrs. Kincaid whimpered, "That's true. Perhaps there's still hope."

I said, "I'm sure there is," and I scrammed out of there as if my skirt were on fire. I didn't even stop in the kitchen to see Aunt Vi. She'd only have scolded me for upsetting Ms. Kincaid, even though Mrs. Kincaid had been upset before my arrival.

Boy, was I glad to get out of there!

Chapter Fifteen

Because the afternoon had been so unpleasant, and that was after two weeks of even worse unpleasantness, I decided to take a trip to Maxime's fabric store to see if I could find any spectacular new patterns and materials on sale with which to update my wardrobe. Not that it needed updating.

Still, the past month had been perfectly horrid, starting with that wretched séance at Maggiori's speakeasy south of Pasadena, up through and including Sam's bargain with me, Flossie Mosser's problems, Billy's illness, and Mrs. Kincaid's hysterical unhappiness. Therefore, I decided to treat myself.

As I drove down Colorado heading to Maxime's, darned if I didn't spot Flossie Mosser walking purposefully on the sidewalk towards Pasadena Avenue. I pulled the Chevrolet to a stop and got out of the car. "Flossie!"

She stopped, turned, saw me, and waved happily. "Hey, Daisy! Wanna come with me?"

"Where are you going?"

"The Salvation Army church," said she, as if she did such things every day in the week.

I gave a mental shrug, figuring it would be cheaper to go with Flossie to the Salvation Army than visit Maxime's and buy material and a pattern for clothes I didn't need. I hurried to catch up with her.

"What's going on at the church?" I asked as I got into step with her.

"I don't know. I just thought I'd visit and see if there's some way I can join."

"You want to join the Salvation Army?"

I guess I didn't hide my astonishment very well because Flossie turned a small frown upon me. "You don't think I should? I thought you was the one wanted me to go in the first place."

"No! I mean yes. I mean I'm only a little surprised is all." Shoot, my big mouth could get me in more trouble than anything else I knew. Well, maybe except for Sam Rotondo. "I think it's great that you want to join." I just hadn't anticipated this since she'd appeared to feel so unworthy the last time we'd spoken.

She seemed mollified. With a satisfied sigh, she said, "Yeah. I think it's the right thing to do. Them—I mean *those*—Army folks are real nice. They didn't even sneer at me or anything for being what I am."

Aha. So Johnny, or somebody, was not only trying to boost her self-confidence but also trying to teach her proper grammar. Interesting. "What you are is a very nice person who's had a rough life, Flossie. You aren't at fault for that."

"Huh. Try telling that to Jinx. He keeps telling me I'm the lowest of the low."

"Jinx is wrong," I said through clenched teeth. "*Jinx* is the lowest of the low, if you ask me."

She flashed me a smile that made her look pretty and young and shy. Boy. And when I'd first seen her across that smoke-filled room filled with flaming youth and jazz music, I'd thought she was old and hard and coarse. It was amazing how far a little honest interest and caring could go to redeem a lost soul. I guess that was the Salvation Army's message and goal in life. I thought Billy should be applauded for suggesting it in the first place, even if he *had* meant it as a joke.

Therefore, instead of visiting Maxime's, I decided to see if I couldn't find something for Billy. He deserved a nice present. Not only had he probably saved Flossie's life, but his own as well, and he'd accomplished both in a very short period of time.

Since Flossie had brought Jinx into the conversation, I decided to be blunt and ask her about him. "So . . . are you going to leave Jinx, Flossie? Your association with the Salvation Army seems at . . . um, cross-purposes, I guess, with your association with Jinx."

Her smile vanished as if it had never existed. "Yeah. I'm going to leave him. Only I have to do it careful, or—"

"Carefully," I said, and then wished I hadn't.

"Huh?"

With an internal smack upside my head for my idiocy, I said, "Carefully is the word you want. You need to plan *carefully*. Not careful. You can *be* careful, but you have to *plan* carefully."

She mulled that one over, and I feared I'd distracted her from telling the story of her escape plan from the miserable Jinx. "Oh. I guess there's a rule for that sort of thing, huh?"

"You betcha. But you said you're planning your escape carefully, right?"

"Yeah. I'm being real . . . careful?" She cocked an eyebrow at me, and I smiled my approval. She went on, "Anyhow, I have to plan my escape carefully, 'cause otherwise he'll get me, and I don't want to be beat up no more."

I opened my mouth to correct her, realized what I was doing, and snapped it shut again.

She understood in spite of my clumsiness. "Any more, huh?"

"Right. Any more."

"I don't want to get beat up anymore."

"Right." Good enough for government work, as my father was fond of saying. "Um, is Johnny Buckingham helping you in this regard."

Darned if she didn't practically start glowing right there on the street. "Oh, yeah. He's such a swell guy. He's real nice, Daisy. I wish I could meet somebody like him instead of bums like Jinx."

"What do you mean somebody like him? You've met *him.* Why would you want to meet anyone else?"

"Well . . ." Now that she wasn't wearing a thick layer of powder on her cheeks, her blush stood out like a red, red rose. "I don't. I really like him, Daisy." She bowed her head. "But I got a long ways to go before I can think about finding a fella like him."

She clearly didn't get my point. "You've already found him, Flossie," I said gently.

"Oh, but—"

"And don't tell me you're not good enough for him, either, Flossie Mosser. You most definitely *are* good enough for him. Why, you'd be a swell addition to his army of folks. Say, Flossie, do you play an instrument or anything?"

"An instrument?" Her big blue eyes rounded, and she gazed at me with puzzlement.

"Sure. For the Army band, you know?"

"Oh." Her face took on an expression of bleak sadness, as if her being unfamiliar with a musical instrument would be the death knell to her interest in the Salvation Army and Johnny Buckingham. "No. I don't play nothing. Anything."

There was definitely hope for the woman. "Well, don't worry about it. You can be one of the ladies with the tambourines. They're almost more important than the musicians, anyhow, because they collect the money after the band plays."

She brightened minimally. "Oh. Yeah. I forgot that part."

"Anyhow, you can sing, can't you?"

"I guess. I don't know no—I mean *any* hymns."

"You'll learn," I told her confidently. The good Lord knows,

I'd learned.

The strains of "Onward Christian Soldiers" smote our ears an instant before the band, led by Johnny Buckingham, turned the corner from Pasadena Avenue onto Colorado Boulevard. Flossie blushed again, and I was pleased to see that as soon as Johnny spotted us, he lowered his cornet and rushed over.

"Flossie! Daisy! It's so good to see you both." His eyes were on Flossie, though, and my hope for her future brightened even more.

"Hey, Johnny."

"Hi," said the now-shy Flossie.

Johnny took her arm. "Say, you two want to go grab a cup of coffee or a Coke or something? It's time the band got back to headquarters, and I'm dry as a bone after playing all afternoon."

I pondered for only a second or two. "Say, Johnny and Flossie, why don't the two of you go grab a Coke. I've got some shopping to do."

So they did. And I went shopping.

I was pretty pleased with myself when I got home about an hour later. I hadn't found exactly what I was looking for, and what I had found was awfully expensive, but I figured that I could save some money, and maybe I could give Billy his thank-you treat pretty soon.

My mood didn't last past the front door, in spite of Spike's happy greeting and my happy response to it. When I stood up, Spike in my arms, I discovered that Pa and Billy and Sam Rotondo were all there waiting for me, and each one of them looked like the face of doom. I stared at the group of the men in my life—Sam was only there because I couldn't get rid of him—and my heart sank.

"What's wrong?" I knew something was wrong.

"Nothing," said Pa.

Another glance at the threesome, Sam and Pa flanking Billy in his chair, had me calling my own father a liar, although that's not exactly what I meant. "I don't believe you. What is it? I can tell something's the matter. You all look like somebody's died." I gasped and cried out, "It's not Ma, is it?"

Sweet Lord in heaven, if something had happened to my mother, I didn't think I could stand it. Life was hard enough already. I couldn't bear to think of a life without Ma.

"Good God, Daisy, get hold of yourself."

This, from Sam Rotondo. I glared at him, furious. "Well, then, tell me what's going on! You three look like a firing squad, and I don't care what you think of me, Sam Rotondo, I do *not* deserve to be executed!"

"For God's sake," Sam said, patently disgusted. "Nobody's talking about executions here. Billy called me at the station and asked me to come over. Maggiori's been trying to get hold of you."

My heart squeezed painfully. I didn't like that expression, *get hold of* me. It sounded ominous. So much for my pleasant mood. Sighing wearily, I dragged Spike and my spiritualist accoutrements to the sofa and sat, plopping my Ouija board and bag of cards on the table beside me. "Oh, joy."

"I told him you'd be home after you went to Mrs. Kincaid's," said Billy. He looked at me accusingly. "Where the devil have you been? I thought you'd be home an hour ago. Did the woman have *that* much to say to the blasted spirits?"

Eyeing him with disfavor, I tried to remember why I'd spent the afternoon scrounging around for a specific present for him. Didn't work. Feeling even more put-upon than usual, I snapped, "I saw Flossie on the street and stopped to talk to her. We walked to the Salvation Army. Then I did a little shopping. Should I have telephoned? I didn't know I had to account for every minute of my time spent away from you." I regret to say that my tone of voice was rather vicious.

Billy's lips thinned. "No, you don't have to account to me for your darned time, Daisy. I just don't like this whole situation."

I sighed, already regretting my temper. "I'm sorry, Billy. My nerves are shot. I don't like the situation, either. Maybe this telephone call from Maggiori will signal the end to everything." Oh, boy, I didn't quite mean *that* either. While I prayed that his speakeasy would be closed and he and his goons driven out of town forever, I sort of wanted to survive the ordeal.

"I hope so," said Billy, sounding as if he'd accepted my apology.

"We all hope so," said Pa. He came over and patted my arm. "It'll be all right, Daisy. You'll see."

"You're performing a valuable service for the citizens of Pasadena, Daisy."

I stared at Sam Rotondo. Then I shook my head hard, sure I'd misunderstood. Had he actually said something nice about me? Wonders never cease, do they?

And then the telephone rang. After all four of us exchanged speaking glances, I rose, set Spike on the floor, and went to the kitchen to answer it. I felt as though I were going to my own hanging.

Sure enough, it was a Maggiori thug. After he'd assured himself that I was I and not some police-planted interloper, and after I'd shooed all our party-line neighbors off the wire, Maggiori came on the wire and spoke to me. I'd have felt important if it had been, say, the king of England or someone like that. As he was only a rather high-level criminal, I saved my awe for someone who deserved it.

"Mrs. Majesty," he said. He had a smooth voice, low and sort of insinuating, if you know what I mean. Oily. The man was oily.

"How do you do, Mr. Maggiori?"

"Swell. Say, Friday would be a good time for doin' another séance here. That okay by you?"

Friday. I wasn't sure I could last that long. "That will be fine, Mr. Maggiori."

"Good. I'll have somebody pick you up at eight."

Pick me up? I hadn't envisioned this scenario. "Um . . . you needn't do that, Mr. Maggiori. I'm sure I can get my friend Harold to drive me there." If the cops were going to raid the joint, I sure didn't want to have to depend on any of Maggiori's employees for a ride home.

"Nuts," he said. His tone was a little less greasy. My mental image was of butter with spikes stuck in it. "I'll have one of da guys pick you up at eight."

I guess one of his guys would pick me up at eight, then. I said, "Very well."

"Bring dat guy Rolly witchya, too."

"Rolly is always with me," I told him, matching oil for oil.

Now here's something silly. I'd invented Rolly when I was ten years old out of whole cloth. Yet every time I told someone that Rolly was always with me—the subject came up occasionally—I felt better, probably because I wished it were true. Wouldn't it be nice to know that you had a friend who *never* let you down or got mad at you or scolded you or any of those things that real people do? Maybe it's not silly. Maybe it's pathetic. Oh, well.

"Good. I wanna talk to my granny."

His granny? What happened to his godfather? However, mine was not to question why. Mine was but to . . . I decided not to finish that particular quotation. I said, "Very well," again and prayed my terror didn't come across in my words. I was attempting like mad to sound arcane and mysterious, but *you* try sounding like an oracle when you're scared to death and see how well *you* do.

My knees felt weak, my eyes were watering, and I was wringing my hands like Lady Macbeth when I got back to the living room where the men in my life awaited me. Even Spike, who was sitting on Pa's lap, appeared to be intrigued.

"He's picking me up at eight on Friday. He wants to get in touch with his granny."

And then I burst into tears.

Chapter Sixteen

Friday rolled around, as Fridays generally do. It came a lot faster than I wanted it to. Bless Harold Kincaid's heart, even though he wasn't allowed to pick me up and take me to Maggiori's new place in Lamanda Park, he at least told me that he and Del Farrington, his gentleman friend, would meet me there. That made me feel slightly better, but not a whole lot.

"Buck up, Daisy. This will spell the end of your involvement with the case," said Harold in a bracing tone. He was always telling me to buck up. Sweet guy, Harold.

"I'll just be glad when it's over."

"And you'll have performed a valuable public service."

"That's what Sam told me," I said miserably. "As if he cares about that."

"Oh, I'm sure he cares, sweetie. He's a copper, after all, and they don't like law-breakers."

A certain edge to Harold's voice made me think suddenly and inexplicably of Oscar Wilde, who had been persecuted for his affection for another man. Were there still laws on the books that rendered such affections illegal? Good Lord, that notion had never once occurred to me before that instant.

"Thanks, Harold. I really appreciate this."

"Think nothing of it, Daisy. Del and I will be happy to give you moral support."

My emotions were truly on edge. My eyes teared up, and I sniffled.

"And for God's sake, don't cry at me!" Harold demanded, sounding pretty much like any other man in the world. Maybe Harold and his ilk weren't as different from other men as people thought.

"I won't," I said, and hung up quickly to make sure of it.

The mood of the whole family was sober that evening. Ma gave me a hug when she got home from work, and Aunt Vi fixed one of my favorite meals: roast lamb.

"Thanks, Vi," I said mistily.

"You're welcome." She didn't sound particularly worried about me, but she gave me a pat on the back, and I knew she was. Aunt Vi wasn't awfully demonstrative. Or, rather, she demonstrated her affections with her cooking, which was fine with the rest of the family, as she was one of the best cooks in the entire universe.

She even baked floating island for dessert. Floating islands are puffs of meringue floating on a sea of cream custard, and I positively adored them. I knew then that she was not merely worried, but she was *extremely* worried.

That didn't make me feel any better since I didn't like worrying my family, but at least I knew they loved me. Billy actually held my hand after dinner until I had to get dressed for the séance.

I chose my costume carefully that night, believe me. The weather had turned chilly again, so I decided on a long-sleeved black dress with a draped neck. A black tie upon which I'd sewn black sequins tied around the low waist, and the skirt of the dress was longer than the prevailing custom for daytime wear, but most appropriate for an evening séance. Black stockings, black shoes, black gloves, and a black hat added the finishing touches to my ensemble. Except for the sequins, I might have been going to a funeral.

As I gazed into the mirror in the bedroom Billy and I shared,

I decided I looked suitably ghoulish. A little pale powder took away any hit of a shine to my face, and a discreet swish of black mascara added the defining touch. I could have passed for a vampire, by gosh. If nothing else about this evening was any good, at least *I* was. I couldn't have looked more like a spiritualist medium if I'd worked at it for years.

Actually, come to think of it, I *had* worked on my image for years. Oh, well. I'd done a darned good job.

When I walked into the living room where my family waited for the dreaded knock at the door, Billy took one look at me, opened his eyes wide, and grinned. "Jeez, Daisy, you look like you're going to your own funeral."

"I *feel* like I'm going to my own funeral."

"You're lovely, dear," said Ma.

"That's my girl," said Pa.

"Mrs. Kincaid would be proud," said Aunt Vi.

Even Spike stared at me with what looked like the canine version of awe.

I love my family.

When I sat in the chair next to Billy's wheelchair, he took my hand again. "It'll be all right, Daisy. Sam promised that he'd take care of you during the raid."

Oh, goody. Since Sam was Billy's very best friend, I didn't say any of the million and three things that instantly popped into my mind. After hesitating long enough to drive the reproachful comments from my tongue, I said, "I'm sure he will." Huh.

We didn't have a clock in the living room, so I'm not sure if it was precisely eight o'clock when the knock came. I stiffened up like setting cement for a second, and I noticed the rest of the family did likewise. Then we all looked at each other, I sucked in a deep breath, and I rose to go to meet my doom. I mean, I went to meet Maggiori's henchman at the door.

High Spirits

I had a little bit of good luck then because it turned out that Maggiori wasn't in the automobile waiting for me. I guess he trusted me not to skip out of our arrangements now that he knew that *I* knew he had me in his sights. Dismal thought. Anyhow, it was only the chauffeur and me in that big black car driving through the dark streets of the city I loved eastward toward Lamanda Park.

It didn't take nearly long enough to get to Maggiori's joint. When the driver-henchman pulled up to the door of the place, I was too petrified to move. I guess the driver thought I was only waiting for him to open the door because he didn't seem to mind that I was sitting there like a lump. However, when the door opened, I knew what I had to do. And I did it.

Funny thing is that as soon as the driver managed to get me inside the place—there always seem to be elaborate rituals involved in gaining admittance to speakeasies, not that I know much about them as a rule—I felt better. The place was packed with people, full of cigarette and cigar smoke, and the band containing Mr. Jackson's son was playing a jolly rendition of "Where Did Robinson Crusoe go with Friday on Saturday Night" on the rise that passed for a stage. The musicians looked happy. The cigarette girls in their skimpy costumes and shingled hair didn't seem to be having a bad time, either. Thank God I didn't recognize any of them from school, or I'd never have lived this down.

I was happy, too, when, after I'd allowed a scantily clad maiden to take my hat, gloves, and coat, I heard a high-pitched, "Daisy!" and I turned to find Harold Kincaid at my elbow. Del Farrington stood behind him, smiling at me with quiet understanding. Del was much less exuberant than Harold, and I know he disapproved of drinking and smoking and speakeasies. According to Harold, he was a Roman Catholic and quite involved with his church, so I imagine he was about as uncomfortable in those surroundings as I was.

"Harold and Del!" cried I in return. "I'm so *glad* to see you here!"

"I'll bet you are," Harold said with a wink. "But we can't stay long. We're going to skedaddle as soon as you disappear."

"Disappear?" I said, appalled.

"You know." Harold nudged me. "When you start your séance."

"You mean you're not going to be there?" Horror crept through me. I don't know why, but I'd expected Harold and Del to be members of the séance group.

"Sorry, sweetie. Stacy isn't here tonight, so I don't have an in."

I glanced around the room, astounded. "Stacy's not here?" That shocked me almost more than knowing I wouldn't have the comfort of Harold's presence during the séance.

"No. She's decided to drive our mother crazy in another way these days."

His comment reminded me that I still didn't know what evil Stacy was up to now. But at that moment I didn't give a rap about Stacy Kincaid. I stared at Harold in patent alarm. "Oh, Harold, I wish you'd be there. And you, too, Del." I didn't want him to feel left out.

Harold leaned over and spoke directly into my ear. If he'd whispered, I wouldn't have heard him because of the general noise level in the place. "I really don't want to be picked up in another raid."

"Oh, but it's all right, Harold," I told him. And I opened my mouth to let him know that Sam was aware that he and Del would be there, but I realized it would be foolish to do so right out loud. "Really," I said weakly. "It's all right." I tried to wink at him to let him know the score, but I've never been very good at winking, and I think he thought I was merely grimacing.

The crowd parted at that moment, sort of like I imagine the Red Sea once parted for Moses, and Maggiori strode down the aisle thus created, straight at me. I very nearly fainted.

Scolding myself for cowardice, I managed a small smile, which was all right, since spiritualists aren't supposed to look happy, I guess because they—I mean we—commune with ghosts all the time. For the first time since I'd started this spiritualist nonsense, I seriously considered getting a job as a clerk at Nash's. Of course, that would mean giving up our lovely home and all that, but at least I wouldn't be at the mercy of Sam Rotondo any longer. Or Vicenzo Maggiori.

Maggiori nodded at Harold. I guess he recognized him as a paying customer. Then he reached for my hand, which I relinquished to him reluctantly. Touching him gave me the jitters. "Good to see ya, Mrs. Majesty. Thanks for coming."

"You're welcome." What was I supposed to have done? Tell him I couldn't perform the stupid séance and have my entire family wiped out if he succumbed to a fit of pique?

"Didja bring that Rolly guy witchya?"

"He's always with me." I'd already told him that. Was the man deaf?

"Dat's right. I knew dat." He let my hand go and rubbed both of his together. He looked mighty satisfied with himself. "Don't the place look great?"

I glanced around. It appeared merely frenzied to me, but that was probably because of my black mood. "Wonderful," I said.

"You want I should get you something to drink before we start?"

"No, thank you." My mouth was dry as the Gobi Desert, but I definitely didn't want to drink anything stronger than water.

"Nuts. I'll get you a ginger ale."

"Thank you. That would be nice. Only ginger ale, please."

Maggiori laughed. "Of course!" He snapped his fingers, and

one of his outriders appeared at his side. They were a remarkably well-trained bunch. I suspect fear of death kept them in line. I know it did me.

"Buck up, Daisy," Harold said as Maggiori turned aside to give a ginger-ale order to his henchman. Harold was always telling me to buck up.

"It's gonna be all right, Daisy," said Flossie, who had appeared as if by magic out of the smoke.

Which reminded me of something. While I was overjoyed to have friends present in this dreadful place, I was actually kind of sorry to find Flossie hadn't already fled from the clutches of the diabolical Jinx Jenkins yet. "Thanks, Flossie. Um . . . how are you doing?"

She looked pretty good. Really, she looked much better than she had when I'd first met her. Her hair was darker and, while she'd dressed appropriately for an evening of frivolity and law breaking, she still retained an aura of near-respectability. It would take a while for her new persona to fit comfortably on her, but she sure was trying to remake herself into the image of an upright young woman.

"I'm okay." She lowered her eyes. "I know you think I shoulda already got away, huh?"

"Um . . . well, no. Not at all."

She knew I'd lied. "Yeah. You do. And I will. But I'm scared, Daisy. Jinx, he's a bad man." She cast a frightened glance into the cigar smoke, looking for Jinx, I guess.

"I know, Flossie." I tried to sound encouraging. "But you have other friends now, too, don't forget."

To my dismay, her eyes filled with tears. "That's one of the reasons I'm still here. I don't want him to do nothing to . . . to anybody else."

She meant to Johnny Buckingham. I sighed deeply. Unfortunately, the room was so full of smoke that the breath I took in order to sigh made me end the sigh with a cough, and my own eyes started watering. Harold thumped me on the back.

Flossie took my arm. "It'll be okay, Daisy. I can't thank you enough for what you done . . . *did* for me. It'll be okay," she repeated, although it didn't sound to me as if she meant it.

Because I couldn't think of anything to say—she might be right about putting Johnny in danger if she left Jinx for the Salvation Army, and anyhow, my lungs were still trying to expel smoke—I patted her arm.

"Here's your drink," said a monster, appearing at my elbow kind of like a mountain emerging from an ocean during an earthquake. By gum, he even carried my ginger ale on a tray. Maggiori's idea of class, I reckon.

"Thank you." I took the ginger ale, truly glad to have it since my mouth was awfully dry, and my tongue had a habit of sticking to its roof.

And then Maggiori loomed large at my side again, and he cocked a bushy eyebrow at me. "You ready to start?" he asked. He sounded polite, but I decided not to test that theory by balking.

"Yes." We spiritualists use as few words as we can get away with when chatting with our customers because we don't want them to get the idea that we're actually just people.

"Let's get goin' then." He looked around. "Jinx! Get yourself over here."

It was then I spotted Jinx. He looked every bit as rough around the edges as he had the first time I'd seen him, and I truly pitied Flossie in that instant. It would be genuinely difficult for her to extricate herself from his clutches. And it's all well and good to say that she shouldn't have become involved with him in the first place, but she'd been only a kid at the time, and kids are often too stupid to realize there's trouble ahead until they fall smack into it. I know this from bitter personal experience.

I glanced at Flossie, who, thank God, didn't desert me. Not that Harold and Del were deserting me exactly, but that's what it felt like. Turning to look at them one last time before I went to the séance room, I felt as though I were leaving my last friends in the world behind, even though that was definitely not the case. Heck, Flossie was my friend, wasn't she? Even if she was entangled with this gang of goons.

With a sigh, I decided I'd be better off not thinking in terms of friends, goons, or anything other than the job ahead of me. Therefore, sticking close to Flossie, I walked through the milling mob to the room where another monstrous mountain of a man stood guard. This latest monster opened the door for Maggiori, who stood aside for me to enter. I took Flossie with me. I don't think Maggiori or Jinx wanted me to, but that's just too bad. I needed her presence just then.

Maggiori had remembered how I worked. The table was round, and there was one cranberry-glass candle lamp in the middle of it. After Maggiori, Jinx, Flossie, and I were in the room, the monster shut the door and stood in front of it. He looked as if he were daring me to try to escape.

"Are there only going to be four of us?" I asked, feeling nervous. I didn't like to perform for so small a group. Mind you, I didn't like too large a group, either, but a particularly small group meant that I had to be more mindful than ever of my act because there were fewer distractions present for the attendees.

"There a problem wit dat?" Maggiori asked, grumbling slightly in his oily base.

Maintaining my serene demeanor through sheer force of will, I said, "Séances work better with six to eight people." I had a dazzling idea then. "Perhaps Mr. Kincaid and Mr. Farrington can join us. They're both excellent conduits."

Maggiori squinted at me. "Huh?"

"They're both receptive to the spirits," I explained. I know, because I've practiced so long and so hard at my craft, that I betrayed none of my inner turmoil. Inside, my heart was hammering like a woodpecker after a grub, and I felt lightheaded.

"Yeah?" Maggiori cocked his head to one side and appeared thoughtful.

"It would be better to have six," I said again, quivering like Jell-O gelatin internally, but sounding self-confident and tranquil. I was actually rather proud of myself for not crumpling into a sobbing heap on the floor of that despicable room.

Maggiori jerked a nod at Jinx. "Go get them faggots, Jinx."

Faggots. Hmm. Maggiori and Jinx could learn a lot about decency and morality from Harold and Del, darn it. I didn't say so. "Thank you."

The room was silent as Jinx went to dig up Harold and Del. He came back alone. "They're already gone, boss."

Curse it.

"Well, grab another couple of people then," Maggiori growled, sounding as if he needed a lube job on his vocal chords.

And it was entirely my own fault. If there was one thing I *didn't* want, it was to irritate Vicenzo Maggiori. I thought about apologizing but decided against it. After all, I was merely performing according to my profession, and if Maggiori thought I was a prima donna, he'd be less apt to call on me in the future.

Not, of course, that there would *be* any future calls from Maggiori since tonight was the end of it all.

That thought braced me minimally as we waited for Jinx to return with two kidnapped customers. I hoped they wouldn't be under the influence of alcohol because it's difficult to conduct a séance, which is supposed to be serious business, with people giggling in the background. Not for the first, or even the thousandth, time, I wished I'd kept my fat mouth shut.

But I needn't have worried—about inebriation, anyhow. When Jinx returned, he bore with him two of Maggiori's ruffians. Both of them looked as if they'd never allow a giggle to pass their lips. They also looked as if they'd rather be shooting somebody than attending a séance, but at least there were now six of us. Goody gumdrops.

"Sit down there and keep your mugs buttoned," Maggiori said to the two men, gesturing at the table. "You, Marco, sit there. Giovanni, sit there."

This meant that I would, again, be seated between Maggiori and Jinx, and Flossie would be one thug down from me on my right. I was glad to know she was there, even if I couldn't hold on to her for support.

"That all right now?" Maggiori asked me. I detected no sarcasm in his voice, although I couldn't be sure.

"Very good," I said, aiming for a mystical tone.

Then I sat, too, and went through my usual rigmarole, telling everyone to hold hands and be silent because the spirits couldn't come unless the mood was properly set. The two newcomers looked at each other and one of them sneered, but they held hands. When I took Maggiori's hand, I felt as though I were gripping a serpent. When I took Jinx's hand, I *knew* I was clasping the paw of a truly evil person. I said, "You may now turn out the lights."

The room went dark.

It didn't take as long to get into the swing of the séance as it had the first time I'd done this for these people, probably because I anticipated the end of it all—one way or another. I still didn't believe Sam was correct in that nothing bad would happen during the raid. All I knew, or hoped for at any rate, was that Peter Frye wouldn't be able to tip off the bad guys that the good guys were going to bust in.

I must say that Rolly had remarkably little trouble communicating with Mr. Maggiori's Sicilian great-grandmother that evening, in spite of the fact that Rolly was made-up, and she was dead, and they both spoke different languages.

See, this is yet another thing I don't understand about spiritualism. Say that it's marginally possible to communicate with someone who lived a thousand years ago, like Rolly was supposed to have done. The English language is different now than it was then, even if Rolly, being from Scotland, would have spoken English, and I don't think he would have because didn't they speak Gaelic then? And these people who claim to raise long-dead Egyptian princesses as their controls, wouldn't said controls be speaking in ancient Egyptian or something?

The whole thing is so clearly ridiculous, it floors me that I still have a job.

However, that's not the point. Rolly and Mr. Maggiori's great-grandmother, whose last name was also Maggiori, although her first name was Bella, were blabbing away like nobody's business when the police *finally* broke down the front door of the joint and screams erupted from the front part of the speakeasy. It was probably a good thing since Grandma Bella had just told her great-grandson that she thought it was a shame he couldn't go into a legitimate line of work, and Maggiori had just uttered a low growl. I don't know why I do things like that. Death wish, maybe.

But that's neither here nor there.

A tremendous crash resounded through the place. We even heard it in the séance room, although it was supposed to be soundproofed. On either side of me, Maggiori and Jinx leaped to their feet.

I think it was Jinx who said, "Shit!"

Maggiori bellowed, "Frye, you're a dead man!"

The door burst open, and instead of one of Maggiori's mugs, a herd of uniformed policemen rushed into the room.

I guess it was Jinx who hauled out a machine gun from God knows where. I only caught a glimpse of him out of the corner of my eye, shrieked, *"Flossie!"* and reached over and grabbed her by the arm. We both hit the floor just as all hell broke loose.

Chapter Seventeen

I've never heard such a racket, and hope never to hear one like it again. Jinx must have been standing right over us when he jammed his finger on that infernal machine-gun trigger because not only did plaster and people start falling like hail, but so did very hot shells which, I presume, were ejected from Jinx's gun.

"Oh, my God! Oh, my God! Oh, my God!" That was Flossie, and I didn't hear her until she was about a hundred "Oh, my Gods" into her litany.

We'd both covered our heads, and I don't know about Flossie, but I started praying like mad. I guess she was praying, too, come to think of it.

I'm not sure how long the chaos lasted. My ears were still ringing when I realized the gunfire had stopped. Plaster dust and smoke and I don't know what all else still filled the air. Through the ringing in my ears, I finally made out the sounds of human voices.

Since I wasn't sure if the voices were coming from the good guys or the bad guys, I stayed down, although I turned my head to see if Flossie was still with me.

She was, which I would have known already, if my brains weren't so rattled. Heck, I still held her hand. She squinted at me through the haze. "You okay?"

I'm sure that's what she said, although I didn't really hear her, due to the aforementioned ear problem. I nodded. "You?"

Inside my head, my voice sounded like I was speaking into a barrel.

She nodded, then winced. There was a lot of rubble on top of us.

And then I felt a large body looming above me. Said large body bent over and grabbed my arm. "Get up, you," it growled.

At first I thought it was one of Maggiori's goons. I staggered to my feet, plaster dust and bullet casings flying far and wide as I rose. It was then I realized it wasn't one of Maggiori's felons who'd grasped my wrist, but none other than Sam Rotondo. In the flesh. From the corner of my eye, I realized another police officer was helping Flossie to her feet. Hmm. Sam hadn't bothered being that gentle with me, curse him.

"S-sam," I stuttered.

"Shut up, you," said Sam.

I was so stunned by his gruff, uncivil tone of voice that I shut up.

What the heck was going on here? I was supposed to be a heroine, wasn't I? You wouldn't know it by Sam's rough handling. He turned me around, grabbed my arms, and darned if he didn't slap handcuffs on me! "Hey!" I bellowed.

He leaned over and hissed into my ear. "Shut up, dammit. I've got to make this look legit. You don't want those goons to think you're in on this, do you?"

Oh. He had a point there.

Thus it was that I endured the humiliation of being handcuffed by Billy's best friend. When my head finally stopped spinning, although my ears still rang, I glanced around the room. Flossie was in handcuffs, too, and she was crying. Poor kid. I shot a fulminating glance at Sam, who still held my arm. He gave me a curt nod, which I interpreted as meaning Flossie wasn't going to be locked up. If I'd interpreted that nod wrong, Sam Rotondo was going to pay dearly.

My eyes watered from the gun smoke and the plaster dust, and I couldn't rub them since my hands were cuffed, so I blinked hard several times and looked around some more.

All things considered, the scenario was promising. Jinx Jenkins was on the ground, blood leaking from a hole in him somewhere—I hoped it was somewhere fatal. He was swearing a blue streak, but the copper who'd cuffed him didn't seem to care a whole lot.

Vicenzo Maggiori stood at the far wall, also cuffed. I hadn't realized a complexion as dark as his could appear so pasty. Several of his underlings sat against the wall, their hands behind their backs, I presume handcuffed, and a couple of them bleeding from various cuts and gashes. The police contingent looked amazingly unscathed, albeit dusty as all get-out.

"Let me go to Flossie, Sam," I muttered under my breath. I could scarcely hear myself and hoped my ears would stop ringing soon.

"Be quiet," he growled.

Boy, that made me mad! "I will *not* be quiet, curse you! You take me . . ." He slapped a hand over my mouth, and darned if he didn't lift me right off my feet and carry me over to where Flossie stood, still weeping pitifully. He dumped me none too gently on my feet, and I'd have hollered at him except that what little common sense I possess came to the fore then, and his comment about not wanting Maggiori to know I was in on the raid registered on my feeble brain.

Therefore, after giving him as furious a scowl as I could muster, I shut up about his brutal treatment of me and started in on comforting Flossie.

"It'll be all right, Flossie," I said, hoping I was right.

"I-I know. I'm just s-so scared, D-Daisy."

"Yeah. I know. So am I."

I glanced once more at Maggiori and his crew. I felt a little better when I saw the calm and collected contingent of uniformed police officers taking care of business in an orderly manner. Sam, I noticed, stood at the far wall, talking to another man in plain clothes. His captain, maybe? Some Pasadena politician? I didn't know, but they seemed very serious as they gabbed. At one point they both glanced at me with frowns on their faces, and my fear spiked.

Sam wasn't going to renege on his promise to me, was he? If he did, what would I do? Oh, Lord, I wished I were home.

But I didn't get home until a long, long time later. In fact, it was the wee hours of the morning before Sam finally drove Flossie and me to my lovely family bungalow on Marengo Avenue. I could hardly walk, I was so exhausted. And not only that . . .

"Darn you, Sam Rotondo, my wrists hurt. I think they're bruised from those stupid handcuffs."

"They probably are," he said with a grunt. "That's what usually happens."

Well, really! "For heaven's sake, we were on your side. I don't know why you had to handcuff us, darn it," I muttered, even though Sam had carefully explained that he'd wanted Flossie and me to look as if we were being picked up in the raid along with Maggiori's folks because he didn't want us to become targets.

Targets. Oh, boy.

"Yes, you do," Sam snarled.

Yes, I did. That didn't make me any less truculent. "And poor Flossie! She doesn't even have a place to stay any longer."

"You'll help her get established," Sam said, as if helping former floozies get established was my trade or something.

"Easy for you to say," I muttered unhappily.

"I'm sorry, Daisy," Flossie said, sounding as miserable as she looked. "I'm *so* sorry."

Then, of course, I felt awful, because I honestly didn't mind helping Flossie. I was only mad at Sam. "Don't worry, Flossie. I don't mind, really."

She whimpered a little bit. She hadn't stopped crying entirely during the several hours since the raid. I wished she would. Heck, I was upset, too, but I'd be cursed if I'd cry in front of Sam Rotondo again.

It must have been close to two o'clock in the morning when Sam's big police-issued Hudson pulled up to the curb in front of our bungalow on Marengo. The only lights on for the length of the street were in my house. And that, of course, meant that Billy, at least, and probably everyone else in the family, were waiting up for me. I darned near lost my resolve and started crying then and there.

Nevertheless, I didn't seem to have a whole lot of options available, so when Sam opened the automobile door, I got out. Flossie stumbled after me. She was a total mess. I suppose I was, too, what with leftover plaster dust and stuff clinging to my formerly beautiful black dress. Even my sequins were dusty. Well, that's not true. They didn't sparkle, but that might have been because we stood on the sidewalk on a dark street in the dead of night.

"You'd better come with us, Sam. You'll have to explain what happened." My voice was cold. I didn't want to ask Sam for any favors. But this wasn't a favor, darn it! He owed Flossie and me an explanation to my family at the very least.

"Of course I'll come with you." He sounded about as outraged as I felt. "What do you think I was going to do? Leave you two here on the sidewalk?"

Actually, after I pondered his question, I realized I hadn't expected him to desert us. I'd be damned for all eternity before I told him so, however. I only sniffed meaningfully.

He said, "Gah!" or something along those lines, spun on his

heel, and marched up the front walk to the porch.

After glancing at each other, Flossie and I followed him. My heart was thudding like a bass drum. I knew Billy was going to be mad as fire when he saw me. He'd anticipated my homecoming several hours earlier, with me not only without Flossie but in much the same condition as I'd exited the house with Maggiori's pet thug at eight. When he looked at me as I was now, he was going to pitch a fit.

Spike started barking as soon as Sam's big foot hit the first step. I sighed. While I loved Spike like the child I'd never have, I did wish his bark wasn't so darned loud. And persistent. The dog could bark for hours if we'd let him, which, naturally, we didn't.

In actual fact, poor Spike only let out about five barks before he yipped and shut up. Poor baby. I suspect Billy or Ma or Pa smacked him, told him to hush, and picked him up.

It was Ma who opened the door, clad in her robe and slippers and looking haggard and worn. My level of guilt soared into the stratosphere. Sam stepped aside to allow Flossie and me to enter the house, and Ma clapped a hand to her mouth and shrieked, "Daisy! What *happened* to you?"

Billy spoke next. "Damnation, Daisy, I thought nothing bad was supposed to go on there tonight!"

Hurt, I cried, "It wasn't *my* fault!"

Flossie said, "Oh, this is all my fault!" and began sobbing again.

I think Pa said, "Hmm," but I'm not sure because too much other stuff was going on.

At least Aunt Vi wasn't there. I guess the woman had done the sensible thing and hit the sack at a reasonable hour.

Finally Sam growled, "Get inside so I can close the door."

I gave him a furious scowl for his efforts.

Billy said, "This is the limit."

I felt like two cents. Maybe less. Definitely less.

"Sit down, ladies," Sam said, indicating that Flossie and I should sit. We did so, on the sofa. Close together. Flossie buried her head in her handkerchief once more. I doubted that the hankie would survive the evening, and I was almost certain I wouldn't.

Billy was in his chair, of course. Ma and Pa took chairs facing the sofa. Sam continued to stand. Bless Spike, he jumped up on my lap. *He* didn't care that I had the remnants of gangster bullets, shattered liquor bottles, and the dust of speakeasy walls on my dress. *He* knew I'd been through a dreadful ordeal. *He* appreciated my helping the police capture a bunch of hoodlums. Of course, *he* didn't know that I'd been forced to do so because I'd been stupid in the first place. Then again, he was an awfully forgiving fellow; he probably wouldn't have minded that, either.

At any rate, I appreciated Billy's dog in that moment and vowed never to live without a dog again. They were ever so much more faithful and understanding than people could ever be.

So, while I petted Spike, and Flossie sniffled into her soaking-wet handkerchief, Sam took the floor. "The raid was a success," were the first words out of his mouth.

Nobody moved or spoke for several seconds until Pa finally said, "Um . . . that's good."

Billy was next. He still frowned murderously—at me, of course. "But obviously it didn't go off without a hitch."

Sam sighed. "No, there was a definite hitch. Jenkins pulled out a Tommy gun."

Billy, agog, said, "A *Tommy gun?*"

Ma slapped a hand to her cheek and said, "Sweet Lord, have mercy!"

Pa whistled.

Flossie uttered a loud sob.

Billy's frown eased slightly, but he still looked angry. "Jenkins is one of the gangsters?"

"Yeah," said Sam. "But he didn't hit anybody."

With a glance at me, Billy said, "Looks like he hit a lot of walls."

"Huh," said Sam. "A *lot* of walls. And the chandelier and the table, and a bunch of other stuff. You should have smelled the booze. Fortunately, Gil Waters winged the bast—uh, the fellow before he could kill anybody."

"Thank God," Ma murmured. She and Pa held hands, and they were both looking at me as if I were their baby whom someone had only barely rescued from certain death.

"I thought there wasn't supposed to be any danger involved in this little adventure." Again, Billy frowned at me. *Me,* of all people!

"It isn't my fault!" I cried, beleaguered to my boots. Well, my shoes, anyway.

"I swear, Daisy, you can get involved in the most—"

Fortunately for me, and perhaps for Billy, too, since I wasn't in any mood to be picked on, Sam interrupted Billy's next statement.

"It isn't her fault, Billy. We all thought the raid would go without a problem. Nobody *ever* gets hurt when a speakeasy is raided. The goons don't dare shoot the customers, so they never haul out their guns. They generally just try to get away, which is what Maggiori had planned to do, only we gagged his contact."

I sniffed. "They pulled out guns this time."

With a scowl, Sam said, "Yeah, *Jenkins* did some shooting this time. But that was *very* unusual. Anyhow," he continued, turning to Billy, "Daisy and Miss Mosser were heroes in the situation. They managed to find out the name of the snitch in the police department, and in spite of their reluctance"—he laid special emphasis on the word *reluctance*—"they distracted the

High Spirits

crooks so that they were totally unaware of the police presence at the joint until we battered down the door."

At the mention of her name, Flossie pulled her nose out of her hankie. "M-me?" she stammered. "What did I do?"

I patted her arm. "You gave me the name of the police rat." I deliberately chose the word *rat*, hoping to make Sam flinch. It didn't work. Figures.

She turned drowned eyes upon me. "I did?"

"Yes, you did."

"Gee," said she. "I didn't mean to. If Jinx finds out . . ."

"Mr. Jenkins is going to be put away for a very long time, Miss Mosser, so I don't expect you'll have anything to worry about from him."

Flossie's waterlogged eyes grew large. "Yeah? You really think so?"

I think Sam caught himself a second before he could roll his eyes. Although I'd never admit it aloud, I didn't blame him a whole lot. Flossie was a sweet kid, but she had the brainpower of a gnat. "He shot at several members of the Pasadena Police Department. We don't look kindly upon that sort of behavior. And that's not even counting the charges against him in Detroit."

"Detroit?" I asked, surprised. "You mean Detroit, Michigan?"

Sam gave me one of his looks. "What other Detroits do you know about?"

Irked, I growled, "Just asking," and turned back to Flossie, who appreciated me. I think she was the only one present who did at that particular moment. Well, except for Spike.

"And Maggiori's facing murder charges in New York City, so I don't expect we'll be seeing very much of him, either."

"*Murder!*" Even though I didn't want to, I gaped at Sam.

Naturally, he smirked. "I told you these guys were no good and that you should stay away from them."

"I thought you're the one who wanted her to hang out with them in the first place," said Billy, noticing a discrepancy in Sam's testimony, if that's the right word for it.

But Sam was uncowed by discrepancies. "As a general rule. Daisy agreed to help us out in this case, but as a general rule, she shouldn't consort with fellows like that."

"As if I would!" I snapped.

"Hmm," said Billy, eyeing me strangely.

"I wouldn't! Darn it, Billy Majesty, you know me better than that!"

He finally admitted it. "Yeah," he said with a sheepish grin. "I guess so."

"You *guess* so?"

I might have pursued the matter, which would have been very unwise on my part, but sometimes I can't seem to help myself. However, Flossie tugged on my sleeve at that moment. I turned to her. "Yes?"

"Um . . . I don't wanna be a bother or nothing—anything, I mean. But, well, I don't have a place to stay or . . . or any clothes, I guess, unless . . ." Her voice trailed off. She looked uncertainly at Sam.

I had a feeling I knew what she was thinking. She didn't want to ask in front of my parents and Billy if she could run and fetch her belongings from the apartment she shared with Jinx. Poor kid. She'd really managed to get herself into a big mess. And she was young, too. I guess one's upbringing has a lot to do with the decisions one makes in life. Flossie had made her Jinx decision when she was no more than seventeen years old. She'd been a baby, for Pete's sake.

Oh, very well, I know. I married Billy when I was seventeen, but that decision was nowhere near as basically bad as the one Flossie made when she linked up with Jinx, in spite of how it turned out. Why, if it wasn't for that blasted war, Billy and I would probably be happily rearing a brood—or maybe one or two—children in Pasadena, and Billy would be employed at the Hull Motor Works as an automobile mechanic. Automobile mechanics made really good money, too. Curse the Kaiser.

Ma, bless her heart, said, "You may stay with us for a while, Miss Mosser." She smiled sweetly, even though I knew she wasn't eager to take on another housemate, and especially one as doubtful as poor Flossie.

"Sure," said Pa, aiming for jollity. "Happy to have you."

Flossie knew they didn't mean it. She looked at me, pain as well as supplication in her eyes.

I glanced helplessly at Billy . . . and then I remembered the perfectly brilliant question he'd asked me that day several weeks ago. I got up from the couch. I'd be happy to say I jumped up eagerly, but there wasn't an eager bone in my body at that moment.

"I have an idea," I said, and limped toward the kitchen and the telephone. There I took the Pasadena Telephone Directory from its little nook and thumbed through it, searching for a name and a number.

Ah, there it was. COlorado 728. I dialed the exchange and gave them the number, thanking my stars that I didn't have to work all night like a telephone operator. *Usually.*

It was very late. If Flossie had to spend the remainder of the night in our house, that wouldn't be *so* bad, but . . .

"Buckingham," a voice rasped into the receiver. He sounded sleepy but not especially surprised. I guess when you're a captain in the Salvation Army, you come to expect telephone calls in the middle of the night.

"Johnny? It's Daisy."

"Daisy? What's up?" He sounded as if my name had brought him to instant attention. "Is something wrong? What's the matter?"

"Well . . ." Now that I had him on the phone, I wasn't sure how to phrase my question.

"Is it Miss Mosser? What's the matter? Damn, I knew I should have rescued her from that situation before now."

He'd said *damn*. For a second, that one solitary fact drove everything else out of my head, which I guess is a pretty good indication of my state of mind.

"Daisy? *Answer* me!"

"I'm sorry, Johnny. Yes, it's Flossie."

He made a sound indicative of shock and dismay.

"No, no! She's all right! She's not hurt."

A huge sigh nearly blew my eardrums out.

"But you see, there was a raid on the speakeasy tonight, and all the crooks were arrested, and now Flossie doesn't have anywhere to go."

"Yes she does."

My heart, being too exhausted to leap, staggered to attention. "She does?"

"Absolutely. Is she at your place now?"

"Yes. She's here."

"I'll be there as soon as I can get some clothes on and crank up the Ford."

I guess captains in the Salvation Army don't make a lot of money. I knew for a fact that Johnny drove an old Model-T Ford with a crank. As I've mentioned before, we used to have one of those until I got the Chevrolet with its lovely self-starter. Those cranks are . . . well . . . cranky.

This was good news, though. On the other hand, I really didn't want to send Flossie into another situation where she'd be living in sin with a man—even such a man as Johnny Buckingham, who was a very good one. "Um, will she be staying with you, Johnny?"

"*Me?*" he cried, as if I'd asked if he could catch flies with his tongue like a frog. "Shoot, Daisy, I thought you knew me better than that."

He sounded so hurt and reproachful, I hung my head. "Sorry, Johnny. It's been a rough night."

"I'll get in touch with Sergeant Dabney. She's in charge of housing accommodations for women who have to leave their homes unexpectedly for one reason or another."

Principally drunken husbands threatening their lives, I supposed. How depressing. Only not in this instance. "Thanks, Johnny. You're a great guy, you know that?"

"It's God, Daisy, not me. If it were up to me, I'd probably be sleeping it off in a gutter somewhere."

And on that lovely note, we disconnected.

I made a brief detour into Billy and my bedroom in order to shuck off my good shoes and slip into slippers. While I was there I grabbed a couple of clean handkerchiefs, thinking that you never knew when they might come in handy, especially during situations such as the one at present visited upon us.

Things hadn't become lively in the living room during my absence, I noticed when I returned thereto. Even Spike was snoring peacefully on the sofa, his head on Flossie's lap. She sat there, head bowed, stroking the pup, looking about as unhappy as a person could look. Billy, Pa and Sam spoke softly together, probably about gin rummy, since they were all gin rummy fiends, and Ma seemed to have sunk into a trance-like condition indicative of too little sleep.

They all looked at me when I entered the room. Except for Spike, who continued to doze. He saved his energy for important things, like people walking by on the sidewalk outside.

"It's going to be all right," I said before anyone could ask a question. "Johnny Buckingham will be here as soon as he gets his Ford cranked to life." I went over and sat next to Spike, which was as close as I could get to Flossie. "He said one of his sergeants will be able to give you shelter until we can get this whole thing straightened out."

She gulped audibly, and I laid a hand on her arm.

"Everything's going to work out all right, Flossie. You'll see. Johnny will make sure you never have to worry about the likes of Jinx Jenkins and Vicenzo Maggiori again."

Although you'd think she didn't have another tear in her, having cried pretty continuously since about nine o'clock the previous evening, Flossie began leaking again. "Oh, Daisy," she whispered. "I don't know how I'll ever be able to thank you. For everything." She sniffled, and I handed her one of my clean hankies.

"It's okay, Flossie. Johnny will be sure that you're safe and have a place to stay and . . ." My voice trailed off because I didn't know what else to say. That Johnny'd help her get a job? That Johnny would find her a place to live? Well, I suppose he might do those things, but I didn't know it for certain, so, recollecting that discretion is the better part of valor—although I don't know what valor had to do with the current situation—I shut up. Mercifully, I might add.

"Thank you so much."

"Sure." I patted her arm some more. When I drew my hand away, I noticed I'd managed to make a handprint in the dust on her sleeve. Oh, boy, the two of us were truly a couple of messes. "Say, Flossie, would you like to wash up a little bit before Johnny gets here? We're both pretty dusty."

"Could I?"

She sounded so pathetic, *I* darned near started crying. "Sure. I'll show you to the bathroom."

I decided that after Flossie cleaned herself up as much as she could, Sam finally left for wherever *he* lived, and everybody in my family went to bed, I was going to treat myself to a long, hot bath with some of those sweet-smelling bubbling bath salts Billy

had given me for Christmas.
   And I did.

Chapter Eighteen

The next morning was Saturday and everybody except Ma got to sleep later than usual. Poor Ma, even though she'd stayed up until almost three in the morning, still had to go to her job at the Marengo Hotel. Fortunately, she only worked a half-day on Saturday.

Billy and I were silent as we dressed and I made the bed. The silence wasn't fraught with any sort of emotion; we were both merely worn out. I didn't even glance at Billy when he opened his dresser drawer, although my heart lurched a tiny bit when I heard the cork come out of his morphine solution. I told myself that morphine was simply a part of Billy's life and that there was nothing anyone, least of all Billy, could do about it. My heart gave another brief ache, but it was too exhausted to ache for long.

When we were dressed, I staggered out to the kitchen and plopped myself on a chair while Billy went to the bathroom. It was around ten in the morning, hours later than we usually awoke and got moving.

" 'Lo, Vi," I said to my aunt, who was preparing breakfast as she always did. We were so lucky to have Vi living with us. "Where's Pa?"

"He went for a walk."

I glanced at the floor, where Spike sat, eagerly waiting for food to drop from heaven. Or me, which was a more likely scenario. "He didn't take the dog."

"He thought you needed the dog more than he did this morning."

My darling father. "That was nice of him." I *did* need Spike, especially that morning. "I guess Ma's gone to work."

"Yes."

Short and snappy. I sensed my aunt wasn't happy with me that morning. I guess Ma or Pa had filled her in on all the excitement. Oh, dear.

My suspicions were confirmed when Vi said sternly, "Your mother doesn't need this grief."

True, but neither did I. Sensing it would be unwise to say so, I aimed for a repentant tone when I said, "I know." In truth, repentance was easy to achieve, since I felt so *very* guilty about worrying my family.

Aunt Vi only harrumphed. Then she placed a plate of waffles and bacon in front of me, along with a sliced orange—we had two orange trees in our backyard, and we had tons of oranges almost all year long—so I guess she wasn't too mad at me.

"Thanks, Vi. This looks delicious."

Billy rolled himself out of the bathroom along about then and came into the kitchen. Vi blessed him likewise. "Thanks, Vi. What's the occasion?"

"According to Daisy's father," Vi said stiffly, "Daisy has helped to capture an entire gang of bootlegging crooks. That detective friend of yours telephoned early this morning."

"Sam?" Billy looked up, surprised. "What did he have to say?"

"He wanted to talk to you or Daisy, but I said you both needed your sleep. So he said he'd come over around three this afternoon to give you some important information."

Billy and I looked at each other, and it seemed to me that Billy was as dismayed as I about this news. I think I whimpered. I know I said, "Oh, no. Now what?"

Billy patted my hand and forced a grin. "It'll be all right, Daisy."

"I doubt it."

Although weary and sorry that I'd put my family at risk, I'd thus far during the approximately forty minutes I'd been awake that day, figured my problems, as regarded bootleggers at least, were at an end. Sam's impending visit not only made me wonder about that, but it successfully killed my appetite. Boy, *that* doesn't happen often. I ate my orange and shoved the bacon and waffles around on my plate for a few minutes.

"Daisy Gumm Majesty, you're too old to be playing with your food," Vi snapped.

I regret to say that I burst out crying and ran from the table, flinging, "I don't *want* to do any more work for the police!" over my shoulder as I did so. Vi and Billy both probably thought I was crazy, although Billy finished his breakfast before he joined me in our bedroom. By that time I was face down on the bed, Spike at my side, wishing I were dead. Again.

"Hey, Daisy, it'll be all right. Sam's probably only going to tell you what they've done with the crooks."

"Huh."

He took the hand that wasn't wrapped around Spike. "Come on, Daisy, get up and get dressed. It's Saturday, and maybe we can take Spike for a walk. The weather's not too cold, and it's sunny out."

Wiping my eyes, I pushed myself to a sitting position, beginning to feel guilty for being such a sissy. Billy was probably right, and Sam was probably going to do exactly what Billy expected him to do. My heart didn't buy it, but I knew I owed it to my husband, the only man I'd ever loved and ever would love, to get control of my emotions.

"Sure," I said, the word as thick as mud. "Yeah. You're right."

Deciding to forego wallowing for another little while, I surveyed my spouse.

Poor Billy still hadn't gained what little strength he'd had before his recent illness, but his color was better, and he seemed to be looking a little healthier every day. A walk sounded like a good idea.

"Let's go for a walk!" I said it brightly so that Spike would understand.

He did, all right. At the word *walk* he bounded off the bed, ran around in a circle twice, and raced out to the service porch where his leash hung.

I sighed. "Just let me get my coat."

"I'll get my jacket," said Billy.

The telephone rang just before Billy, Spike, and I got to the front door. I glanced back at Aunt Vi, indecisive.

Vi didn't suffer from such wishy-washy sentimental claptrap. She waved us off imperiously and said, "I'll tell whoever it is that you're not home." Then she added, "And that you *won't* be home until Monday morning. In fact, I'll tell everyone who calls that."

An entire weekend free. Sounded like heaven to me. Provided, of course, that the telephone call was for me. As I opened the front door and pushed Billy's chair through it, attempting to hold Spike at bay at the same time—he always lunged for the wide open spaces as soon as they were revealed unto him—I heard Vi say, "Mrs. Majesty is unavailable until Monday morning. Please telephone again then."

Billy chuckled. "Saved by your aunt."

"Thank God for aunts."

Therefore, it was with a relatively light heart that I pushed Billy's chair down the ramp on our front porch that fine morning in early March. Spring was just about to burst forth, and I no longer had to consort with bootleggers and gangsters. Sure, I

247

still had an ill husband, a sick father, and a whole host of nutty clients—and Sam Rotondo—but I was used to dealing with those things. It was the criminal part of my life I was thrilled to be rid of.

"Oh, Daisy!"

The warbling cry came from across the street when I was not more than a house down from our bungalow. It was more difficult to convince Spike to stop than it was to halt the forward motion of Billy's chair, particularly since we had one of those newfangled wheelchairs that Billy could operate himself via the oversized wheels. Therefore, I only had to struggle with Spike in order to see who had hailed me thus.

"Mrs. Killebrew!" I was surprised to see our across-the-street neighbor waving at me.

She came over to us and, avoiding Spike through some means known only to her, she grasped my leash hand. "Oh, Daisy, I can't tell you how much Jerome and I appreciate what you've done for us!"

Jerome was her husband, but that's about the only part of her speech I understood. I opened my mouth to say so, when she rushed on.

"I just think you're wonderful, and I wanted you to know it. I'm baking a chocolate cake right now—it's in the oven—and I'll bring it over as soon as it's frosted."

"Uh . . ." I was, as they say, at a loss for words.

Billy said, "Thanks a lot, Mrs. Killebrew."

Bursting into tears, Mrs. Killebrew flapped her hand in the air, whipped out a hankie, and said, "No, no. It's we who should be thanking your heroic wife."

And she dashed back across the street. I stared after her, completely baffled. Then I looked down at Billy, who was likewise impaired.

Not so Spike. He wanted to *go.* So we went.

High Spirits

Our walk was interrupted another couple of times by neighbors, however. They all came up to thank me. For what, I didn't know, although I suspected it had something to do with the raid on the speakeasy.

"Shoot, Billy, I hope word hasn't gone around that I've been consorting with those horrible people at the speak."

He shrugged. "If it has, it looks as if folks don't mind."

Neither one of us could figure out how anyone could have learned of my involvement so fast, although we didn't dwell on it a whole lot. We walked clear around the block that day, which isn't as meager a walk as it might sound, since those were long blocks. It felt good to be out and about on a gorgeous day instead of crammed into a stuffy, smoke-filled speakeasy. I felt free for the first time in a month, at least. And Billy was as healthy as we could expect him to be, although not forever, I hoped. He might even begin trying to walk again one of these days.

Thus it was that I felt relatively rested and happy when Sam Rotondo showed up at our house, as threatened, at about three o'clock that afternoon. It was he who explained our neighbors' odd behavior.

"You didn't read the papers this morning?" he asked incredulously after he'd parked himself on a chair in the living room with my family and me scattered here and there in the room, staring at him. He looked pointedly at Pa, who grinned sheepishly.

"I didn't want to spoil the surprise, so I hid the paper."

"Huh. So that's why I couldn't find it," muttered Billy.

I seldom glanced at the newspaper, so I hadn't missed it.

Sam held up the morning's copy of the *Pasadena Star News*. To my utter horror, a big black headline across the top read: LOCAL PASADENA MATRON FOILS BOOTLEGGERS.

My mouth fell opened and stayed that way. It was probably

249

just as well, or I'd have screeched at Sam.

Sam didn't seem to care. "Listen here," said he. " 'Local matron, Daisy Gumm Majesty, wife of war hero William Majesty, assisted the Pasadena Police Department in the arrest of several criminals who have been operating a speakeasy in various locations throughout our fair city and surrounding areas. Before Mrs. Majesty agreed to assist with the investigation, the police department had been stymied in their attempts to capture the vicious gang.' "

"Good Lord," I whispered, more appalled than flattered. What would this do for my business? What would this do to my family? What would this do to *me*, for crumb's sake?

Relentlessly, Sam read on: " 'Hailed as a heroine for undertaking such a hazardous endeavor—' "

I squealed an incoherent protest. It was an undignified noise, but I couldn't help myself. It *had* been hazardous, blast it! Even the newspaper said so. Then I buried my face in my hands.

Sam read even *more:* " 'Detective Sergeant Samuel L. Rotondo, who worked closely with Mrs. Majesty during the execution of this case, hailed Mrs. Majesty as a true heroine.' "

"*Ohhhhh!*" Me, again. And I really didn't like that word "execution."

" 'The acting Chief of the Pasadena Police Department, Mr. O'Dell, declared that the department intends to honor Mrs. Majesty with an award for meritorious service, as well as present to her the reward that attaches to the capture and conviction of the criminals.' "

A word in that part of the narrative caught my attention, and I stopped moaning. Looking up at Sam, I said, "Reward?"

He grinned. He would. "Reward. There's a big reward on these guys. One originating in Detroit and one from New York City."

My entire family, including Ma, who'd napped after return-

High Spirits

ing home from work, turned to stare at me. I stared back, only managing to whisper, "Oh, my."

"Mind you," Sam said, cautioning me not to become too ecstatic, "you won't get the reward until the creeps are convicted."

I said, "Oh." I still couldn't quite take it in.

"However," he went on, "the Chief wants to have a ceremony next Wednesday at one-thirty. All the papers will be there, and you're going to get a certificate suitable for framing to hang on your wall."

I swallowed hard, something ugly having occurred to me. "And you're sure none of Maggiori's associates will come after me with Tommy guns? I've heard these guys are vicious." Heck, I'd seen how vicious some of them were with my own very eyeballs.

"They won't dare. You're a heroine. If they go after you, their bosses will be furious. The gangs don't shoot women."

"That's not what I've heard," I said darkly. In fact, the reason I stopped looking at newspapers was that I got tired of reading about all the innocent victims of these so-called gangs back East.

"Well," Sam said, amending his statement. "They don't go after women *on purpose.*"

Somehow that didn't make me feel a whole lot better, although that other word, *reward,* softened my worry some.

Billy took my hand. "Hey, Daisy, this is good! I didn't realize what an important thing you were doing. Sorry if I was crabby a couple of times."

Turning to gaze at my husband, I thought, *a* couple *of times?* I said only, "Thanks, Billy. I was really scared."

He pulled me into a hug, which surprised me almost more than anything else that had happened to date. "I'm sorry, sweetheart. I know you were scared."

And then everyone except Sam stood up and rushed me. I was overwhelmed with hugs and congratulations from Ma and Pa and Aunt Vi, all of whom beamed fondly at me. Poor Aunt Vi told me she'd been fielding telephone calls for me all day long, and that I'd probably be spending all of Monday on the 'phone.

I didn't mind that. In spite of my remaining misgivings, it appeared that my misery was *over*. And evidently it wasn't merely over, but I'd come out of the whole thing smelling like the proverbial rose. It truly boggled my mind.

My mind being boggled did not, however, prevent my entire family and me from piling into the Chevrolet and riding up to City Hall the following Wednesday afternoon at one-thirty. There, while flashbulbs went off all around us, one of the two men who were handling the affairs of the police department since the resignation of Chief McIntyre, Captain Louis O'Dell, handed me a lovely parchment certificate acknowledging my "bravery and valiant efforts in service of the citizens of Pasadena, California." Wow. I never in a million years expected anything like that.

The two acting police chiefs, Captain O'Dell and Mr. Harley Newell, both shook my hand. The mayor shook my hand. Sam Rotondo—who shocked my socks off by appearing in full uniform for the ceremony—shook my hand. A whole bunch of other people shook my hand, too, and my picture showed up in both the evening editions and the morning editions of all the newspapers. The neighbors not only brought chocolate cakes, but flowers and presents and all sorts of other things. My business, which was already good, boomed until I wasn't sure I could handle it all.

Boy, you just never know about these things, do you?

I didn't discover what had thrown Mrs. Kincaid into a tizzy

about Stacy until we attended the engagement party for Miss Florence Mosser to Mr. Johnny Buckingham, which was held in the Fellowship Hall of the Salvation Army Church about three weeks after I'd been feted by the city fathers.

The whole family attended this function, too. I was ever so happy for Flossie and Johnny, who looked great together. Flossie had a glow about her I never expected to see, and she looked positively charming in her Salvation Army uniform.

As soon as she saw us enter the room, me pushing Billy's chair, and Ma and Pa and Aunt Vi trailing behind us, Flossie squealed and rushed over to us. Her easy tears were flowing, but since she didn't wear makeup any longer, they didn't stain her cheeks—devoid now of any hint of bruising—with dark streaks.

"Oh, Daisy, I can't thank you enough for what you've done for me!" said she.

Johnny was hot on her heels. "And I can't, either. You're the best, Daisy." He shook my hand warmly once Flossie released me. She'd had me in a bear hug for a second there.

"Shoot," I gasped—Flossie's bear hug had been fierce—"I didn't do anything, really."

They both said, "Ha." I guess they didn't believe me. They were captured by well-wishers then, and my family and I proceeded merrily into the room.

And then I nearly fainted dead away. "Billy!" I whispered, agog.

"Good God," said he, similarly afflicted.

"What's the matter?" asked Ma, oblivious.

Well, that's only because she didn't know Stacy Kincaid. Aunt Vi, who had spotted the same phenomenon Billy and I had, sat with a thump on one of the hard benches. "My word." A mistress of understatement, my aunt.

But there she was. Stacy Kincaid. In the uniform of a Salvation Army minion. A private, I reckon, unless there's a rank beneath private.

But that's unkind.

But . . . Stacy Kincaid?

She gave me a little finger wave and a smile, and I smiled back uncertainly. Then she crooked her finger, inviting me over to where she stood.

Billy and I looked at each other. Then he grinned.

With a big sigh, I said, "Well, I guess it can't hurt. Too much."

Oddly enough, it didn't.

Mrs. Kincaid told me the next time I visited her to read the cards or the board or whatever idiocy she wanted done that day that she was pleased Stacy no longer frequented speakeasies.

"But I must say, Daisy, that I didn't know the Salvation Army was what Rolly meant when he said something dreadful was going to happen to Stacy if she didn't change her ways."

Some people are never happy.

I received the reward money, quite a bundle, by golly, around the middle of April. I didn't tell anyone about it because I had a surprise to spring on my family. I was lucky when the funds finally came because by that time a good deal of progress had been made in the area where my interest lay.

Sam Rotondo, who seemed to live at our house, Pa and Billy were all sitting around a card table in the living room, playing gin rummy, Ma and Aunt Vi were chatting at the dining room table while Ma embroidered a handkerchief, and Spike rested happily on Billy's lap when I opened the front door.

"Hey, Spike," I said when heads turned toward me. "You're falling down on the job."

"I told him it was you," said Billy with a smile for me. He'd been very nice to me in recent weeks, and I appreciated him for it.

High Spirits

"That accounts for it, then."

"He's a good boy," said Billy in that silly voice people use on dogs. Me, too. I'm not denigrating it or anything; I'm just reporting.

"I have something for us," I said as I turned around and picked up the parcel I'd lugged up the front porch steps. I fear the grunt I made while doing so was rather unladylike.

It did, however, prompt Sam and Pa to get out of their chairs and hurry to the door.

"What is it?" asked Pa, curious.

"You'll see. Take it inside and put it . . ." I looked around, hoping for some free space. The only flat space was the card table. What the heck. "Put it on the card table."

"But . . ."

"Put it on the card table," I repeated ferociously.

So Sam put the parcel on the card table.

"Ma and Aunt Vi, come here!" I called.

They did.

So I stood back, planted my fists on my hips, smiled hugely, and told Billy, "Open it."

Paper crackled before the first gasp went up. It went up from the men, since neither Ma nor Aunt Vi knew what Billy had just revealed. I wouldn't have, either, if I hadn't listened to the men in my life ooh and aah over radio signal receiving sets for a couple of years now. This one was a beauty, too, made by a company called Westinghouse, and came complete with a wooden cabinet and a head seat so that Billy could listen to whatever was being transmitted. I still couldn't quite figure that part out.

"The man at the store said that pretty soon more than one person will be able to listen at a time. This thing here . . ." I pointed at what I hoped was the proper place on the machine. ". . . is where you're supposed to be able to plug in what he called a microphone. He said that invention is only months away. That means that everyone in the room will be able to listen." To what, I hadn't a single, solitary clue.

Silence greeted this announcement. I stood there, nervous as a cat, although I'm not sure why. Worried that my gift wouldn't be appreciated, I reckon.

"My God, Daisy," Billy whispered, awed. "I don't know what to say except . . . thank you."

I relaxed. He liked it. That was the only important thing. I didn't care what anyone else thought, although, I noticed, as I glanced around the room, everyone else looked to be pretty much in awe, too.

"Wow," said Pa.

"How kind, Daisy," said Ma uncertainly.

"Laws a mercy," said Aunt Vi. I think she'd said that one before.

"Well, I'll be damned," said Sam Rotondo.

He would.

ABOUT THE AUTHOR

In an effort to avoid what she knew she should be doing with her life (writing—it sounded so hard), for several years **Alice Duncan** expressed her creative side by dancing and singing. She belonged to two professional international folk-dance groups and also sang in a Balkan women's choir. She got to sing the tenor drone for the most part, but at least it was interesting work. In her next life, she'd like to come back as a soprano—and maybe as someone who longs to do something that makes money.

In September of 1996, Alice and her herd of wild dachshunds moved from Pasadena, CA, to Roswell, NM, where her mother's family had settled fifty years before the aliens crashed. She loves writing because in her books she can portray the world the way it should be instead of the way it is, which often stinks. She started writing books in October of 1992 and sold her first one in January of 1994. That book, *One Bright Morning,* was published by HarperCollins in January of 1995 (and won the HOLT Medallion for best first book published in 1995). Alice hopes she can continue to write forever!